There was
on his face.

◇

Almost a softness, but there was still that hard line to his jaw. His eyes went down to her mouth.

"What we are up against is greed," Edward said, stretching his arm sideways along the back of the sofa, sure and decisive in relaxation as he was in action.

"Greed?" Fanny said.

"And something else . . ."

"What?" She turned. He seemed very close. As Fanny fixed him with her green eyes, he didn't move. His arm was still stretched along the back of the flowery chintz, his long legs stretched on the Turkish carpet in front of him.

"Don't you know?" Was he teasing her? It was difficult to tell with men like him.

"No." There was no point in pretending.

"I thought you understood these things." The room was perfectly quiet. Still the same unexplained note in his voice. He lifted a hand, touched the still damp loop of her hair, and unexpectedly let his hand fall to her neck. "I meant"—his whole body moved nearer—"this." The next moment, his lips were on hers . . .

◇

Golden Dolly

Lizbie Browne

PAGEANT BOOKS

♪

PAGEANT BOOKS
225 Park Avenue South
New York, New York 10003

Cover artwork by Hector Garrido

Printed in the U.S.A.

First Pageant Books printing: October, 1988

10 9 8 7 6 5 4 3 2 1

Golden Dolly

Chapter One

They called it the Summer of the Sovereigns. 1814. A summer of the most charming suppers and balls all over London. The war in Europe was over at last, and Lady Oxford's waltzing parties swarmed with foreign princes and victorious generals. Metternich and Talleyrand. Alexander, Czar of Russia, bristling with gold braid, and the king of Prussia dazzling them all to death in his blue regimentals with the silver embroidery. There had never been a more delicious season.

Except in Wentworth Street, where the widow Milbanke was hovering between bouts of melancholy and hysteria, and where her younger children spent most of the day tormenting their tutor, and where Miss Fanny Milbanke, sitting staring out of the window at black iron railings, had that moment decided that matters could not continue to get worse.

The reason for her gloom was the impending visit

of Mr. Clarence Stanhope. Fanny heartily wished she could escape the dreaded encounter. Her mother was astonished at such ingratitude. "Mr. Stanhope is not obliged to call, Fanny." Mrs. Milbanke fiddled with the bow on her cap. "I hope you will be civil to the gentleman: I do not know why you dislike him. I find him excessively kind."

"Mama," Fanny said, "he is licentious. Everyone says so. And he is fat and old, and he wears his morning coat too tight."

"He has helped us a great deal since our misfortune . . ." Mrs. Milbanke ferreted for her handkerchief. "Since your poor father died I have tried to spare you knowledge of our financial rigors, Fanny. I do not expect you to share in my distress. I daresay you do not care! But—"

"Mr. Stanhope brought us a brace of pigeons last week and a picking of grapes on Tuesday," Fanny said. "It is not a fortune. It cost him nothing. Oh, and the checkered ribbon for your bonnet. We must not forget the ribbon."

"That was to go with my purple silk. Because he admired it. I was very much flattered." Mrs. Milbanke sighed at the memory. "I think he is quite an admirer, Fanny. It was kind of Cousin Caroline to send him. I find her most amiable."

Fanny considered this. "But we do not know my cousin Caroline," she said. "My father did not keep in touch with that branch of the family."

"To be sure, Fanny, you are your father's child!" Mrs. Milbanke displayed her irritation. "Stubborn: He was stubborn, too. Now, had he only listened to my brother's advice, we should not be in such dire straits . . ."

To this Fanny replied with only the lightest of sighs. Against her mother's tongue, her father had been her only ally. She still felt the loss of him dreadfully—his quiet affection, his dry asides.

"I shall be very glad to see Mr. Stanhope, at any rate," her mother said. "I expect you will sit there like a dumb thing as usual. I should be obliged if you would try to look more . . . pretty, Fanny. A smile would help. You look more pleasing when you are animated."

Fanny was not a conventional beauty. In fact, she had no reason to believe she was a beauty at all. Her brown hair was drawn back into the fashionable Grecian knot. Wispy ends strayed around her forehead. But her light brows were so fine as to seem almost unnoticeable. The pink of her upper lip matched the faint color in her cheeks, but hers was not a face that invited attention. It was a face that belonged to a girl of some character, but one might be forgiven for not observing that fact. At first view, at least, only the steady green eyes, the lift of a square chin, gave any notion of Fanny's strength of mind.

She would be twenty in a few months. If her father had not died, and if they had not had to move to this disagreeable little house in Wentworth Street, the summer might have held more promising prospects: riding and dancing and visits. As a matter of fact, she did not care about the lost pleasures. They were a sacrifice that she was prepared to make. It was her mother's constant scolding and continual abuse of her father's memory that made Fanny despondent. And callers like Mr. Clarence Stanhope.

He arrived promptly at eleven. A florid gentleman with a heavy, jowly face above a big, puffed body, he stood by the fireplace tapping his boots with his malacca cane, and again Fanny wondered why he was there. He pandered to her mamma's little vanities with unparalleled ease, but every now and again, Fanny fancied he threw an attentive glance in her own direction. Never open stares, but they made her feel uncomfortable.

"And how is dear Cousin Caroline, sir?" Mrs. Milbanke began to use her society voice. "Well, I hope? I wonder she don't come up to town for the season. I am sure it is pleasant in the country at your brother's place, but you must own that all London is *en fête*. And *très, très charmant.*" The society voice had to be duly larded with the fashionable French phrases. "I confess, I could not stay away, if it were me."

"Lady Caroline dotes on the country, ma'am. And then, of course, she has not long been married to my brother, George. No more than a twelvemonth. I'm sure I need not remind you of the joys of marriage?" His gaze flicked over to Fanny.

"No need at all, sir." Mrs. Milbanke's voice quivered with emotion. "I had all the comforts of a long, happy marriage. Ask Fanny. She will tell you."

Fanny fixed her eyes on the railings and hoped that he would not. Her father, could he have heard the conversation, might have had some remarkably wry comments to make on the delights of marriage to such a woman as her mother. Nor, for that matter, could she imagine what joy Cousin Caroline could take in being married to a man twice her age, even if he did happen to be a baronet. Especially if Sir George Stanhope should resemble his brother in the least particular.

So Fanny said nothing. She smiled faintly. If she acted dimwitted, she thought, he would not bother to address her.

"We had a place in the country once." Mrs.

Milbanke's handkerchief was out again. "The world was brighter then, Mr. Stanhope . . . We are forced to live quietly now. My girls' prospects are sadly diminished!"

"Which is exactly why I wished to confer with you, ma'am." Mr. Clarence Stanhope spoke smoothly. His gaze rested on Fanny, then moved back to her mother. "I have an offer to make. It concerns your daughter, Fanny. Lady Caroline was most particular that I should see you as soon as possible."

"An offer? Lady Caroline?"

"A very generous offer, madam, if you will allow me to say so. Not that you wouldn't be doing Lady Caroline a favor at the same time."

"A favor?" Mrs. Milbanke repeated. "But what is the offer, sir?"

"Lady Caroline has adapted herself amazingly to life in the country." He rolled smoothly into the story. "She finds Cranthorne exactly to her taste. Nevertheless . . . there are times when she would wish for a little company. Cranthorne Hall is somewhat isolated and the neighboring families a trifle older than herself. I will be frank, ma'am—Lady Caroline would take it as a compliment if your daughter, Fanny, would come on a visit. She is aware of your present . . . troubles. She hopes for the satisfaction of offering you some small aid."

"Fanny? Visit Cranthorne?" Mrs. Milbanke was temporarily surprised into silence. Then she said, "Do you hear that, Fanny? Is it not excessively kind?"

In vain did Fanny try to shake her head, in vain attempt to signal that she had not the least intention of visiting Cranthorne. Her father would not have approved at all. And Fanny always experienced misery in the company of total strangers.

"Of course, it is a day's journey. We should find her a suitable traveling companion," Mr. Stanhope said. He moved to the narrow window, where his great bulk suddenly blocked out all the light. "Caroline would hope to have your daughter for most of the summer. I am glad you seem favorably inclined to the proposal." Then he added, "If I am not mistaken, that is very fine lace you are wearing, ma'am. Very fine indeed. Nothing more becoming than fair lace at a fair neck. Nothing at all."

Mrs. Milbanke's look was of flustered bliss. "My sister sent it me from Bath, sir. She assures me it is the latest pattern. I have been trying to make Fanny trim her blue gown with the remains, but she is a stubborn girl. She tells me she prefers the gown without. I cannot understand her."

"Miss Milbanke assumes her own style." Mr. Stanhope flashed Fanny a leering sort of smile.

Fanny said, "It was not so huge an argument, sir. Mamma exaggerates." She looked across at him and thought, He tries to curry favor with both of us. There is something peculiar about that. And about him. It was not all the gossip she had overheard about his lechery, his string of mistresses and general dissipation. It was not even that stout, overindulged stomach or the watery blue eyes flicking all over her. It was, she decided, that slight softness in his voice when he thought he was flattering her . . .

I won't go, she thought. They can't make me. My father would have hated him, too. They have no right to decide it without even asking me. I will deal with Mamma when he is gone.

The morning had begun with an altercation. It ended with one, too. After Mr. Clarence Stanhope had gone, Fanny allowed her true feelings to emerge.

"I don't choose to visit Cranthorne," she said. "I am not acquainted with Cousin Caroline. I do not wish to be acquainted."

"Fanny!" Mrs. Milbanke went into the attack. "I don't understand you! I find it an excessively good offer. You are not nearly so grateful as I expected—"

"I do not wish to visit strangers."

"You cannot refuse. It will be most uncivil. Though I suppose that would not concern you!"

"I cannot be concerned about people I do not know. I shall not go."

"Impertinence, miss! Shall not go, indeed!" Mrs. Milbanke laughed shrilly. "I daresay you have no idea of the expense you put me to here? I daresay you do not want to know! I never heard such nonsense. You are perverse, miss! It is easy for a girl of twenty to shrug off wealthy connections—oh, yes, very easy! You have no idea, have you, what a wealthy man Sir George Stanhope is? He could have bought up your father a thousand times over. He is a man of great property and ten thousand a year. And you would spurn their help? Mr. Clarence Stanhope is a fine gentleman, too. A gentleman of some taste and with many connections . . ."

"I do not care for Mr. Clarence Stanhope. I have said it before. I do not know why he comes. I mistrust him."

"Mistrust?" Mrs. Milbanke went into a storm of sarcasm. "Mistrust? Then I daresay you will finish up a crabbed old maid! I suppose you think yourself a perfect judge of gentlemen, miss? I suppose you have been so much in society that you have known thousands of them? Well, I do not know where you expect to find yourself a husband, if you are so very choosy! I do not expect you to find one at all—that is my opinion, if you are asking for it. Well, I hope you will not have cause to regret your decision, Fanny, that is all I can say . . ."

It was not all she could say, however. It was very far from all. Mrs. Milbanke's tongue, once it began, was virtually unstoppable. And that was why, two weeks later, Fanny was forced at last to accept the invitation to Cranthorne. A charming letter from Cousin Caroline, arriving soon after Mr. Stanhope's visit, brought all Mrs. Milbanke's arguments back to the boil. Fanny was equal to her mother's nagging for more than a week; she bore more exhaustedly with the monstrous scolding for a few days more, and at last she admitted defeat. Nothing—no visit or prospect—could be worse than her present sufferings in Wentworth Street. A letter was promptly sent to Cranthorne Hall: Fanny relished the idea of a summer visit, was looking forward to making Cousin Caroline's acquaintance, and would delight in the freshness of the country air after the heat of London. She would come on the twelfth, if that was convenient . . .

It was forty miles from Wentworth Street to Cranthorne along the Oxford road. Fanny had a dry day for the journey, but they seemed an interminable time on the road. The coach was stuffy and badly sprung. Dust got in all the windows, even though they were tight shut. Mrs. Payne, the widow of a clergyman and Fanny's traveling companion, had insisted they stay shut because of her rheumatics. She was an enormously large lady dressed in black satin that reeked of stale odors. She fancied herself an invalid and constantly complained of her bones.

Outside, fields, parks, an occasional cottage lurched by. Fanny had not the least idea where they were by midafternoon. Almost half a mile away was a muddle of gray roofs and the chimneys of a large mansion half hidden by some trees. A child stood on a hedge and frantically waved.

"Stamford Parva." Mrs. Payne must have read Fanny's thoughts. They were not far from Cranthorne, at any rate. Stamford was the nearest hamlet, Lady Caroline's letter had said.

They lurched on around a sharp corner, then down an unpleasantly steep hill. The wheels shuddered and drove up a cloud of dust as the brakes went on. Fanny heard a confused noise of dogs barking, then caught sight of a cart of chickens straight in front of them.

One more shudder. They seemed to be slithering sideways on toward the ditch. "If they are not careful . . . ," Fanny said, craning her head. "If they don't—"

The great jolt, when it came, tossed them all sideways against the doors. It was perhaps lucky for Fanny that she landed on top of Mrs. Payne and not underneath. She scrambled up, relieved to find that no one was hurt, though the coach was now pitched into the ditch at a ninety-degree angle and wedged there with its outer wheel spinning. Mrs. Payne had been winded, to judge from the wheezing sounds emanating from her corner. The gentleman on the other side was recovering his hat. The coachman, a long, shambling fellow, came round to the far door and grumblingly set about trying to heave them all out.

His commentary was graphic and accompanied by foul breath. "Turning into the farm, says he." He dragged Fanny out onto the heat of the road. "No warning of any kind, mind you! And chickens all over the place and two thumping hours, I shouldn't wonder, to get us back on the road."

Fanny stepped back. The coach was thoroughly embedded, the horses restless. Chickens were still leaping about. A red-haired youth had come out of the farm entrance and stood watching the scene.

The coachman had hauled out Mrs. Payne. He was sluggishly offloading baggage onto the road. "You'll have to wait for the phaeton from the inn. The boy's gone to fetch it. Best stay there till the work's been done."

Mrs. Payne glared at him. "This is a pretty fair mess!" she commented. "I am expected in Oxford. It is a wonder we were not all killed!"

Fanny had a sudden idea. "How far is it to Cranthorne Hall?" she asked the red-headed youth. To tell the truth, she found it bliss to be out in the fresh air.

He looked at her a little oddly, she thought. "About a mile or so," he told her. "See those chimneys behind the trees?"

"Then I shall walk across the park." She made an instantaneous decision. "Is it possible?"

"Follow that track through the woods." He was still staring at her.

"Walk?" Mrs. Payne said. "My dear, you must not think of it! There is no haste, is there? I promised Mr. Stanhope—"

"I shall walk," Fanny repeated calmly. "They will be a half hour bringing the phaeton. It's such a lovely afternoon. I hope the rest of your journey will be uneventful, Mrs. Payne. I shall tell them how kind you were."

The coachman touched his hat to her as she climbed through the stile. On the left side of the parkland there was a river and a small lake in the distance. No, more like a largish pond, Fanny thought. On the right was a group of giant oaks and a winding stone wall.

After so many hours cramped up in the coach, she stepped out quickly, sniffed at the fresh sweetness of the air, and looked at all the sheep grazing quietly beyond the belt of woods; she found them bliss. And the silence! A silence broken only by the small twitter of birds or a thin bleat in the blue distance. Things unimaginable in the streets of London. There was another joy, too: being quite, totally alone.

I suppose she'll write and scold me for walking it. Mamma! thought Fanny. But she doesn't know yet. Perhaps no one will tell her.

At first the sunlight almost hurt her eyes, but once she was in the wood, the filter of leaves took off the glare. A squirrel darted away. She'd frightened it. Mamma will have a small fit when she hears about the coach. Let her, I don't care. She's not here. She can't do a thing about it. She can't say a thing . . .

Which way now? The narrow track divided in front of Fanny. Up to the deeper part of the wood, or back down to the lake? Up, of course. The climb made her legs ache. She stopped at the top to regain her breath; she wasn't used to such strenuous exercise.

She was on the point of moving again when she heard the horse approaching. A pale chestnut coming down through the trees, keeping to a light, steady canter. As it came lower, it advanced more rapidly. Fanny saw the rider—a man with a clear-cut profile and very straight black hair. He still kept coming, blundering down through thin branches and undergrowth. Coming closer—too close for comfort . . .

Then two things happened at once. A light wind caught at the muslin of her skirt and hooked it up around a sapling twig. In an attempt to free it, to draw it back out of the rider's way, she let go of the bonnet she had been carrying. The wind took that, too, right out into the path of the horse.

Grab it—reach for it—quick! It was a purely instinctive reaction.

But before she had taken two steps, the horse whinnied, reared sideways. Fanny's small yelp of fear went unheard. As she pressed herself back out of the way, the rider shot forward, flew through the air, hit the undergrowth with a sturdy thump, and slithered another yard before coming to a halt.

The horse was gone. Already it was halfway down to the lake.

"Jupiter's jackstraws!" cried a male voice, husky with fury. He was alive! And heaving himself back onto the track, he crouched there for a minute on his haunches, getting his balance back, his dark eyes fixed on the ground in front of him. He muttered a string of invective she could hardly credit. Then he got up, swaying a little on his feet.

His blue coat was torn across the shoulders and one sleeve was ripped at the elbow. Cream riding breeches clung to his powerful thighs, mud from the track plastered all over them. There was a long scratch on his cheek, which was bleeding a little.

Fanny came out onto the track and braved him. His words had made her cheeks burn. "I . . . I'm sorry. Very sorry."

"Sorry?" His face was pale and savage. Making no apology for his language, he demanded to know what she was trying to do. "Didn't you see me coming?" he demanded.

"Yes," said Fanny. "But you were coming too fast."

He straightened at that. The smile that lit up his

face was incredulous. "Oh . . . I was coming too fast, was I?"

"Yes." Her heart hammered, but she stuck to her view.

"And what if I tell you you're trespassing? That I don't expect to find young ladies wandering all over my park?"

"I was not wandering all over it," Fanny said. "I was on my way to Cranthorne Hall."

"Cranthorne?" His tone changed. Sharply, he said, "Why are you going to Cranthorne?"

Fanny colored. "I do not think that your business, sir." She was pink and flustered, but she stared him out.

"You are on my land."

"If I am, I am sorry for it. It is not my fault the coach went into the ditch. They told me I could get to Cranthorne this way." Now it seemed the most dignified thing was to explain about the mishap. "It was a great deal too hot and dirty on the road," she finished. "And it seemed foolish to wait on and on when I could walk to Cranthorne in a half hour."

"You still did not answer my question." His voice was abrupt. His eyes went up and down her face. "Why are you going to Cranthorne?"

Suddenly Fanny was tired of his ill manners. She looked him straight in the eye. "Lady Stanhope is my cousin. I am invited to stay."

She thought afterward that there was something positively strange about his reaction to that simple statement: He said nothing, not a single word. Fanny waited. Then, almost churlishly, he turned on his heel and went off down over the slope to the lake without a backward glance. As if he would have cut me dead, she thought. Yet swift as his departure had been, it had not been so quick as to hide his reaction.

"He looked scathing," she said aloud to herself. "And disdainful. I never had anybody look at me like that before." Then, "I am glad he came off his horse. It will teach him a lesson. He should not be so vastly unpleasant."

The house looked solid, a mansion snugly facing south in the center of a grove of oak and beech and chestnut.

Fanny had resolved not to be too nervous. She had been reasoning it out all the way down. At least she was out of reach of her mother's tongue for a time, there was no obligation on her to be here forever, and a change of surroundings might be good for her spirits. Wentworth Street had been dismal without her father. It was now more than a year since his death, but his many kindnesses, the pleasure they had taken in each other's company, all his loving ways were far from forgotten. Yet it was necessary to live for today. Always to be harking back to the past was productive of nothing. In short, Fanny was young and sensible and determined to make the best of life.

She walked across the gravel. The gardens were suitably trim. There was no one about. A wheelbarrow had been left at one corner of the portico. Fanny skirted it and went on round and up the steps. The bell tinkled faintly when she pressed it. She leaned against a stone pillar and waited for someone to come. As she waited, the sun went behind a cloud.

It looks sad, she thought, for some reason. It was all right when the sun was shining. I expect it is just an impression.

Chapter Two

A manservant in a striped waistcoat and a white apron opened the door. While he went to acquaint someone of her arrival, Fanny was left in the middle of the black-and-white-tiled hall, under the sweep of a great staircase. She looked about her.

It was cold in here after the heat of the park. There were heavy oil paintings in gilt frames on the walls. Huge, trapped landscapes. Then stiff family portraits and even stiffer horses. A whiff of wax polish, and dust from a sagging tapestry at the far end. A solid marble fireplace in the left hand corner and a side table with painted china against the wall. Houses were sometimes like people, she thought. They stayed in the style of fifty years back and stifled change, stifled the occupants sometimes.

It's me—I'm imagining things, Fanny thought.

At the far end of the hall, a door opened. A maid in a cherry-colored dress scuttled out, followed rapidly by a young woman with light, curly hair— rather boyish-looking—a pale gown, and frank, honey brown eyes.

"Fanny—my dear!" A cool, young voice. Cousin Caroline? "What a dreadful thing to happen!" Obviously it was Caroline. "Colman was about to send someone out with the phaeton. My dear, you must be thoroughly fatigued."

"No," Fanny said, "I have a sound constitution."

Lady Caroline laughed. She looked a little nervy, Fanny thought. "You will not have it much longer," she said, "if you are obliged to be out in this heat." With a cool hand, she touched Fanny's arm. "I am so glad you have come. Tea, I think, in the drawing room, Céline."

15

The door to the drawing room was open, and
when she saw it, Fanny wished she had not come in
so wild from the park. More splendid marble fireplaces—two of them—and deep carved friezes all
round the room, a painted ceiling. It looked rich.
Very rich. Daunting. Lady Caroline must have seen
Fanny's face. "Wait till you see the ballroom," she
said. "It is even more grand. It gives me the fidgets. I
can never wait to get back to my little breakfast parlor. But it is cool in here, so we will sit in state for
once."

Fanny chose a chair by one of the fireplaces. It
wasn't comfortable; she sat on the very edge. Space,
oceans of space, stretched between her and the other
side of the room where Caroline sat. Caroline had an
extraordinary face, Fanny thought. Very white skin;
huge, startling eyes.

Her smile was beautiful, very warm, very quick—
as quick as the rest of her movements. She said,
"Don't feel awkward. You will get used to the
house."

Fanny let her hands relax. "There is so much space
here after Wentworth Street," she explained.
"Mamma is very unhappy there. We are all on top of
one another. It makes her disagreeable sometimes."

"I'm sure it must." Caroline sounded sympathetic.
"But you will not need to worry about that for a
while. We shall see that you have a most enjoyable
stay."

It was all right, Fanny thought. They would be
friends. Already she was feeling more comfortable
in the room.

Lady Caroline said, "I'm so glad you were allowed
to come. You can't know how delightful it will be to
have someone young to talk to." Her profile was
perfect as she bent to pour the tea. "I said to Sherry,

I cannot imagine why the two halves of the family never speak to each other. It is ridiculous. Sometimes these things spring up and no one knows why. Don't you agree?"

Fanny smiled. She said, "My father would never say much about it. I always imagined it was some old quarrel between brothers. Who is Sherry?"

"Sherry?" A quick laugh. "I forgot. You know nothing about us. Sherry is Mr. Sheridan Crawley. He is a friend of my brother, who is now gone back to sea. My brother was here until only last week. When he left, I begged Sherry to stay on and keep me company until you arrived. And how was Clarence? I have not seen him this last month."

Fanny did not know how to answer this. She bent and picked up her cup so as to hide her true feelings. "He was quite well, I think."

Fanny was quite prepared to unpack her things herself when they came up, but a maid arrived to do it for her—the dark-haired French maid called Céline, who had come with Lady Caroline from the place in Piccadilly and who found country life extremely trying.

"I didn't know Lady Caroline ever lived in Piccadilly," Fanny said idly. "I thought they lived in Brighton. Or was it Bath?"

"M'lady was there only a little time." Céline's voice grew more rapid, implied the social whirl and great events and boredom. She shook out a shawl and screwed up her dark little face. "Me? I hated to leave."

"You don't like it here?"

"Is so dead. Always fields and sheeps and . . . and servants more stupid than sheeps!" Céline stuffed the shawl into a cupboard. "I want to seize

them and throw them! M'lady, too. She tells me not
to say so, but it is the truth, so I do not care."

Fanny looked at the brass-handled chest, the old-
fashioned chairs by the bed, the watercolors of
Stamford Rectory, and imagined the girl was exaggerating. The French did. Everyone knew that.
Cousin Caroline had appeared perfectly happy. In
the mirror reflection, Fanny studied Céline. She
looked the flighty type. Feckless. She's a gossip,
Fanny thought. And she looks as if she has a spiteful
side. I shall have to take care what I say to her. My
clothes don't impress her, that's for sure. Not half
grand enough.

"That is all?" Céline said, taking the last brush
out of the trunk.

"That's all. Thank you."

"Do you want me to do your hair?"

"No. No, thank you. I can manage by myself."

Céline smiled, a perfunctory, careless little smile.
Her eyes were like a cat's, slanting and watchful.

"What time is dinner, Céline?"

"At six. You will hear the bell."

"A whole hour, then. I shall rest for a bit." Suddenly, the tiredness hit her.

At dinner, Fanny met Sir George Stanhope. He
was worse—much worse—than anything she had
vaguely expected. She was shocked, though she
tried not to show it. She knew him to be almost
sixty years old, but if anything he looked older.
There were stories he had been exceptionally handsome as a young man. Remnants of his looks remained—the blue eyes and solid jowls—but his fea-
tures were blurred by the weight he carried. He
smelled of whiskey and cigars, and his manners
were alarmingly coarse. He had a tendency to thump

on the table and bawl for whatever he wanted from the servants. He spoke in the loudest, most vulgar country accent, and his waistcoat buttons were half undone. If Sheridan Crawley hadn't been there in the next chair to help interpret, Fanny didn't know how she would have gone on.

Sir George had flung some incomprehensible question at her that made no sense at all. It sounded like, ". . . hosses . . . in the sayson . . . running out, d'ye?"

"No need to look so scared," Mr. Crawley leaned over and murmured in her ear. "He wants to know if you ride?"

"Oh . . . is that what it was?" Fanny was wildly grateful. And she liked the look of Mr. Crawley's smile and his handsome blue eyes. She answered Sir George as best she could, then whispered to Mr. Crawley, "I shall get used to him, I expect. I had no idea what he was saying."

"The horses understand him," Mr. Crawley said. "That is the main thing."

"The horses . . . ?" She saw that he was laughing. There was a layer of discomfort about their making fun of their host, but Mr. Crawley's smile was infectious.

"Sir George prefers horses to people," he told her sotto voce.

"Colman!" Sir George roared at this point. "What's wrong with the damned beef? It has no taste! Damme, it's a fine lookout when you can't get a decent piece of beef at your own table."

"Take it away, Colman, and bring the lamb." A light, soft voice. Caroline's voice. She was doing her best not to look uncomfortable. "Perhaps, George, it is a little overdone. Fanny, my dear," the soft voice went on. "You must fill me in on the new London fashions. We get so out of touch in the country. I have a woman who sews for me and pretends to know what is à la mode in London, but she will never acknowledge she may be a little behindhand. Tell us what is new this summer."

A clatter of cutlery. Fanny eyed Sir George nervously. He was pushing his plate away and reaching for the wine bottle.

"The . . . the thinnest muslin," she began hurriedly. "So very fine, Mamma says it is almost shocking." Was it going to be all right? She thought so. Sir George was silently pouring wine into his glass. "It . . . it is come from Paris, I believe."

"A pox on your French," Sir George growled. He had knocked back the claret in one go and his voice was rising. "I hope they go rot!" He slammed his glass down on the table. "Talleyrand and Bonaparte and the lot of them. They are no better than dogs! They will never beat us in any war . . ."

"George . . . dearest . . . will you take some of the mutton?" Lady Caroline's voice slipped in gracefully and quickly. "It may be more to your taste. Fanny, we will walk in the morning, if it is fine. We will take the lane to the village. It is not much of a place, but the views are quite sweet. And after being shut up in town all these months, you will find it a great pleasure . . ."

Her smile was so civil, so sweet; she so easily made light of Sir George's bullish manners that for a moment Fanny almost forgot the first acute moments of raw embarrassment.

It is astonishing she stays so calm, Fanny thought. I could not do so. Why did she ever make such a match? Did they force her into it? She surely could not have chosen such a . . . such a boorish old

monster! With a shiver she turned her attention
back to Mr. Crawley and asked how long he had
known Lady Caroline's brother.

The evening was an odd experience. After dinner,
they sat and talked in the drawing room. Fanny
played on the piano a little at Caroline's request;
Sheridan Crawley told them a string of silly stories
about his childhood in Ireland. Sir George drank,
dozed off, woke up at intervals and launched into
more confusing tirades, first about the Corn Law and
then about some battle or other near Madrid. One
thing Fanny was certain of was that he drank far too
much. One could see it in his face, in the high color
and the mottled cheeks.

It was the reason for half his sanguine outbursts.
They ought to stop him, she thought, looking at the
whiskey glass on the arm of his chair. He'd had far
too much for one evening—why don't they stop
him? She daren't, I suppose. Look at the size of him.
The servants will have to cope with him later.

But Fanny's apprehensions turned to pleasure and
surprise when Mr. Crawley seemed to single her out
for very particular attention, offering to cut off a
lock of his hair for her after she had admired its curl.
He added that he could have it put in a locket, if she
liked, as the poets did, so that she could wear it
round her neck and languish over him in his absence.

Fanny laughed. "I'm not the languishing kind,"
she told him.

"What? Never languish?" Playfully, he gazed at
her. "You've got to languish, you know, when you
fall in love. Haven't you never been in love?"

Fanny gazed right back at him. "Not that I can
recall. Is it obligatory?"

"Not obligatory." He laughed. "Just vastly entertaining."

"Don't listen to Sherry," Caroline said. "He's a frightful flirt. No girl ought to be allowed within a mile of him. I am always being forced to reprimand him."

"For what?" Crawley demanded.

"For coaxing the ladies into losing their wits over you."

"Their wits? I never knew a woman who had any." His gaze was wickedly straight. "Present company excepted, m'lady. I've known them to lose other things. Their memory or their virtue—but never their wits. Even when seized with the wildest of passions—"

"I will have nothing more to do with this argument," Lady Caroline told him. "You are too unkind." She looked fond, but candid. "And you are shocking Fanny. She is not used to your nonsense."

Mr. Crawley turned to Fanny and took her hand. Her heart hammered. He said with exaggerated relish, "Fanny, say it is not true . . ."

Sir George snored. The snore ended in a little snort. It changed the tone of the proceedings entirely.

"Sir George is on my side," said Mr. Crawley drolly.

Fanny wanted to giggle. Caroline looked at him. Clearly, it made him feel guilty and penitent.

"I'll get out the cards," he said.

"I wish you would."

"We'll play at whist," he said. "Fanny won't mind if I cheat now and then, will you, Fanny?"

"Why do you need to cheat?" Fanny asked.

He brought the cards back. He smiled a smile of

pure charm. "Because I like to win," he said. "Don't you?"

"Sherry!" Lady Caroline's voice cut in with a warning shot. She looked even more cross with him.

"All right. I'll behave."

He wasn't really wicked, Fanny thought. Just amusing. What was wrong with that? For the rest of the evening, she tried not to look at him too much, keeping her eyes down, concentrating on the cards. But it was novel to be flirted with by an amusing young man. In London there had been so few amusing young men—particularly any who noticed her.

She felt a slight pang, though, whenever she looked at Caroline. Pity filled her. How dreadful it must be to be completely out of range of handsome young men. Trapped in marriage with an old horror like Sir George . . .

"Fanny, it is your play . . ." Caroline's voice, light and patient.

"Yes . . . yes, of course . . ." Scarlet-faced, Fanny turned her mind back to the cards. Caroline couldn't read her thoughts, could she?

The one thing she must never do was show any pity.

She took out a card and put it on the table. She glanced at Caroline. Tomorrow it won't seem so grotesque and unnatural. I'll get used to it. And there won't seem such an odd atmosphere. I'm exaggerating because I'm tired.

She fell asleep as soon as her head touched the pillow, and dreamed she was still shaking around in the coach and that a great dray horse was kicking at the side of it loud enough to break the door in.

The thumping had just stopped when she woke up. Then it turned into muffled voices outside her bedroom door. For a moment, she just listened. What time was it? Two o'clock? Half past? She hadn't been asleep more than an hour.

Perhaps it was servants. At this hour? Or dogs. Dogs didn't talk. Swiftly, but silent enough to listen on the way, she pulled on a wrapper and went to the door. Quickly she opened it.

The valet and Sir George were standing in the passage side by side. No, not standing. Sir George was half slumped over the valet's shoulder. Candlelight wavered, too shaky to reach the ceiling.

"Fanny, don't be alarmed." Caroline's voice came out of the darker patch. "We were just . . . just trying to get him to bed."

The darkness lightened. Fanny saw her for the first time and stared. Somehow, blood had gotten on Caroline's forehead. She said, "What has happened?"

"Nothing. It's nothing. A . . . a slight accident." Caroline moved her hand and then Fanny saw the bruised cheek.

"An accident?" she said.

"Yes. An accident. I . . . I slipped on the stair."

Fanny's gaze turned toward Sir George. "Did he do it?" she asked faintly.

"No. No, of course not." Too swift an answer, though. Caroline's candle moved farther away so that it lit the ceiling, the paneling, Sir George's red fist, the valet's shirt.

"He did, didn't he?" Fanny insisted. "He struck you." Instinct told her.

"Fanny, you mustn't think . . ."

"He's been drinking all evening."

Sir George mumbled something incoherent.

"Fanny . . ."

"Yes?" Fanny wished her knees would stop shaking. She had never come into contact with violence before.

"Do you wish to help me?"

"Yes. Oh, yes . . . You know I do."

"Good. Then go back to bed."

"But—"

"But nothing." Caroline reached out. A quick hand touched Fanny's cheek. "Forget what you've seen."

"But I can't forget. Why do you . . . ?"

"Fanny . . . please." The candle swayed.

She looks exhausted, Fanny thought. Near to collapse. "But why can't I . . . ?"

"My dear . . . Not now. It is two in the morning. I am not much hurt. There are things you don't— can't understand. He is not a bad man . . . at the bottom of it all. Go back to bed. That is how you can help me. James . . ."

The valet shifted his weight, heaved Sir George, none too easily, another yard along the passage toward his room. Caroline moved, too. But Fanny heard the last, almost inaudible sigh that escaped from her as she followed her husband. "Sometimes I think I shall never leave this place alive . . ."

Céline came in to wake her in the morning. "What time is it?" Fanny mumbled.

"Just past nine."

"How dreadful!" She shot up fast, then, and first heard the dogs. "What's all that noise?"

"It's the hounds," Céline said. "They meet here today."

Below the window, dogs strained and swarmed over the loose gravel. Hounds yelping and baying as if bursting to take off. Through the crowd of grooms and their governors, Fanny saw another brilliant blue day. Dog-days, she thought. The idea pleased her, made her smile.

Servants, boys, one or two scarlet jackets. Then she saw Sir George waving his crop at one of the dogs. He looked hale, alert enough this morning, the exertion perhaps concealing last night's excesses. Fanny's smile died as her anger rekindled.

I wonder how Caroline is this morning? I wonder if she will come down?

Then she saw the brown chestnut again. The sun was so bright, she had to shield her eyes. Yes, it was the same one. And the same rider. The man she had unseated yesterday. She watched him come up the broad drive. A big man. Top hat, blue jacket with a velvet collar. The man who had been so very disagreeable.

"Who is that?" she asked Céline. "The man riding up to the house?"

Céline said, "That is Mr. Edward Knight." The dark face grinned. "He is good to look at, no?"

"Where does he live?"

"At Leigh Park. On the other side of the hill." Céline laughed. "M'lady does not like him, but for me he would do very well."

Some people have strange tastes, Fanny thought. Then she noticed someone else, the red-headed youth who had directed her to Cranthorne. "And who is the boy behind him?" she asked. "The one with red hair."

"That is Bob Steadman. He is Mr. Knight's groom. The sister of the boy is a maid here. She is with them, too. Look—" Céline pointed. "Susan. M'lady has trouble with her. She would get rid of her if she could, but Sir George will not allow it. He keeps her on because his first wife was fond of her."

Susan Steadman had red hair, too. She had run

across to her brother and seemed to be talking to him with some force. As Fanny went on looking, Sir George crossed the two or three yards that separated him from Edward Knight and was doing what he had not been capable of doing last night: reaching up to pump his neighbor by the hand. At the sight of the older man, Edward Knight found a smile and a warm greeting.

As he dismounted, there was a swirling movement among the dogs that made him turn his head, look up, and see Fanny and Céline framed in the window. Fanny found herself unable to look away. He didn't either. He saw her nightgown, her untidy hair. Was his gaze noting any of it or looking right through her?

How cold and peculiar he is, she thought, drawing back. But then what could one expect if he was a friend of Sir George's?

I've as much right to be here as he has. I won't allow him to intimidate me. And it's stupid to feel he's so hostile toward me. He doesn't even know me. Fanny resolved not to think about Mr. Knight again.

Chapter Three

When she had finished breakfast, Fanny found Lady Caroline alone in her small sitting room. Caroline with her pale face bent over her needlework and a small, purplish bruise on the side of her cheekbone.

"Good morning," she said by way of opening. "I'm late. I'm very sorry. I overslept."

"You were tired after the journey."

"Yes. A little." Fanny hesitated. Was it better to pretend she had not witnessed the scene last night? Probably not, she decided quickly. Better to be direct than to tiptoe around the place pretending. She eyed Caroline's bruise. "Do you have a headache?" she asked. "You look very pale."

"A headache? Not much of one." Caroline sighed and made a brave, comic face. "You are kind to inquire, Fanny, but I would really rather pretend it had not happened."

A small silence followed. Fanny sat and stared at the pattern on the wall. The sitting room was on the ground floor, on the left of the hall. It was connected to the rest of the house by an anteroom with a small writing desk and it had formerly been the coachroom. But now it was newly papered to Caroline's taste with a trellis design of roses.

Fanny said, "I will not speak of it again, if you do not want me to—but it distresses me to see you ill used."

"Fanny—" Caroline was clearly embarrassed. Her eyes flickered down to the work in her hand. "There is nothing I can say . . ."

"It should not be allowed. Something should be done." But the more Fanny said, the more difficult it became. Caroline's tranquillity was vanishing by the minute. Her needle was stabbing into the work. Her breath was shallow and her fingers shook.

Was that why they wanted me here? Fanny wondered. To console her? To be around in the house with her in case he abuses her?

"All right. I'm sorry. We won't talk about it anymore." Fanny's tone was soothing. The conversation came to a full stop. She searched around for something to start it again. "I saw Mr. Edward Knight outside before breakfast." She gazed out at the sunshine. She could see all the way down across the park. "What kind of gentleman is he, in your estimation?"

A pause. "Mr. Edward Knight?" Caroline sounded startled, so startled that she forgot her distress. "You do not know Mr. Knight, Fanny, do you?"

"I . . . no. Yes. At least . . . there was a slight accident yesterday."

"An accident? When? Do you mean the coach?"

"No. Not exactly. But it is connected with the coach. I was walking through the woods on my way here and . . ." Fanny looked down, then up, then confessed the whole story. "I did not tell you before," she said in a rush at the end. "I thought you might have been . . . Well, I did not think . . . I was afraid you might be cross with me."

"Cross with you, Fanny?" Now there was amusement in Caroline's throaty voice. Also an audible note of curiosity. "What did you make of Mr. Edward Knight?"

"I did not like him. I found him most detestable." Her cheeks colored up as she said it. "I am sorry if he is your neighbor and a friend of Sir George's, but it is the truth."

"You are right. You should not say it," was the rather wry reply. Nevertheless, Caroline sounded somewhat pleased at Fanny's opinion. "Mr. Edward Knight is a very fine gentleman and he is, as you say, a great friend of Sir George's."

"But you do not like him either," said Fanny. "I can hear it in your voice."

"Then you hear a good deal too much." Caroline put down her work and rose from her chair. She was making an immense effort, Fanny saw, to be light-hearted and gay. "Come . . . we will walk as far as the shrubbery. It will work up an appetite for luncheon. We are to be a fine company tonight for dinner—did I tell you? I have invited Sir William and Lady Austen. And Mrs. Rushworth and her daughters . . . and Dr. Baillie. And then there will be the detestable Mr. Knight and his sister, so you had better put away your opinions about the gentleman, for a few hours at least . . ."

The air on the terrace was warm and still. The climbing roses filled the air with heavy fragrance.

Fanny thought, She dislikes him even more than I do. She's awfully good at hiding it, though.

That evening, Fanny felt apprehensive: Was she a little shabby? She tried to reassure herself that her yellow spotted looked like fine French muslin and that the gray slippers were not worn at the toes. She slipped downstairs and into the drawing room as unobtrusively as she could. There had been so few formal evenings since her father's death, she'd almost forgotten how to behave.

Sherry found her in the alcove by the door. "Fanny, what are you doing skulking there in the corner?"

"I'm not skulking." She felt scared that someone would hear him. "I would just much rather stay here than have to talk to people."

"I believe you would." He took her arm. "But you are being selfish. You do not consider others at all. Why should I have to talk to these fusty old dowagers when I can feast my eyes upon you?" He propelled her around the piano and toward the center of the room.

"There is not much to feast on." Fanny's voice was nervous. "You will probably go very hungry."

"Let me be the judge of that." His thumb moved up and down her arm. "So . . . tell me what you make of our company," his voice said in her ear. "And then we will compare notes. Don't you think Lady Austen looks a little like a camel?"

"Which one is Lady Austen?"

"Guess."

It wasn't difficult. Lady Austen had to be the haughty female in brown seated next to Caroline. She was peering around the room through her lorgnette, seemingly entirely self-contained.

"Which one's Sir William?" Sherry asked.

"Her husband?" Fanny looked around. "Is he near her?"

"As far away as he can get, I shouldn't wonder."

Fanny's eyes surveyed the room. "The little man with white hair."

"Right first time. He looks a little jaundiced tonight from a cross in love."

"In love?" Fanny said.

"Yes." Sherry looked confiding. "He is mad about some filly he found on a stay in Bath. He threatens a duel with some officer over her."

"I don't believe you!"

"Fanny . . . !" Bright blue eyes gazed back at her. "Are you calling me a liar?"

"Yes . . . That is, no . . ." Fanny didn't know whether to laugh or not. And her pulse was unsteady. Sheridan Crawley in teasing mood was rather too much at close quarters, in his plum velvet jacket with two rows of brass buttons. "It just doesn't seem very likely," she countered. "He is very old and quite fat."

"My dear Fanny, that don't stop the passions." His smile was playful.

"Well, it ought to," Fanny said.

"Quite right," he said, his eyes moving over her face. "Quite right. Pity it don't work that way."

I ought to stop him saying all these improper things, she thought. He's doing it on purpose to make me blush. He's a little wicked—but not too much so. He does make everything feel like fun. There's nothing much wrong with that.

"Fanny, you must come and be introduced. You must not let Sherry monopolize you." Caroline's throaty voice swept through the room. She seemed lit up tonight. She had done something to the bruise to make it not so noticeable, Fanny saw. Now she was swooping down on them like a slender, perfumed bird, making a point of chastising Sherry in front of the company. "There are others who want to talk to Fanny, you know, my dear Mr. Crawley." Fanny was drawn over to the fireplace. "Fanny, this is Dr. Baillie. He is quite an expert on ancient Greek temples, only do not start him off on it or he will be going on for hours . . ."

Edward Knight and his sister did not come in until dinner was served. He looked as grim as usual, Fanny thought. He settled his sister in a chair at the other end of the table. Miss Knight looked a pleasant sort of young woman with an abundance of soft, reddish hair. Everyone spoke to her.

Mr. Knight had been placed next to Caroline.

Fanny glanced along the table now and again. She felt sorry for Caroline. It was obvious that he was solidly ignoring all her attempts to amuse him. If he ever did that to me . . . Fanny thought. If he came as a guest to my house, then the least he could do was to attempt politeness, and not sit there like a dumb thing. Like a cold, dark slab of granite.

Some of her indignation must have showed. Sherry said, "Something is worrying you."

"I feel sorry for Caroline," Fanny admitted. "Mr. Knight seems impervious to her conversation."

"Caroline is used to it," came the sardonic reply. "Mr. Knight does not approve of her."

"Not approve of her?" Fanny put down her fork. "Why not?"

Sherry laughed. "Mr. Knight belongs to a particular sort of the landed families. They do not like newcomers marrying into them." He made a comic face. "Unless, of course, they come with money. Now if Sir George had found a nice little heiress with a fat fortune, they might have made an exception. But Caro hadn't a bean. So . . ." He spread his hands.

"But that is preposterous!" Fanny was furious. "He thinks our family inferior, just because our fortunes are diminished? What right has he . . . ? Mr. Knight is a fool and a humbug!"

"I would not say so to the gentleman's face, if I were you," Sherry murmured.

"Why not? Does Caroline have to simply swallow his arrogance?"

"She will not show him that she cares," Sherry said casually.

"Then I pity her, indeed!" Fanny said. "Why, he has no idea . . . ! Does he know, for instance, how . . ." She stopped. Perhaps Sherry didn't know about the scene upstairs last night. Perhaps he had taken Caroline's excuse about slipping on the step at face value. Fanny took a sip of wine. Maybe Caroline wouldn't want the truth told.

I don't wish to add to her problems, Fanny thought. There is her pride to consider, after all.

"Our family is as high as his," she finished rather tamely. "Anyway, why does he bother to come, if he does not approve of her?"

"He and Sir George are regular old cronies. Haven't you noticed?"

Back in the drawing room when dinner was over, Fanny's indignation was in no way abated, but she covered it with a smile and endured a whole half hour on the sofa with a Miss Petley, whose brother had been a nabob in India. She was rescued at last by Caroline, who wanted to introduce her to Lady Austen.

"So this young lady is your cousin?" Lady Austen eyed Fanny up and down. "You look very young. Sir William, do you not think so?"

"Fanny is nineteen, almost twenty," Caroline told her. "And we are great friends, are we not, Fanny? Fanny is a very comfortable sort of girl to have in the house, Lady Austen. Yesterday she walked all the way through Leigh Wood when the coach went into the ditch, and she was still in good humor."

"I heard about that," Lady Austen said. "Yesterday was hot. The cream all went sour. When I was a girl at Throxton, one of the grooms died of the heat. Dropped down like a stone in front of the buggy. They threw a bucket of water over him, but of course it was no use. Are we to play at cards? The evening is going on. Miss Knight is to be my partner. We understand each other."

Over cards, Fanny was able to study Louisa Knight more at her leisure. She did not in the least resemble her overbearing brother. In fact, Fanny even felt a degree of sympathy with her for having to live with the gentleman.

Miss Knight's sprigged cotton pleased Fanny. So did her voice and the sparkle in her brown eyes when she apologized to Lady Austen for having such a regular bad hand. Fanny was bound to smile, too, when Miss Knight told Dr. Baillie it was a mercy they played only for half crowns and not for guineas, or Edward would have to be responsible for all her debts.

I should like her, Fanny thought, if it were not for her brother. I'm surprised she allows him to behave as he does.

"Lady Austen will be angry if she loses," Sherry whispered from behind Fanny's chair. "She will tip up her cards in a minute and pretend it was an accident and call for some music. What are you thinking about, Fanny? Or shouldn't I ask? I don't much care —I shall ask anyway."

"They were dull thoughts," Fanny said. It was wrong of her to feel so pleased that the handsomest man in the room should be hanging over the back of her chair. Secretly, though, she was enormously flattered. "I was admiring the fringe on Miss Knight's shawl and wondering if Sir George ought to sit down before he falls down."

Sherry had a bad effect on her. He made her say things she would never say to anyone else.

Sir George's voice roared out almost at once. He said, "Dammit, Edward, I don't mean to get rid of the horse yet!"

A little hush. The conversation started again. Caroline did not seem to have noticed the interruption too much. I should notice, Fanny thought, if I were married to him. But Caroline carried on talking calmly to Mrs. Rushworth. There was strangely little contact between her and her husband sometimes. Tonight they were like separate poles in the same room.

"A ride is good for the constitution," Sir George went on. His face was very flushed. As he moved to the fireplace, he was unsteady in his gait. Edward Knight moved, too, following him across the room.

"You should give it a rest for a week or two. Go out in the chaise." Mr. Knight turned as he spoke and his eye fell on Fanny. Fanny sat there and looked back at him. He was strikingly dark, yes, but so arrogant. She let him go on staring at her and at Sherry and refused to be intimidated by it.

"Why, dammit?" Sir George exploded. Fanny wondered if she would ever get used to the sheer volume of his voice. "Why shouldn't I go on riding Horatio?"

"He is getting too strong for you," Edward Knight said.

"You mean you think I'm getting too weak to handle him?" Sir George refilled his glass. Whiskey spilled over the polished wood. "Say what you mean, young Edward. You needn't beat around the bush. But I don't need any of your advice!"

"Nevertheless . . . I hope you will take it." Edward Knight's voice had a strong, powerful insistence. He looked tough and harsh and very sharp.

To Fanny it sounded almost like a threat. I wonder if he has ever smiled in his life, she thought. She looked at the set of his back: strong and straight, but as stiff and set as a brick wall. Perhaps he has bruises all over it from his fall yesterday, she thought hopefully, and perhaps they are all very sore. That is what he deserves.

Sherry was right. Lady Austen lost at cards and called for music. The Misses Rushworth were earnest and determined on the piano, if not talented. When Caroline asked Fanny to fetch some cigars from the library for Sir William, she was pleased to escape for a moment.

She found the cigars in a box on the library table. The curtains were undrawn, the moon rising through them. The piano tinkled faintly in the distance, across the hall, but nothing disturbed the brilliant moonlight out in the garden.

Fanny did not know how long she stood there, two minutes or ten. There was such a peacefulness about the room, the grounds. Then she stiffened at a noise from the hall.

"Susan!" The tone was urgent, husky. Edward Knight's voice.

"Sir?"

"Here—quickly! Before anyone comes."

Fanny crept to the half-open door and stood mesmerized behind it.

"Sir—I was trying to get to you. They kept me busy in the kitchen." Susan Steadman's voice sounded breathless, almost scared.

"Things are worse, aren't they?" Edward Knight said. "I don't like it."

"Nor I, sir."

A door banged somewhere. The voices stopped, then spoke again in hoarse whispers. "The girl . . . ?" Edward Knight said. "Where does she fit in? What's she here for?"

"She was sent for," Susan told him. "That's all I know."

"The connection is real. She has nothing. Her father died penniless last July. I investigated the whole family after the marriage."

Fanny's heart pounded. Me. He's talking about me! About my father. And Susan Steadman's spying for him. Why? Why should she?

Susan's voice said, "She's nothing to worry about. Meek and mild. A bit birdwitted I think. I saw her yesterday. She don't say much."

"She's very young." Edward Knight's voice was ironic. "Gullible, do you think? Can be used in some way?"

"I don't know, sir." Another noise. "Somebody's coming!" A note of panic. "I'll have to go . . . they'll see us."

"See Bob when you go home on Sunday," he told her. "Don't forget."

A sudden emptiness. They'd gone. Fanny's legs took a long time to recover. She touched the door gently, pushed it slightly to make sure it was safe. Yes. No one there now. Only a servant passing through the green baize door at the end. She realized, I'm the only one who knows what's going on. He resents Caroline more than anyone could guess. Much more. He's planning to do her damage in some way. But what could he do?

He couldn't really cause trouble for her, could he? It seemed crazy. Not so crazy, though, when you knew he'd even been making inquiries about her background. Only someone completely determined —or obsessed—would do that.

The music had stopped. Fanny realized suddenly how long she had been gone from the drawing room. They'd be coming out looking for her if she wasn't careful. She slipped back into the company as quietly as possible and put the cigars on the small table next to Sir William. Everyone was moving toward the cordial and biscuits laid out in the corner.

Edward Knight was standing on his own by the piano. Fanny thought, Why don't I just go up and ask him what he thinks he's doing? He looked so intent, so impeccable in his starched white cravat and his dark coat. Yet she still had the feeling she might have dreamed the conversation she had overheard out there if she just blinked her eyes and started again.

"We are immensely lucky to have the Misses Rushworth to play for us, Mr. Knight," Caroline said, coming across him as he was just standing there. Being astonishingly nice to him, Fanny thought, considering his demeanor.

"Oh, immensely," came the reply like a shower of hailstones.

No doubt he was snubbing her again. Fanny listened to his insolence and knew she couldn't ignore it. She took a deep breath and her face went very shiny. "I think the music was delightful," she said pointedly. "I never heard such singing, even in London."

"London . . ." he said, putting on deliberation. "Then I see we have an expert in our midst." He paused for effect. "And which part of London would that be, Miss Milbanke?"

She wanted to say, Don't you know? You've been prying, haven't you? But she didn't quite dare. Her voice was defiant. "Wentworth Street," she said.

"Ah . . . Wentworth Street!" His manner showed that he despised the sound of it.

"Yes. It is on the very edge of Kensington. Near St. Luke's Church."

"Near St. Luke's Church?" He folded his arms. The smile, when it came, was horribly mocking. "Then I'm sure you must be right, Miss Milbanke. We are not qualified to quarrel with the opinions of Wentworth Street. Or St. Luke's Church . . . I would not dream of it."

He was detestable, Fanny fumed in her room that night, crossly pulling the pins out of her hair and remembering the relish with which he had taken apart her musical pretensions.

She remembered Sherry's words. "The landed families do not take kindly to penniless newcomers."

So who cares what they take to, she thought. I don't care a jot for his money or his pretensions. That man must think he's some kind of a god.

There was one aspect of it that bothered her, however. Should she warn Caroline that he was in league with Susan, before he made real trouble for her?

I suppose they think she married him for his money? Any amount of money wouldn't make up for what she has to put up with. No, I won't tell her about Susan yet. It will only upset her more. I'll wait a day or two and see how things go on.

There was a tap on the door, but it wasn't Céline. It was Susan Steadman. Fanny reacted quickly, saw her chance.

"Come in, Susan," she said. "It is Susan, isn't it? You can help me with these fastenings."

Close to, the girl had broad shoulders, a blank face, raw red hair. Fanny thought, So she thinks I'm meek and mild, does she? And birdwitted? She'll find out!

She gave an exaggerated yawn. "My, I'm tired!"

Then, with apparent artlessness, "How long have you worked here, Susan?"

"Since I was thirteen." The girl's voice was as blank as her face. "Ten years."

"You were here before Lady Caroline came, then?" Keep it casual.

"When I came here, Lady Anne was my mistress." Hard edge to the voice, hard green eyes.

"Lady Anne was Sir George's first wife? Is that right?" Things were beginning to emerge. Old loyalties that died hard. Reasons for Susan's antagonism. Caroline had taken her mistress's place. For some reason, Fanny felt inwardly relieved. If there was a reason, it removed some of the chill from a frightening situation. "And you were fond of her?"

"I loved her." The girl gave a wickedly sharp tug at one of the fastenings. "She would turn in her grave if she could see him now."

Edward Knight, too. The thought went through Fanny's brain: if he had been as fond of the first Lady Stanhope, then snobbery is perhaps not all of it. Stop making excuses for him. There are no excuses.

Fanny said, "Where did Sir George first meet my cousin? I never heard."

"In London," Susan said sourly. "His first and last trip there."

"Last? It may not be his last."

"It will be." A tug and a wrench.

"You don't know that."

"I do!" There was a harsh note in the girl's voice.

"Thank you, Susan. That will do." Fanny had had enough of her roughness and her sharp comments. There were other things she wanted to ask. If Sir George had always been such a heavy drinker, for instance. And why the girl stayed at Cranthorne if she resented Caroline so much.

Not too much. Not all at once. Better to pump some of the other servants instead. Take it very slowly.

No need to make a cake of oneself.

Chapter Four

It was probably because the house in Wentworth Street had been female dominated of late that Fanny always found herself so nervous in Sir George's company. His loud, eccentric behavior startled and frightened her. His bellow echoed through the rooms so, especially of a morning when his perusal of yesterday's morning post had finished and his riding boots were on and the Madeira for luncheon had not yet come up from the cellars to dull his spirits.

She came across him quite suddenly one morning in the drawing room. She was waiting for Caroline to come down, as they intended riding together. Fanny wore her charcoal-colored riding dress. She walked in without thinking, and by the time she had seen Sir George over by the writing desk, it was far too late to escape.

He had just knocked over a pile of papers, letters or something. The curse that followed made Fanny jump. She tried not to look frightened because she sensed it would only make him worse. "Always

cluttering up the damned place with this and that!"
he growled. "Wasn't like it in my father's time. Kept
enough space for a man to walk through, then . . ."
His breath came short; his face this morning was a
bluff, weatherbeaten red. He turned and looked at
Fanny. "So you're off riding, miss? Fine morning!
Fine morning! I'm off out myself. Down over Leigh
Wood to Parson's Meadow. Join me if you like," he
said bluffly. "Fine day . . . Fine ride!"

Fanny started picking up the papers. "I . . . I
have to wait for Lady Caroline. I rather think she
intends a less arduous ride."

But just at that moment the valet came in. "Lady
Caroline sends her apologies, miss. She has a bad
head. She will not be down this morning."

"Oh. Oh, dear." Fanny looked at Sir George, then
away. Sir George banged the desk shut and she
wondered uneasily if she was seeing the reaction of
guilt in him. There was always a slight feeling of
contained violence about Sir George.

"Better come with me, then?" He squinted at her
through thick eyebrows. It was an abrupt invitation,
but the gruffness did not sound unkind.

She said, "I . . . Perhaps Mr. Crawley would
want me to wait."

The valet said, "Mr. Crawley went off early, miss.
He has gone to visit a friend at Lowton."

"Oh. Oh, I see." She felt disappointed, but could
not show it.

There was no point in waiting, then. She felt
obliged to ride with Sir George. He had to be helped
into his saddle outside by Morton, the head groom.
"Fine day, Morton," he said vaguely. "Pretty good
morning!"

The groom agreed. His eyes warmed to the old
man. It was odd how the servants stayed so fond of

him, Fanny thought. She remembered how long most of them had been there, practically all their lives, and decided it was not perhaps so puzzling after all; one could learn to live with anything.

They rode two, three miles in a huge loop out around the park. Looking down across, Fanny saw the soft valley unfolding in front of them. Such a morning! Sir George was right. So blue, yet hazy. She kicked the gray into a canter. If he goes ahead like that, she thought, he will lose me.

She kept to the dry mud track, drawing rein as they went down across the wood. Leaves, greenly touching, looked alive in the sunlight, like shivering moths rustling and fluttering and about to take off.

Sir George was heading, still at a lumbering gallop, along the lowermost slope of the wood, some fifty yards in front. He was taking the hill at an angle and at a speed that Fanny would never dare attempt. Suddenly he turned and yelled something back at her, but she could not catch it and it was clear he wasn't going to slacken his pace. Fanny watched him, fascinated. He would never attempt to take that bank at the bottom, would he? Surely not . . . ? Was he mad?

There was a ditch at the bottom. He was heading straight for it. As he approached it at an angle, he let out a hoarse, exhilarated, "Halloo!" and the hand holding the whip came up and flailed at the air.

He can't. He won't make it! Fanny turned her head away. She didn't want to see the fall when it came.

No crash. No cry.

She turned her head back and looked. He was over the bank and galloping full pace across the meadow on the other side. After the first relief came a kind of irritation. When she caught him up, two minutes later, she let it all out.

"Was that sensible?" she demanded.

"Took your time, miss!" His face was mottled, but it wore a triumphant smile. "Came through the gap, did ye? Didn't fancy the jump?"

Fanny just looked at him. "That was an outrageous jump to take," she told him. "You might have been killed!"

"Made that leap almost every single day of my life, miss! Every day since I was twelve years old." The blue eyes twinkled. "Frighten you, did it?"

"Yes. It did!"

"Adds a bit of spice to the morning," Sir George said.

"I don't think I care for spice," Fanny told him, "thank you very much."

He tried to keep the ravaged grin off his face, to look merely casual. "Better not look next time," he said.

"I didn't look this time." She didn't want to smile back. She wondered why, out here, there was something almost endearing about him, and decided it was probably because Caroline wasn't around to remind her of his misdeeds. She certainly didn't want to let a pleasant ride on a beautiful morning make her forget what he was like after a few glasses of Madeira. Out here, though, one could see what he might have been when he was younger and more sociable. She analyzed this change in her reactions with faint surprise and felt somewhat confused.

Sir George was ready to go on. "We'll have to go around by the lake. And we'll call on Edward before we turn back."

"Oh, but . . ." Fanny panicked. She did not want to call on Edward Knight. It was the last thing in the world she wanted, but Sir George wasn't listening. He was already cantering away across the field and she had no choice but to follow him.

Leigh Park was a long, honey-colored house with tall chimneys and a long terrace covered with stone urns and flowering shrubs and pear trees trained up the walls.

Fanny was acutely aware of her windblown appearance, her hair half falling down from the gallop and the streak of dried mud on the toe of her boot. Louisa Knight looked pleased, however, when they were shown into her sitting room. She made a great fuss of welcoming them and sent for some tea.

"I am so glad you came," she said. "It is exactly what I was hoping for. Edward will be in in a minute. He has been to look at the timber, but I heard him come back. In the meantime, I shall consult you about our new Turkish carpet. Do you think it will do? Edward left the choice to me and I never can make up my mind."

The carpet was very pretty, Fanny thought, in shades of pink and red. All in all, it was a very pleasant, tranquil sort of room. Not so grand as Cranthorne by half, but perhaps more comfortable. If this was Miss Knight's taste, then Fanny approved. There was a small chess table in the corner, with candles behind it. A little refreshment table over by the door. Paneled white walls and china in the glazed cupboard and a sofa that was loosely rumpled, though newly covered in chintz.

Even Sir George appeared to scale down his volume to such a tranquil setting. As though he had tried all the chairs in the room and knew his favorite, he made for the one by the window and dropped into it with a satisfied grunt. He wiped his face with a large pocket handkerchief. "Fine day, Louisa! Pleasant ride, but devilish hot! Still, it's always restful in this house."

It was weeks later, letting her mind wander back over the sequence of events, that Fanny remembered the significance of that little phrase, "in this house." The emphasis he placed on one word passed unnoticed at the time. Sir George pushed the handkerchief back into his waistcoat and let his head drop back onto the cushion as if suddenly exhausted.

"Woke up with an infernal headache," he said. "Something I ate. Thought the fresh air would cure it. Can't tell if it did or not."

"You should rest more," Miss Knight responded. "At your age, you need rest."

"Damme, what good's rest?" he growled.

"It would do you good. You look tired. You will be knocked up, if you are not careful."

This seemed to amuse him, but his laugh was harsh. "I am knocked up already."

Then he knows what a state he is getting himself in, Fanny thought. Why does he do it?

A small pause. Louisa Knight sat looking at him, but she said no more. To Fanny she said, "Are you enjoying your visit to Cranthorne, Miss Milbanke?"

"Yes. Yes, it is delightful." Fanny glanced again at Sir George. He was sitting, head back, staring silently out of the window.

The door behind them opened and Edward Knight came in. The pale sitting room made him look darker, taller than ever. In one strong glance, he took in the scene. He said, "Sir George . . . Miss Milbanke . . ." His expression was unreadable. He came right over and stood by the sofa.

"Good morning." Fanny returned the greeting with what she hoped was cool nonchalance.

"You came across Parson's Meadow," he said. "I saw you from the coppice." He looked at Sir George. "You went over that bank again like a man possessed."

"Indeed, he did!" Fanny said. She caught Mr. Knight's glance and immediately looked away. "I told him how dangerous it was. I thought he would break his neck!"

"It wouldn't be any surprise." That was irony in Edward Knight's voice. But his eyes were on Fanny's face with an expression of—what? Puzzlement?

"Edward!" His sister was mildly disapproving.

"You told him the same thing yourself two weeks back."

"I told him to be careful."

"That is the same thing."

"It is not the same thing at all," Louisa Knight told him. "I choose my words more gently than you."

So she did stand up to him sometimes, Fanny thought. She wished Mr. Knight would stop staring at her, though. Why did he scrutinize her so? It made her hot and flustered.

They drank tea, and afterward Sir George insisted on playing a game of chess. The table was drawn up to the fireplace. Sir George sat on one side, Edward Knight on the other. It seemed a regular habit of theirs.

While the game progressed, the ladies talked. Fanny heard about Miss Knight's father, who had died five years or so back; about his sister, Lady Mellor, who sometimes came to stay and upset all the servants. About the latest ball that had been held at the Assembly Rooms at Lowton in April, after which everyone went down with some mysterious ailment; and about Edward's last visit to Bath and his opinion of the new pony they had just bought for the barouche.

Edward's opinions entered into Miss Knight's conversation a great deal. It was evident that in his sister's eyes, at least, the gentleman could do no wrong. Fanny could only think that sisters were often apt to be a tad biased and totally blind to their brothers' faults.

"Cornered!" Sir George roared at last. "I have you cornered!"

"Not . . . quite." Edward Knight leaned over the table and moved his bishop. His gaze, dark and intent, came up to meet Fanny's.

"Dammit, boy! Why didn't I see that?"

"You didn't look," Edward Knight said, still staring into Fanny's face. Fanny veered between wanting to look away and the urge to stare back. She could feel her colors begin to rise. She was baffled by his expression. She did not really care what he was thinking, but she wanted to know.

"This is a pretty kettle of fish!" Sir George grumbled. His red, puffy hand moved clumsily toward his cup, made it rattle, shoved it away. "Your brother's a ruffian, Louisa. I'll have a glass of brandy and water, if I may. It clears my head."

"Have some more tea," Edward Knight said. He signaled to his sister and the tea was quietly poured.

"Tea?" Sir George coughed and spoke derisively. "Milksop stuff! Can't stomach it. I'd rather have brandy."

"There's none left." Edward Knight set the china cup firmly before the older man. "Tea. It's your move."

For the first time Fanny found herself approving of Edward Knight's toughness. It needs somebody to be firm with him, she thought, looking at Sir George. That did not mean to say that she liked Mr. Knight any better, just that he had the necessary hardness of nature to deal with the man.

Sir George wasn't used to people denying him. He didn't like it at all. He didn't want the tea. And for one second, Fanny thought he was going to give the teacup an ill-natured swipe and knock it off the table. But the moment didn't come. He just flung Edward Knight the deepest of scowls, with no more commotion.

"You're a cool young puppy," he muttered gloomily. "Like your father before ye. Deuced if I'll come again, but we'll finish the game . . ."

It turned out to last another hour. Miss Knight showed Fanny the gardens below the terrace. "We shall have fine apricots if this weather goes on," she said as they came back up the steps and through the open windows. "Dawkins says they will need another week or two. Would you think it a great bore to come and dine one night, Miss Milbanke? I've enjoyed our morning."

"I wouldn't think it a bore at all," Fanny answered instinctively. She liked Louisa Knight, she decided. She was very easy, very straight, and Fanny found herself regretting that they had to leave so soon. The trouble was, one couldn't feel entirely pleasant and comfortable with Miss Knight's brother in the same room.

There was a movement from the other end. Fanny turned to look and saw that the game was over.

"Who won?" she asked.

"Sir George did," said Edward Knight.

"Had you today, boy!" Sir George was shambling around the room looking for his crop.

Louisa laughed. "Edward does not often lose."

I bet he doesn't, Fanny thought. I bet he hates to lose any kind of battle. He has that look about him.

"When are you coming to dine?" Louisa went on. "I shall send a note to Lady Caroline asking when it will be convenient."

Edward Knight said abruptly, "Don't forget we dine with the Austens on Friday."

"To be sure." Louisa smiled. "But we must arrange something very soon."

Fanny said, "I should very much like that. Goodbye, then. And thank you."

"It was our pleasure," said Louisa Knight.

Fanny glanced at Edward Knight. He looked, as always, very formal. What do I do? she thought. Do I shake hands with him and smile sweetly and thank him for his kind hospitality, even though he's been about as kind as a hedgehog? She compromised. She smiled sweetly, held out her hand, and said, "Goodbye, Mr. Knight. I am so sorry you lost at chess."

He looked at her for a few unnerving seconds, at her wide green eyes, her round cheeks flushed by the sun. He took her hand briefly, then he smiled. "Perhaps I'll win next time."

Fanny wondered if the smile was genuine. She decided not, because it had seemed so warm and dazzling, and he obviously wasn't a warm sort of man. Its effect on her had, for a moment, been quite powerful, but it only made her more determined to keep up her guard.

I won't change my mind about him. That's probably what he wants. He needn't think I'm so gullible, Fanny thought. The word still stung. There was still Caroline to consider.

* * *

When they got back to Cranthorne, there was a
new arrival: Mr. Clarence Stanhope. His baggage
was all over the hall and the servants were scuttling.

It was from this point on, Fanny decided later,
that the whole atmosphere of the place changed.
Clarence's presence altered a house, and not for the
better. He perverted people, brought out all their little faults, just as he had seemed to encourage her
mamma's vanity. It was his forte.

He came out of the morning room as Fanny passed
in through the hall—exactly as if he had been lying
in wait for her. "Why, it's dear little Fanny!" he said
in that obnoxious way of his. "You have had a long
ride!"

"I . . . I didn't know you were coming," she
blurted out. Why did he always make her feel like a
silly chit?

He stood there grinning. "Pleasant surprise,
then?" Laughing at me for some reason, Fanny
thought. He sounded freer here. He knew she was
wary of him, and without Mrs. Milbanke around to
impress, he could indulge himself making Fanny
squirm. "And how was the ride?" he asked.

"It was very enjoyable."

"You've been gone three hours, the servants said."

"I . . . we stopped at Leigh Park."

"Leigh Park?"

A change of expression, to one even less pleasant.

"Yes. We rested and took tea. Sir George played at
chess. He won."

"Won, did he?" That horrid laugh. Open mockery, more sarcasm. "D'you hear that, Caroline?
George won at chess."

Caroline came out through the morning room
door. Her bad head must have gone. She looked all

right, at any rate. Perhaps a little flushed, fevered up
in some way. Her eyes did seem glassy, her manner
strained. Fanny thought Clarence had probably flustered her, too.

"So you stopped at Leigh Park?" she said to
Fanny. Bright, but forced. She was cross. Or worried. Or both.

"Yes. I hope you don't mind. Sir George insisted."

"No matter." Caroline gave a light laugh. "As you
see, we have another guest. Clarence is come to stay.
It was quite unexpected. He hired a hackney coach
to drive down from Oxford. But then, Clarence is
like that . . ."

Is she scared of him, too? Fanny wondered. She
seems so nervous. Overstrung this morning.

The door from the stable room slammed open. Sir
George leaned heavily against the door frame and
glowered at his brother. In Wentworth Street, Fanny
had gotten the impression that all was sweetness
and light between Clarence and Sir George. It was
obvious this was far from the case.

"So you've turned up again, have you? Like the
damned bad penny?" Sir George said viciously.
"Come to see if I can do you another hundred or
two? Eh?" In his tone there was real loathing. "So
who's dunning you this time? Had to get out of
town quick, did you?"

Clarence went on grinning. "What a welcome
. . . brother, dear! Is that the very best you can
do?"

"How much is it going to cost me? Eh? Eh?" Sir
George's face grew redder and redder. "How much?
That's what I want to know."

"Why, George—are you offering to settle a few of
my debts?" Clarence said.

His brother sounded apoplectic. "I told you the

last time . . . it's the end! No more! Colman, bring
the brandy! I'll be in the library." The older man
pushed past them all, found the library door, and
slammed it tight shut against him.

Fanny looked at Clarence's grinning face and for
the first time felt a real dart of sympathy for Sir
George. Clarence had positively enjoyed stirring him
up. Clarence would drive anyone to drink. Was that
part of the reason for Sir George's condition? The
hall was left in a shadowy undertow of malice. How
did Caroline stand it?

Clarence said to Caroline, "You'd better tell him
about the girl."

Caroline said, "The girl. Susan. Yes. Yes . . . I
will do it now."

Fanny said, "What about Susan?"

Caroline said hurriedly, "One of my rings was
missing this morning. Céline had her suspicions. She
went off to look. It was found hidden in Susan
Steadman's room. I have sent her off. Sir George will
have to listen to me now. There can be no arguments
. . . the girl is a thief."

Chapter Five

Clarence Stanhope knew how to stir muddy waters. All the sediment of silent conflicts and petty jealousies that lie just under the surface of any household. It wasn't always what he said. Sometimes his mere presence in a room was enough. Without doing a great deal himself, he edged others toward foolish words and actions. He was a catalyst. That was the opinion formed by Fanny soon after his arrival. She disliked him more than ever.

Quickly, the house changed. People changed. Doors slammed, voices were raised, the servants looked harassed. Sir George became even more aggressive. Even Caroline grew sharper—her tongue seemed to develop a cutting edge.

Breakfast was always a coming-and-going sort of a meal. If Clarence had gone out early to the stables or somewhere, it was a blessedly quiet time. Luncheon, too, was light. But at five every evening, there was no escape. One was pinned down for almost two hours in the company of Clarence Stanhope, and wine usually added to his queer, ogling gaze. Fanny would swear that he amused himself at her expense simply because he knew she was the one most vulnerable to his double entendres. And there was nothing she could do about him at all.

"So, you're enjoying your stay in the country, Miss Milbanke?" he began one night when the neck of venison had been placed on the mahogany. "My dear Caroline, you are to be congratulated! Your cousin has an uncommon fine complexion with all this air. I like a pretty complexion. The ladies in Park Lane would be envious, would they not?"

"Clarence, don't tease so." Caroline laughed.

"Fanny is blushing. You have made her uncomfortable."

"Is that so?" He was smirking over the table at her. He hadn't smirked so much at Wentworth Street, Fanny thought. There he had kept himself in check for the sake of appearances. "You ain't blushing, Fanny, are you? My dear Caroline, you would not blush at such a compliment, would you? It would take more than that to make you blush."

"I am not nineteen," Caroline told him. "I am a married woman of twenty-nine and I do not succumb so easily to the wiles of the tongue."

Clarence burst into a horselaugh. "A married woman, ma'am? Why, in town they are the easiest . . . they are the first to fall! They are cleverer at hiding things," he explained. "That is all. That's what it comes down to, eh, miss?"

"I think it most unkind of you to say so," said Caroline. But as she spoke, Fanny could see she was not so unaffected by Clarence's tasteless remarks as she made out. A slight flush stained the edge of her cheekbones. Her fingers touched at the lace on her shoulders. She was not so perfectly easy after all, yet she rallied with a brilliant smile. "You should take a wife of your own, my dear Clarence, and then you might learn to think differently."

"A wife?" Clarence clasped a plump hand to his forehead. "Pray, what sport is there in that, ma'am?" A short pause. He looked at Fanny. "Could you find sport in marriage, Miss Milbanke?" he inquired. "Well, you'll find out one day, no doubt . . ." And then he started laughing again.

Caroline came up to Fanny's room to soothe things over, after that particular episode. She knew Fanny was not fond of the gentleman, she said. Anyone could see that. But she must not mind Mr.

Clarence Stanhope's little jokes. He was not so bad as he seemed—he had merits that should be taken into account. Clarence was . . . had been . . . feckless. No one could deny that, but there had been occasions when he was extremely kind to her. Occasions when . . . when Clarence might be needed . . . She could not say more . . .

"What occasions?" Fanny said. She saw Caroline's face and almost wished she hadn't asked. "Caroline, why did you marry him? Sir George?" she said, all in a rush. "He is an old man. He drinks all the time . . ."

"My dear, I wish you wouldn't . . ."

"I try not to be curious. But it will be easier if I know."

A small silence. Caroline sat looking down at the floor. Then she seemed to come to a decision. She sighed. "George came to London after his first wife died. Clarence brought him up to town. He was very lonely. I met them both at one of Kitty Kinnaird's routs."

"Was that when you lived in Piccadilly?" Fanny asked.

"Piccadilly?" Caroline turned her head. "No. No . . . no. We lived in Lockyer Street at the time . . . though we had moved around a great deal. Who told you I lived in Piccadilly?"

"Céline."

"Ah, Céline!" Caroline said. "I expect you misunderstood. Her English is so peculiar sometimes. Sometimes I cannot collect half what she says when she goes on so fast." She laughed. "As I was saying, I met George and Clarence at this rout one evening. Clarence—well, you know Clarence—he came right up to me and got Kitty to introduce us and then after that, he introduced me to George." She looked

almost wistful. "You could tell George was lonely.
He was all out of things. But he was quite sweet
. . . excellent ton. He wasn't half so bad then as he
is now. We got on quite well . . . at that time. I did
not know how things were going to turn out, and
when he begged me to marry him . . ." Caroline
looked down at her hands. "I know you will never
understand. The age difference . . . it was there,
but he acted so charmingly." She looked straight at
Fanny. "There is another element which I suppose
you should know. My father wanted it, too. He was
very domineering, and he was deeply in debt. He
put pressures on me, extreme pressures. And Sir
George promised to set things all straight for him. I
am not proud of that, Fanny. It should not have
been of account, but it did, in the end, make me give
in. I . . . I thought it for the best . . . though I do
not expect you to see it . . ."

There was a pause, a silence. Fanny remembered
the pressures her own mother had put on her to
come to Cranthorne, keeping on and on until she
had got what she wanted. She felt such a dart of
sympathy, she did not know how to express it.

She took Caroline's hand. "It's all right. I do understand."

"My dear Fanny . . ." Words seemed to fail her
for a minute. "I have suffered—I admit it. But sometimes, things just have to be endured. There is no
other way." She looked taut, but under control.
"And Clarence, though a little . . . free . . . now
and again, can be a help in difficult moments. Do
you understand?"

"I think so," Fanny said with some difficulty.

"Then you will come downstairs again? Not sit up
here on your own?"

"I'll come down. It was wrong of me to rush off and leave you."

"You are a comfort to me, Fanny." Caroline kissed her softly on the cheek.

It was not only Fanny, though, who suffered from Clarence's foul tongue. Poor Sherry took the brunt of it, too, she noticed. He was too good-natured to say so, but she sensed that there were reasons for him to spend more and more time watching her sketch in the garden or accompanying her on morning walks. Clarence drove him out. Clarence's mocking tongue, with all its nasty innuendos, was often too much even for Sherry.

Fanny now and then allowed herself to believe that Sherry was nurturing a romantic attachment to her. She had thought about it again and again and had decided that Sherry's blue gaze was fixed on her more often than strictly necessary. There was no need at all for him to be so impetuous as to pass the opinion that the green ribbon she sometimes wore on her bonnet was exactly the same color as her eyes. Or to let his hand settle on hers in front of the servants when he offered to carry her books and paints down to the summerhouse for her.

In the clear light of morning, she ridiculed the notion as a foolish fancy. She was always glad to see him, however. She liked him instinctively. She did not have to watch what she said to him as closely as when she talked to others; she felt they understood one another and had a great deal in common. Only she wished he would stand up more to Clarence's baiting.

"My dear Sheridan," Clarence said one morning, coming across the two of them in the garden together. "What a romantic pastoral! The young lover

seated on a rustic bench beside his fair maiden . . .
All we need to complete the scene is a lute. Do you
play the lute, Miss Milbanke? No? Then we must
leave it to your swain." He did not wait for her reply. He was studying her sketchbook. "A skillful
hand!" he went on. "Don't you think so, Mr. Crawley? Makes the old house look quite imposing! My
dear fellow, you are such a dandy this morning!
With that new cravat . . ." His hand whipped out
to touch it. "And the new style of curls! How could
the ladies be expected not to fall? Eh . . . ? Eh?"

Sherry did not reply. He went on watching Fanny
sketch as if Clarence was totally invisible. "It is a
charming sketch," he said at last. "I could not do
half so well."

"Ah, but you have other talents." Clarence
mocked slyly with that dissolute grin. A pudgy hand
was laid on Sherry's shoulder. "Mr. Crawley dances,
ma'am, like a butterfly. The first fling of music . . .
and off he goes! And he's the wit of the coffeehouse
and handles a pistol like . . . like Mars! Ain't that
right, dear boy?" The hand flipped again at the cravat. Clarence was enjoying himself. "The ladies all
adore him! I wonder he ain't found himself some
nice little heiress by now. Yes . . . indeed! Some
nice little, pretty little golden dolly with ten thousand a year, to keep him up in all his delicate luxu-
ries . . ."

Sherry was stung by that. She knew he was. She
saw his hand clench and unclench as if he would
have liked to use it. But all he said was, "That window is not quite right, Fanny. It is heavier than the
rest."

"I think you are right." Fanny put down the pen-
cil with an extra bright smile. "But I've decided that

is enough for this morning. I shall put it right tomorrow—come to it with a fresh eye."

"I expect she'll give it to you as a souvenir if you play your cards right," Clarence said to Sherry. "Think you'd like to keep it? Why, you're warm, man! Sweating . . . Sun too hot for you? Here . . ." He slipped a handkerchief out of his pocket, pretended to wipe Sherry's brow. "You know what it is—too many dandy clothes! Still, play your cards right and she may give you the little souvenir . . . Eh?" And he went off, laughing all the way to the house.

Fanny said, "That man is a monster! Why didn't you answer him back?"

At first he didn't seem to hear her. He was watching Clarence cross the drive. Fanny couldn't read his expression, but whatever it was, it cleared at last. He said, "What?"

"Why didn't you answer him back? I should like to."

"It's not worth it," he said. "Shall we walk to the lake?"

"The lake?"

"Yes. It will be cooler there." His smile was there again. It was all right. He took her arm. "Leave your painting things on the bench. We'll come back for them later."

Sherry was so easygoing. If he couldn't avoid Clarence's jibes, he would simply ride them out. Fanny supposed that was how he came to be dragged down to the alehouse in the village one night with Clarence. There was a room up above that was used for gambling—the kind of place that Clarence naturally made his way to. Fanny learned about the episode when she heard the servants talking. She walked in through the back hall one morning while they were polishing the gentlemen's cloakroom adjoining the conservatory. Betty, the upstairs maid, had her back to the open door and was saying, "Mr. Colman says they were gambling all night. And Farmer Mugford was on his way back from market with a couple of hundred in his pocket from two good riding horses he'd sold, and a fat lot of good it done him, because he lost most of it to Mr. Clarence."

"Up to his old tricks," Mrs. Hurst's voice said. Mrs. Hurst was the housekeeper, and she was hidden from sight somewhere inside the room.

There was a longish pause before Betty's voice started again. "And then he went and lost twenty guineas to that new gamekeeper of ours, Deacon. And Mr. Clarence accused Deacon of cheating and there was a devil of a row kicked up at about four in the morning—a real old brawl starting—only Mr. Sheridan got him out of it and practically had to carry him out to his horse and force him to come home."

Sherry? Fanny could hardly believe it. Sherry . . . down at the alehouse with Clarence in some sort of row? It took five or six seconds for it to sink in. It must be some mistake.

"Won't be the first time they've had to bring him home," Mrs. Hurst said.

Fanny felt blank for the rest of the day. But even supposing it was true, she thought, she could imagine how it had happened. She remembered how easygoing Sherry was, letting Clarence get away with the most disobliging behavior rather than make a fuss. He would have been forced down there by some means. If Clarence set his mind to a thing, one didn't stand a chance.

The following day, Fanny came across Mrs. Hurst sitting mending the curtain in the dining room, and under pretense of making light conversation, Fanny asked if Sir George and his brother had been close as children.

"When they were very young, perhaps," Mrs. Hurst said. She took up the fringe of the drape and put a stitch into it. "But Mr. Clarence was always leading them both into trouble. He was the younger by five years, but very precocious." Mrs. Hurst rolled her eyes. "And then there were all the girls . . . Chased them in droves, Mr. Clarence did. And they all went for him. But Mr. George," she said, "bore no resentment. Always an obliging child . . . an obliging young man, and always good-natured."

Fanny could scarcely imagine Sir George young and good-natured, but then the brandy, she supposed, generally disposed of the latter to a great extent. And he hadn't been so bad at Leigh Park the past week. Compared with Clarence, she was compelled to admit that he seemed an angel. Sir George might drink, but he wasn't capable of mischief. That was the difference between him and Clarence.

There was something else that she wanted to ask. Something seemed to have been hushed up; no one ever said anything about it. "Mrs. Hurst, what happened to Susan?" she said. "Susan Steadman? I heard she had been dismissed—nothing else."

"Susan?" Mrs. Hurst's face changed. "She's gone to Leigh Park."

"To work?"

"Yes. To work." Mrs. Hurst sewed on.

"But if she was a thief . . . ," Fanny said hastily, "aren't they worried about taking her in?"

"It seems not." Mrs. Hurst's face didn't give anything away.

"But it seems to me . . ." Fanny frowned. "Was there any doubt she had taken the ring? Anyone else who might have stolen it?"

Mrs. Hurst simply said, "It was found in her room."

"Caroline said she would far rather not have had to turn her out. But what else could she do?" Fanny felt oddly disconcerted that Susan had gone to Leigh Park.

A pause; a silence. Mrs. Hurst's attention seemed all to be fixed on her work. Her mouth was pursed. Was she holding something back?

"Do you think she stole the ring, Mrs. Hurst?"

The shrewd eyes above a bolster of a bosom appraised Fanny. The mouth pursed again. "She's a strange girl," she said. "One on her own. Nobody ever knew what she was thinking." It was no answer.

Fanny had one last attempt. "What do they say in the village?" she asked. "It's a small place. It must have been difficult for her."

"The Steadmans are well respected." Mrs. Hurst gave a small nod as she snapped off the thread. "Well respected," she added as an afterthought. She gave the heavy curtain a last inspection and picked up her scissors. Fanny heard her last comment on the subject as she bustled out of the room. "Truth will out in the long run. Isn't that what they say? Oh, yes, it will out. I've no doubt about that . . ."

Fanny was left sitting there alone.

Caroline sat with her work at the little table in her sitting room the next morning. Fanny fiddled with a knot in her cotton and fumed inwardly because she could not get it out. Caroline never got her work into a mess. She took the most abundant pains with her stitches and examined them meticulously in the light every chance that she got. Beside her, Fanny always felt clumsy-fingered and stupid and wished she could present a more elegant figure. They both looked up when there was the sound of voices out in the hall. After a moment, Clarence came in.

"The trunk that was lost has arrived," he announced. "There are presents for the ladies."

"Presents?" Caroline said. "Clarence, what are you thinking of?"

Clarence dispensed parcels with imperious ease. "The newest things from Pall Mall," he announced. "That'll be something for you to flaunt yourself around the country in . . . eh, miss?"

The first parcel Caroline rummaged into revealed a froth of white silk—a thin, hazy gauze of it. She gave a little shriek. "Clarence! You have surely gone mad?" She held the silk all around her and danced over to the window. For a moment, she seemed to have forgotten anyone else was there. Her eyes were sparkling; she looked like a slim, rapt child. "This will outdo Miss Knight's frumpy dyed stuff, will it not? And that dreadful old brown holland she wears when she calls . . . !"

Fanny was startled not so much by the words as by the tone that she uttered them in, and as if suddenly sensing the surprise, Caroline said, "That is very wrong of me." She picked up another parcel and dropped it in Fanny's lap. "But one must be silly sometimes. It is a relief . . ." She was composed again. "Go on, then! Open yours, Fanny, and then you can be silly, too, and I shall not feel so bad. I would guess it is a bonnet."

She was right. Fanny's present was a delectable straw bonnet trimmed with a wide yellow ribbon and miniature rosebuds. She looked embarrassed and a little prim.

Caroline said, "Well—put it on."

"Later. I'll try it later."

"Fanny, it is very pretty. Don't you want to try it on?" Caroline said.

"She would put it on if Mr. Crawley asked," Clarence drawled. "Shall I fetch him?"

"Clarence, behave yourself!" Caroline frowned at him and said, "She is shy. Run along and try it on in your room, then, and see if it will suit."

The bonnet did suit. It framed her pointed face and threw a delicate, speckled shade over her eyes. Fanny wished it had been given to her by someone else, and then she could have worn it and enjoyed it without any credit going to the odious Clarence. She untied the ribbons and pulled it off.

Momentarily, she wondered where Sherry was. She wished he would suddenly walk in. They always had such natural conversations. Where did he go on his long morning rides? Why wasn't he around this morning when she wanted him? She supposed she had better go down or else Caroline would come looking for her.

She drifted as far as the top of the stairs. The hall was immense, the cool black-and-white marble floor stretching back behind the staircase for what seemed like miles. The servants were all at the back of the house preparing luncheon. That faint snoring sound coming from the library was Sir George. Clarence had riled him at breakfast, and presumably he had already taken to his comfort. Fanny didn't actually see the door open from Caroline's sitting room, but Caroline's voice, quiet and cutting, spoke from the doorway.

"You must be more circumspect! I wonder you don't see all the damage you might do. It will be much the best if you go straight back to London. I will send for you when you are needed. It is what we arranged."

Clarence said, "I'm in your way, am I?"

"You know what you are . . . You cannot keep out of trouble. Fanny dislikes you."

"Dear little Fanny . . . !" Nasty man! Nasty false voice.

"Yes . . . dear Fanny. We need Fanny. And that brawl in the alehouse . . . it was stupid! Needless."

"It put me into funds," Clarence said.

"Clarence, you are a fool!" Who would have thought Caroline could find that biting edge to her voice?

"Thank you, my dear." Clarence could be cold, too. "A fool who was good enough to introduce you to my brother. And who, if you will excuse my saying so, may yet—"

"M'lady?" It was Colman coming out from the baize-covered door to interrupt.

"Yes, Colman. What is it?" She spoke to him sweetly, calmly. Fanny saw only the tiniest movement of her hands, her eyes.

"The crystal, m'lady, that was broken yesterday. Mrs. Hurst said you would choose what was to replace it."

"I will be there in a minute . . ."

When Fanny came down, all seemed back to normal. Caroline was extra sweet to her, if anything. "How was the bonnet?" she inquired gaily.

"The ribbons exactly match my yellow."

"He chose well, then?"

"Yes. He chose well."

"So Clarence is good for something?" Caroline made a joke of it.

Fanny looked at the beautiful, agile face and thought of an actress she had once seen at Drury Lane. The same easy mobility of expression, the power to size up an audience's emotions and react accordingly. Probably, if one was in Caroline's position, one would need to develop all the skills of camouflage.

Clarence, she thought. I hope he does go. I wish he would. He spoils everything. Changes everything. I don't feel half so easy with Caroline as I used to and it's all his fault.

An invitation duly came for them to dine at Leigh Park and a date was fixed upon. Sir George was not to accompany them as it turned out. The evening before, he had met with a slight accident. In coming down the dim part of the stairs to see where Betty was with his jug of water and his magnesia—he had suffered of late, with a certain weakness of the stomach—his foot caught in a loose corner of the carpet and down he went like a weight of bricks. Then he lay shouting weakly for help for a good ten minutes before anyone heard him, and had to be lifted back up to his bed, weakened and half dazed.

"His movements of late have been so . . . erratic." Caroline looked thoroughly ruffled and bothered by the incident. She came especially to Fanny's room to pour it all out. "He will be laid up two days or so, Dr. Baillie says. Of course, he is not young. He will not moderate his . . . his life."

By that, Fanny knew she meant his drinking habits. "Can't you . . . can't anyone make him listen?" she asked.

"You have seen him, Fanny. You can see how it

is." Caroline shrugged, then shook her head helplessly. "We have all tried."

"Can't you try harder? Forbid him to drink?" She thought of Edward Knight's toughness that day at Leigh Park.

"You don't know . . ." Caroline walked up and down. "We have tried hiding it once or twice . . . I have told the servants."

"But at dinner . . ." Fanny thought how loaded the table was with wine and spirits every night.

"At dinner it is difficult," Caroline said. "When there are guests . . . we cannot keep him away from it. Or put it away. It cannot be done . . . altogether."

Privately, Fanny thought there were a great many ways it could be done, but it was not her place to say so. Not here. Not now, while Caroline was so distressed. "At least while he is laid up, it will be easier," she said.

"If they obey my orders," Caroline said.

"They?"

"The servants."

"But I'm sure . . . I mean, they must . . . surely?" Fanny was surprised.

Caroline said, "Most of them. Some are more sly. Sir George gets around them. They do it for the best of reasons, I suppose . . . out of misguided loyalty. Like that girl, Susan."

"Susan Steadman?" Fanny said curiously. "Did she not do as she was told?"

"Never! Unless it was Sir George doing the telling." Caroline found a painful smile. "That was why I was glad, in one way, to be able to get rid of her. She would do anything he asked. She was helping to kill him."

"Kill him?"

"Yes, Fanny. That is what I am afraid it will come to." Caroline's tautness finally turned into tears. "This accident . . . There have been others. I do not know where it will end. I can't say it's a perfect marriage—indeed, sometimes I think it no marriage at all—but I get so frightened." Then with an uncharacteristically frenetic gesture, she clutched at Fanny's arm. "You will stay with me, won't you? I can talk to you. Tell you things I could never tell to anyone else."

"Of course I'll stay." Fanny was touched. Curiously, she said, "Did you know Susan Steadman is now at Leigh Park?"

"Oh, yes. I knew." Caroline's face was bitter. "It was to be expected. They would take in anybody if they thought it would thwart me."

"I am sure it is not like that. Not on Miss Knight's part, at least," Fanny said. "She is quite genuine, I think."

"It is how she wants to seem." Caroline thrust Fanny's offer of a dry handkerchief away and stood up as if to go. "Sir George would not allow the magistrate to be called in about the stolen ring. Did you know that? Because the Steadmans have lived in the village forever and ever, they can do no wrong. Oh, yes—they all stick together well enough if they are born and bred into the place. It is only newcomers like us whose word is not to be believed." She brushed away all Fanny's attempts at comfort and slammed out of the room.

Chapter Six

Clarence was not to be among the party to dine at Leigh Park either. He returned suddenly to London that same morning. Perhaps this was the reason for the wild bout of gaiety that assailed Fanny at ten minutes to four that afternoon, as she and Sherry set off to walk across Leigh Wood. They were to dine at five. Caroline was to ride to Leigh Park in the carriage, but she had encouraged Sherry and Fanny to walk.

She did not intend to join them, she said. She knew they would enjoy the walk more without having an old married lady limping along in the rear. Fanny rather thought it a deliberate ruse to give her and Sherry more time on their own.

She found the idea of a tête-à-tête with Sherry somewhat disturbing. She had a pretty good idea that he was pleased to be alone with her, however. As they set off from the flower gardens of Cranthorne up over the low, rolling slopes of the park, Fanny sensed that he, too, felt relief at leaving Cranthorne. And Clarence . . .

The faint haze of pearl gray clouds may have been gathering over behind the village in the distance, but Fanny didn't see them. She glanced at Sherry now and again, and tried to give sensible answers to his discourse about the previous day's trip to Langham to see his friend, Brandon, but when the conversation dropped a little at the top of the hill, she decided to ease her unaccountable flutteriness by some questions of her own.

"I believe Caroline said your family is in Ireland?" she said. "That is a long way from here. When was the last time you were home?"

"It is quite some months," Sherry said.

"Then your family must miss you? You are the second son, I believe? Caroline said so." She glanced across at him. "You see, we have had some interesting gossips."

Sherry smiled, but she could see he looked a little uncomfortable. "Oh, it was nothing to your discredit," she told him teasingly. "Everything she said about you was excellent. She admires you a great deal. You were to enter the dragoons, she said, but circumstances forbade it. Now you are to decide between the law and the church. Am I right?"

"You are right." Sherry looked at her as if she might bite him. He did not seem to expect her to know quite so much. "I am still making up my mind. It has not all been straightforward. My father's estate was a large one, but there have been . . . difficulties." He told the story quickly and not altogether happily. "When my father died, my brother inherited the larger part. When we were younger, we were friends. Absolute friends. But as we grew older, he seemed to change. He took up gambling. In short, when he had charge of my father's funds, he began to run through the estate like water. He is not interested in my prospects. I cannot rely on him for support. Therefore we are . . . not close. I should not be welcome at what was once my home."

"But how can that be?" Fanny was shocked. "Can you not go to the law? Make him provide for you?"

"You don't know my brother, Fanny. He is not to be trusted. I am ashamed to say it, but it is the truth. There were some unguarded phrases in my father's will that could be interpreted by clever lawyers just as they wish."

"Indeed?" They were walking slowly. Fanny

stopped and looked up at him. The wind stirred her hair. "But it's not fair at all. It should not be allowed."

Sherry said, "It's the way things are. I'm resigned to it. At first I was bitter . . . but now the only thing I care about is my own reputation. In providing a case for his lawyers and filching half my inheritance for his own gains, my brother has called my integrity into question. I will fight for that, but nothing else. The money is a mere trifle . . ."

Fanny said, "You still should not allow it. Indeed, you should not!"

Sherry smiled a crooked smile and abandoned the subject abruptly. "How that bonnet sets off your face," he said softly. He waited a minute and then took hold of one of the ribbons. "I've never seen you look so pretty."

It was the bonnet Clarence had given her. After he had left Cranthorne, she had had a struggle between her conscience and her vanity, and vanity had won. The compliment made her color up. She was a jumble of shyness and exhilaration. "It is such a relief that Clarence is gone," she said. "I hate having him hanging around."

"Clarence?" He answered her almost absently. In the soft light of late afternoon, his chestnut curls framed the handsome face. He didn't want to think about Clarence either. "He is a nuisance sometimes."

"He's more than that. He's vile!" Fanny's face showed her feelings. "He treats you so badly . . . Why do you let him?"

"He's Sir George's brother." He still had hold of the ribbons. He was regarding her slowly with the soft glimmer of a smile. "Don't let's talk about Clar-

ence. Fanny . . . what if we took it into our heads
to stay here? What if we missed that dull dinner?"

"I . . . I do not think it would please them." Fanny's heart was hammering madly. She had gone very
pink.

"It would suit me," he returned lazily. One hand
moved down, almost touched the pulse in her
throat. He sighed. "But I suppose you are
right . . ." Then, "We shall just have to walk as
slow as we can. Of course," he added as if it had
been an afterthought, "we could get lost. Getting
lost might be rather fun."

"I don't think we ought to get lost either." A
glance up into his eyes. Oh, dear . . . that was a
mistake. She felt her legs go.

"Don't you?" He was smiling.

"No. No, I don't . . ."

He was still smiling when he bent his head and
kissed her. And when the kiss slowly ended, he
whispered, "Don't look so startled. Has nobody ever
wanted to kiss you before?"

"No. That is . . . yes." She made a small hopeless movement with her hands and head. "How
should I know? It's hardly the kind of thing you can
ask, is it?"

"Isn't it?" He was still teasing. Then he kissed her
again and went on kissing her until she was collapsed into his shoulder. "You can ask me," he said.
"I wouldn't mind. I've been wanting to kiss you for
weeks . . ."

They walked the rest of the way so slowly that
the whole party was assembled in the drawing room
at Leigh Park as they crossed the lawns to the house.
Even Caroline's voice was sharp as they were
ushered into the room by the maid.

"We quite thought you were lost!" she said. She was smiling, but there was something about her expression, the gleam of her eyes, that told Fanny she was unaccountably annoyed.

Fanny crossed the room, aware that all eyes were on her. "It was such a delightful afternoon," she said, "we quite forgot the time." Her cheeks were flushed, her eyes shining. "I'm so sorry, Miss Knight. You must blame me. It was my fault. I wanted to see the boathouse by the lake."

"It does not matter in the least," Miss Knight told her. "The beeches are lovely at this time of the year. I was admiring them myself only yesterday. And you are not late. Bates will be another ten minutes before he calls us."

During dinner, Fanny was animated. Guilty at having offended Caroline by allowing her to be stranded without moral support in the enemy's camp, she set out to be as delightful company as she could, thus, hopefully, putting Caroline back into her usual good humor.

She coaxed Dr. Baillie into telling her about his Grecian temples, had a long discussion with Louisa Knight about the poems of Mr. Cowper, told Mrs. Rushworth—who was squeezed into lavender satin and sweating profusely—what lovely stitchwork there was on her gown and what an elegant needlewoman Caroline was; and she even tossed a small smile in Edward Knight's direction now and again, though she had not the temerity to address him directly.

Mr. Knight was seated opposite her in the square, paneled dining parlor and Fanny could not help noticing, while the general conversation was going to and fro, how frequently his dark gaze was fixed on her. He scarcely spoke a dozen words to her, but she still found herself puzzling about his looks and his behavior.

The looks were not so arrogant as before, but neither were they completely amiable. She fancied there was again some kind of special question in them, but she could not imagine why he was observing her so closely. Undoubtedly, the effect of them disturbed her. That surprised her, because she kept telling herself she did not give a jot what he thought. In an effort to shake off the power of his gaze, she turned away to Caroline.

Fanny said, "I did not catch what you were saying about music. Something about some Italian songs, I think?"

Caroline replied, "I was telling Lady Austen about the masquerade held at Lady Oxford's town house last week. It was in all the papers and the talk of the town. Lord Mountjoy was dressed as a Bohemian bandit and is to have his portrait done in Turkish riding dress, they say. And Lady Newcombe was attired in a page's costume. The music was all the new Italian stuff. My dear Fanny, wouldn't that be a delightful evening? All that music and dancing?"

Fanny said, "Not at all. I can't think of a more painful way of spending an evening."

"But Fanny, the waltzing . . . !"

"I can't waltz," Fanny said. She made an apologetic face. "The last time I was forced onto the floor, I tripped someone up." She smiled across at Sherry, quite surprised at her own honesty in owning up to it in company. But at this exact moment, she felt very high, quite exhilarated and daring. How lovely it felt to have been kissed an hour ago by the handsome young man on the other side of the table. And no one else in the room knew, only the two of them. How lovely and how . . . secret.

Sherry was looking back at her. His eyes appreciated her. It was like being warmed right through. She felt glowing; too much so. She'd better calm down or they'd all notice.

Fanny was certain that Caroline had noticed already. It was absurd to feel she disapproved. After all, hadn't she been the one to insist on them walking over here together? Perhaps it was because she was stuck next to that camel of a woman, Lady Austen, with her imperious nose, and with no chance of relief for another two courses.

Fanny could tell that Lady Austen did not think well of the dress that Caroline was wearing. It was the cream silk, very thin and diaphanous, that Clarence had brought her from town and, if truth were known, Fanny could see herself why Lady Austen thought it unsuitable. It was very . . . well . . . revealing around the breasts; and in the first light of the candles and with that brooch of brilliants for extra effect, it made Caroline look—for a moment— quite different.

It didn't really do for a country dinner. It was too exaggerated, too fashionable. It showed off her figure, but it made her look somewhat forward. Her eyes too brilliant.

I am surprised she did not see it herself, Fanny thought. I ought not to be thinking this; I don't mean to criticize.

"So how are you getting on with your new magnolia?" Louisa Knight asked Lady Austen.

"Not too famously. The dry weather seems to be crisping it up," Lady Austen said with some displeasure.

"That is a shame," Miss Knight commiserated. "You took such pains with it, too."

"Fanny and I were remarking on our roses yesterday," Caroline interrupted. "We thought we had never seen any so huge. Did we not, Fanny? We have so many beds of them, Lady Austen, at Cranthorne. In a couple of months, I am going to have them all cut back. It's the only way, I believe. The other Friday, we spent half the day at the garden. I quite forgot the time, talking it all over with Barnes. Barnes is our head gardener, you know."

Still half-detached, Fanny thought, But she hates anything to do with gardening. I never knew her to mention it once at Cranthorne. Every once in a while, she mused, looking at Caroline, you embroider things a little, make breathless comments about things you know nothing about. Why couldn't Caroline see that trying to curry favor and put on airs with these people merely made her look foolish?

"How is Sir George?" Mrs. Rushworth said loudly. "I hear he's had some sort of accident?"

"Oh . . . a little fall. Nothing too bad." Caroline gave them a curtailed version. "The house needs some renovation, you know, in places. I keep telling him so. There are corners—like those stairs—where the servants are sometimes lax. I made Colman nail down that carpet to see that it will not happen again. Poor George . . . !" She laughed in a self-conscious way. "He does not see as well as he used to, you know. It will only keep him indoors for a day or two."

"Was there no one around when it happened?" That was Edward Knight's deep voice from across the table.

"No one," said Caroline, looking defensive. "It's not possible to be with him at all hours of the day."

"I shall ride over to see him tomorrow morning." The look Edward Knight gave her was a long way from an expression of sympathy. Fanny wondered if he blamed the accident, unfairly, on Caroline. And she wondered whether she could hear that note of hidden sarcasm in his voice or if it was not so pronounced this evening. She decided it was probably still there. He hadn't softened any in his tone; only his eyes, when they suddenly met her own, seemed a fraction less hostile.

Caroline said, "I am sure Sir George will be delighted." The words sounded absolutely correct, the tone wrong. But she had cause to be bitter toward them, Fanny supposed. It was true, she thought, that Edward Knight was her enemy. Louisa? No, Louisa was too genuine to be anyone's enemy. Fanny remembered Caroline's light mockery of Louisa's clothes the other day at Cranthorne. She shouldn't have done that. It wasn't very fair.

"Edward, Mr. Crawley's glass is empty." Louisa's voice chimed in on Fanny's thoughts. "Miss Rushworth, will you have another ice? They are very refreshing on a summer's evening, don't you agree?"

Fanny was in the small back room changing out of her slippers and into her shoes for the journey home, when Edward Knight came to find her. She was the last one to come out; she had had trouble with one of her heels.

The voices of the company murmured and moved around the corner in the front hall, taking a leisurely leave.

"Miss Milbanke . . ." His voice took her by surprise. "You have everything you need?"

She wondered why he hadn't sent one of the maids. "Yes. Yes, thank you." She'd looked up with a start. "The heel of my slipper broke. I'm afraid that is the end of them."

He stood there watching her, but he didn't seem concerned about the slipper. "Sir George—did you see him today?" The question was abrupt.

"No . . . no. Not today. He is laid up in his room."

"How bad was the fall? Do you know?"

"No. Not really. I only know what they tell me."

What was he going to say next? Was he going to say anything? She wished he would. She couldn't get by him, even if she wanted. He was blocking the doorway. But they couldn't just stand here all night, in this silence.

Fanny said, more out of desperation than anything else, "You take an uncommon interest in what goes on at Cranthorne."

"I take an interest in Sir George's health."

"You seem very concerned about him, then."

"I am concerned."

A short pause. Fanny said in a low voice, "And I suppose Susan is not there now to pass it all on to you?"

He was surprised. "What do you know about that?"

"I saw you together. I overheard. The night you dined with us. I . . . I was in the library fetching something. You did not know I was there."

"So . . . you heard, did you?"

"Yes." Fanny looked at him. "I heard all your opinions about my family."

"I am sorry for it," he said slowly.

"I expect you are." Her voice was ironic.

"You heard more than you bargained for?"

"Yes."

"I wouldn't have wanted to hurt your feelings."

"Wouldn't you?" Fanny said.

"Don't you believe me?"

"Not very much." Another silence.

He folded his arms. "I suppose you have heard that Susan is now here with us?"

"Yes." She studied his face. "You must be very sure of her honesty. You don't seem to me to be the philanthropic kind."

"Don't I?" That almost amused him. She saw his mouth twitch.

"Not at all. So . . . did Susan steal the ring?"

"No. She didn't."

"Caroline says she did. Why couldn't she establish her innocence?"

"Perhaps the dice were loaded against her," he said.

"What does that mean?"

"Never mind." He shook his head. "I suppose you think me an ogre because I was sharp with you that first day?"

"I didn't care for your tone. That's true."

His mouth twitched. "I didn't care for the hardness of the path. I'm too old for coming off my horse. You were lucky I didn't say more. I might have broken my neck."

"Then you would not have been able to say anything." It was out before she could stop herself, but she immediately thought, You should not have said that, Fanny.

There was a considerable silence. Then sounds of movement came around the corner, voices formally rising. He regarded her steadily with the first glimmer of a smile. "I begin to wish I had said more."

Fanny wondered if she could inch past him, but decided, looking at the size of him, that she could not.

His tone changed and he said, "You wanted to know why I was so concerned about Sir George. He has been like a father to me. Louisa has told you, I think, that we lost our own father."

"Yes. I . . . I'm sorry." There was, in her face, when it came up to meet his, nothing remarkably different. "I should have remembered." But behind the bare words lay a great deal more, an instinctive sympathy.

"The phaeton is ready, sir."

"Thank you, Jane." Speaking to the parlor maid behind him, he never took his direct, brown eyes off of Fanny's. "How long do you stay at Cranthorne? When do you go back to London?"

"To Wentworth Street?" She made the most of that stroke. "I do not know. I was invited to stay the whole summer."

"Why is that, do you think?"

"Why?" It was a very peculiar question to ask. "For company for Caroline, I suppose."

"Is she so lacking in company, then?"

"I don't know!" He was beginning to exasperate her again. "Clarence Stanhope kept calling. He said Caroline needed company."

"Ah . . . Clarence. I thought so!"

"And they thought it would help my mother, too." She looked him straight in the eye. "As you so carefully found out, we have been in difficult circumstances this last year."

"Philanthropy, then?" As he chose the word deliberately, his voice was soft and sardonic.

Fanny felt her temper slipping. "Perhaps!" she said swiftly. "On my cousin's part, at least." Her colors were coming up. "Do you know what she has had to put up with? How Sir George treats her? You would pity her more if you did. I know you resent her being there. You think she is not good enough for your landed families . . ."

"Is that what they told you?"

"It is what Mr. Crawley told me."

"Ah . . . the estimable Mr. Crawley . . ." His voice was still soft.

"Yes, the estimable Mr. Crawley!" Fanny glared at him. "He told me you were a cynic."

"Did he now?" He kept on looking at her. "And of course you believe every word Mr. Crawley says?"

"Yes, I do." She kept her voice low, controlled. "But as you are obviously prejudiced against him— and against my cousin—I shall not stop to argue with you." She tried to push past him then.

"I don't want to argue with you either." His arm reached out, blocked her way. His hand gripped her arm, held her for a moment. "I just want you to think about how things are at Cranthorne. You seem to me a sensible girl . . . sensible enough to use your eyes and your ears."

"Are you asking me to spy for you?" Fanny stared at him. "To take Susan's place?"

"No. Did you tell your cousin what you overheard?"

"No. I was going to, but then Susan left and I thought it best to leave it alone."

"Good. Then don't tell her."

"I shall if I want to!" She tried to pull herself away from him.

"You won't if you've got any sense." He was still gripping her like a vise, but he was thinking of something else. "So it was Clarence who came to get you down here?"

Fanny said, "Look, I don't know what any of this is about, but—"

Edward Knight said, "They're clever. Cleverer than I thought."

"What are you saying?" Fanny asked, bewildered.

"I'm not sure. Not exactly. But do something for me, will you? I don't want you to spy. I do want you to keep a sharp eye on Sir George. Stop him drinking, if you can . . . as quietly and unobtrusively as possible. It's very important."

He was always so sure of himself, Fanny observed, he didn't even question that she would do as he asked. He let go of her arm, and touched it again more gently when he saw her rubbing it where he had gripped so hard. Then he turned on his heel and went.

Fanny had just gotten back to the main hall when the disturbance first made itself known. A man came floundering in through the front door, a servant or groom or something like that; his legs, encased in rough cords, were collapsing underneath him.

"For heaven's sake, Jenkins!" Edward Knight got him to a chair. "What is it? What's happened?"

"It's Bob . . . Bob Steadman!" Jenkins's voice was weak. Big hands clenched and unclenched. "Shot. He's been shot. Some blasted poacher got him down by Parson's Meadow."

"Got him?" Edward's voice was sharp.

"With a shotgun."

"A shotgun?"

"Yes . . ." Jenkins said. "He's had it, Mr. Knight. Caught it straight in the head, see. He's dead, sir. I couldn't do nothing for him."

Chapter Seven

Fanny heard, the following morning, the full story of Bob Steadman's fate. Rumors had filtered through to Taff Jenkins, the gamekeeper at Leigh Park, that some poaching had been going on, over the last few weeks, up in Leigh Wood. Occasionally of late, Bob Steadman had been in the habit of going out with Jenkins late at night, when the area up above the lake needed watching. Bob knew every inch of that territory, as he had since he was a boy. Bob had always been an open-air sort of lad. There was nothing he liked better than a good trek out around, even in the dark.

That night in particular, there was a white moon. Bob could see fifty yards or so in front of him with the sharp vision of a young man. He had seen something move down by the bank at the bottom and had gone on ahead, being swifter of foot than Taff Jenkins. The two did not think there might be any danger. Poachers, if they heard you coming, usually got out of the way smartish. The secret was to catch them at it, come on top of them before they smelled you.

Bob had known how to track quietly, but there must have been more than one of them. And rogues from outside, at that. Local men wouldn't be using a gun. They knew how to set snares, how to work in silence. A gun told the whole world someone was there, and nobody from the village would be such a fool.

Taff Jenkins had been halfway down the slope when he heard the shot. Then Bob's cry, almost at once, and a slithering sort of noise that was branches and undergrowth being flattened. Bob had fallen another twenty yards or so from where his stick had been found.

Bob's face was not too badly disfigured. They had caught him from behind, and the shot that had not gone into his head had caught him in the shoulder and the heart.

"They legged it!" Jenkins kept repeating. "They shot him and legged it. There wasn't nothing I could do, except get him back home."

There were garbled rumors in the village of strangers who had been seen in the area over the last few days—a seaman found drunk over by Langham Abbey and a couple of gypsies or peddlers or some such dirty rogues—mostly exaggerated and for the greater part at second hand.

Fanny was startled by the depth of her own shock. Her feelings surprised her. She had scarcely known Bob Steadman; she had spoken to him only once, that first day. But she had liked the look of him; very young, very straight and wholesome. Sometimes one could sum a person up at a glance. Then there was Susan and her family to consider. Two nasty shocks for them in as many weeks. Fanny would have given anything herself to stop thinking about Bob's death. And if she could not banish it from her mind, what must it be like for them?

Edward Knight rode over to Cranthorne at noon, the day after. He looked cold and hard and intimidating as he came into the house. Even Sherry noticed it, Fanny knew, by the way he glanced over instinctively to Caroline: as if Edward Knight had brought the chill of death into the room with him and Sherry had felt its full power.

Mr. Knight was blunt, to the point. "I have just called at the Steadmans'. They are pretty cut up."

"But, of course . . ." Caroline was sitting on the

sofa. As he looked at her, the sun came out and blazed through the window and onto her pale gold hair. "Sir George . . . all of us . . . would wish to express our sympathy."

"The funeral is to be on Monday."

"It is a very shocking thing," Caroline said. A pause. "Very shocking." Another pause while the clock ticked. "Is there . . . does anyone have any idea who did it?"

"Not at present. The magistrate is gathering what he can. They will want to see your gamekeeper—Deacon, I believe his name is? He has told someone in the village he was out by the coach road and saw someone running away just after eleven."

"Deacon?" She seemed distracted. "Yes. Yes, of course. Someone can find him if it will be of any help."

"I believe it will," Knight said, looking across at Fanny. "And he may wish to speak to others in your household. They may have heard things, witnessed something . . ."

"Is it likely?" Caroline asked coldly.

"I don't know." He stared her out.

"Is it necessary?"

"I believe so."

"But I cannot think . . . I mean, they are all quite upset. I do not wish them harassed in any way. What are they likely to have witnessed? They were none of them in the vicinity," she said with a heightened voice.

"The sooner they get to the bottom of it, the sooner things will be back to normal."

"You may be right." Reluctantly, Caroline agreed. "Even so, I hope it will not be prolonged. The house is unsettled enough . . ."

"It should not take long," Edward Knight told her.

The look he gave Fanny made her feel, for no reason, defensive. He seemed to have nothing more to say, either to Caroline or Sherry or herself, but he still didn't go. He stood there where he had planted himself on the carpet in front of the fireplace, while the rest of them sat uneasily in a semicircle around the low table.

"Will you take some refreshment?" Caroline was reluctantly playing hostess.

"No. Thank you." Elaborately, he refused. "I came also to ask how Sir George is."

"He is better. He will get up later."

"Perhaps I might go up and see him?"

"If you wish." Fanny watched her signal to Sherry to ring for the maid; she paused while he rang and sat there, with a faint smile, waiting.

"So Clarence is gone back to London?" Edward Knight said.

"Yes." Caroline's great hazel eyes gazed back at him.

Fanny looked all around the room thinking that she positively wished he'd go. It was an uncomfortable, scary conversation. He'd said such scathing things the other night. She felt herself start to sweat and grow fidgety. She thought, If this awful ritual goes on much longer, I'll get up and leave.

Caroline said, "He had some business, I believe."

"When did he leave?"

"Yesterday morning."

Sherry shoved his hands in his pockets and said he wondered if it would rain. Having to sit through this kind of icy formality wasn't his idea of a good morning, either. He started to tap his foot.

When the servant came, it was a relief. Edward Knight bent his head to them and followed her out.

"My head aches," Caroline said petulantly as soon

as he was gone. "It is all this disturbance. Fanny, run up to Céline and ask her to get me something. She will be in my dressing room."

"Do you want me to wait and bring it down?"

"Yes. If you like." Caroline nodded, waved her hand, not caring one way or the other.

Fanny had to pass Sir George's bedroom on the way to the dressing room that divided his quarters from Caroline's. She neither stopped nor listened on purpose. It was just that his door had been left ajar and, in moving along the passage, she could not miss hearing the voices.

"Edward . . . ?" Sir George's voice, old and muffled. "You will see the boy's family is all right?"

"I have already been," Edward Knight told him.

"Bob was a good boy. It is a damned shame . . ." The older man's voice caught and broke.

"Don't upset yourself," Edward's voice said, low and clear. And gentle. Fanny caught her breath. Who would have thought he could sound so gentle? "It can do no good. Just get yourself well. I will see to everything."

Fanny hurried on down the corridor thinking she almost wished she hadn't heard. It unsettled her more than she wanted. They'd sounded so close. Like father and son, as he'd said. She thought for the first time how complicated people were. How one never knew them at all or else only the bits on the surface. And in the thinking there was only confusion and worry. She didn't know what to believe anymore.

It was an unpleasant few days. Fanny did not go to the funeral. Sir George represented the household, and a crowd of the servants. But Mrs. Hurst, when she came back, described it all in graphic detail.

"A touching sermon," she said. "The Reverend Dodds can be poetic when the occasion calls."

"How did Susan take it?" Fanny asked.

"Susan?" Mrs. Hurst paused over the bed linen. "She's not like the rest of them. Her poor mother was taken with the faints . . . tears streaming down her face and collapses on the church floor. But Susan . . . She's so quiet that sometimes you think her a bit queer in the head. All Susan did was stand there and stare at the church wall. Stare and stare . . ."

"Poor thing," Fanny said.

"Yes, poor thing. I believe it will all have to come out, though, in the end. Can't bottle it up forever. Terrible close, those two were. Susan and Bob. Come up together, do you see—they were much of an age. Oh, yes . . . it will come out sooner or later."

It was because Fanny went down with a summer cold and Caroline was taken with a fit of calling on the neighbors that Fanny got to talk to Susan Steadman herself.

"Are you sure you won't come to the Austens'?" Caroline asked before she set out one morning.

"Not today. Next week I shall be fit." Fanny's head was all stuffed up; she would not last ten minutes in company.

"You will not mind if I leave you?" Caroline moved to the end of the bed, took off one glove, put it back on again, looked . . . fiddly.

"Of course not. I shall find a book. Or something. I ought to write to Mamma."

"She is well?" Caroline wasn't really interested.

"As well as can be expected," Fanny said. "Knowing Mamma. I hope you enjoy your visits."

"I would rather stay home," said Caroline. "Lady Austen is a dragon."

"Then why go?"

"They get so finicky if one doesn't." Silence. Caroline's voice fiddled around, too, when she was in this mood. "I shan't stay long. But then there are the Rushworths and Captain Wetherby."

Fanny thought, Why cram so much into one morning? She said, "Why don't you space them out?"

"I want to hear the gossip, I suppose. What else is there to do? Anyway, Sherry is coming. He will keep them amused."

Sherry had made no more moves to talk to Fanny alone since the walk to Leigh Park. She wondered vaguely if she had let him be too forward, wondered if he was aware of it and had drawn back, perhaps, because he knew it was not good form. He has regard for my reputation, she told herself. I think he would notice things like that, if it mattered to him.

He puzzled her sometimes. That day on the way to Leigh Park, he had seemed ardent. Yet since then, his conversations with her had come in fits and starts. Lively nonsense now and again, nothing serious. And in between, he seemed unaccountably languid. Lazy, almost. Fanny was disappointed—she owned it—but she was determined not to let it show.

He was sensitive, under all the tomfoolery. That was Fanny's opinion, after she had considered it a little. He was deeper than he would like people to think. She liked that. She liked it a great deal. Very well, she thought. We will wait and see. Wait until he feels the time is right. I am sure that's what it is. He is only biding his time . . .

Fanny thought the round of visits might restore Caroline's good humor. Her mood this last couple of days seemed to be suspended between abnormally high and low spirits. She had a quick nature. She could be exquisitely good company or right down in the doldrums. Perhaps she is sickening from my cold, Fanny thought. That is probably the cause.

The room was extremely warm even with one of the windows pushed open. She read for a while, but her head got more and more stuffed up, which was how she came to the sudden decision to walk down to the village. She could call at the apothecary's and get some new soap. All at once, she needed to get out.

The apothecary, however, was closed up. Perhaps he was ill, too.

She was just turning away down the street, when she saw Susan Steadman come out of an alley. Fanny was shocked by the girl's appearance. She had seemed in fair health when she was at Cranthorne, but now there were great hollow rings around her eyes. Her red hair had a yellowish, thin look.

"Susan!" Fanny called out, and crossed the street on purpose. She tried a tentative smile. Pity for Susan caught at her and made her start frantically talking. "I wanted some soap from the apothecary's but it's all shut up. I've had the most dreadful cold. How are you, Susan? You've lost such a lot of weight. No, Susan—don't go!" She grabbed at the girl's arm. She said, "I'm sorry . . . I was so sorry about your brother."

"Yes, well, you would say that, wouldn't you?" The words were bitten out.

"But I am sorry. Don't you believe me?"

"There's a lot of folks saying they're sorry that think otherwise."

"Oh, no, I'm sure you're wrong!" Fanny was shocked. Even making allowances for the girl's grief, one couldn't let that go. "I do understand how you feel . . ."

"You don't!" A flare of the pale eyes.

"No, you're right. I don't." Fanny acknowledged it. "I can't possibly know . . . but I'm trying . . ."

"Don't bother!" Susan pulled her arm away. "There's one thing . . ."

"Yes?"

"They'll pay for what they've done. That they will! He told me so."

"Who?" Fanny's voice stayed deliberately calm. "Who will make who pay?"

"Mr. Knight."

She idolizes him, Fanny thought. He's like some kind of god to her. I suppose it's because he believed in her. It's what I would feel if I were really in trouble and somebody helped me. She said, "Susan, I'm glad you have a new place. My cousin . . . Lady Caroline feels very bad about—"

"Her?" Susan turned on Fanny. The words were spat out once more. "It's a bit late, isn't it? Her? She comes here without a penny to her name . . . clinging on to what she can get . . . married to him secretly in London! And what's happening inside twelve months? He's falling all over the place and drinking himself into his grave . . ." Susan's voice was harsh with anger. "She's a low, common thing and that's the truth of it! Carrying on under his nose and thinking we see nothing. But Sir George is a good man and they shan't destroy him. Not like they destroyed my brother . . ."

So grief could make one completely crazed, Fanny

thought, after she had watched Susan rush off down the street. Or perhaps if one hated somebody as much as the girl apparently hated Caroline, one hung everything else that happened onto that hatred, found it a relief, tidier somehow, to have all the bitterness in one place.

Fanny took the long way back. The wind was beginning to rise. It caught at the great trees in the park, swished through them, combed them this way and that. Fanny looked at them and thought, It would have been better if the marriage had not taken place. Not only for Caroline, but for Sir George, too. He is not the horror I took him for at first. Just a sad old man who has made a mistake and has taken to drink to try and cure it.

Who am I to judge either of them? How do I know what I would do under the same circumstances? I wouldn't have married for convenience. Not even to get Mamma out of money troubles. Marriage is too big a step for that.

Behind all Fanny's excuses, an element of judgment was creeping in from time to time. Reluctantly, she saw that Caroline had faults, which she could see more clearly when away from the house on her own: a cutting tongue on occasions. Did she use it on Sir George in private? A touch of vanity. And a levity that sometimes masqueraded as gaiety.

Stop it. Stop thinking about her like that.

What did Susan mean when she said Caroline was carrying on behind her husband's back? The wind caught at Fanny from behind. She hung on to her skirts and lengthened her stride.

Edward Knight, coming around the corner from the opposite direction, took her by surprise. "Miss Milbanke," he said.

He was alone. She almost wished she had kept more alert; then she might have avoided him. He spoke while they were still ten yards apart, in a deep bass voice with no smile in it.

Fanny said, "Mr. Knight! I was walking back to Cranthorne."

"Then you are going the long way around." He stopped and stood there beside her. "Do you know the way?"

"I think so."

"This track takes a mile loop before it goes back to Cranthorne." He looked at her. "Are you alone?" Was that slight sarcasm in his eyes? "Mr. Crawley is not with you?"

"No."

"Good. Then we can talk. We were interrupted the other evening."

Fanny pulled a leaf off one of the branches and stood there pulling it to bits. She decided on boldness. "I won't discuss my cousin. Or her marriage. It's not fair to her. It is not a happy marriage . . . I own that. She may regret the day she left Lockyer Street. Sir George may regret it, too—"

"Lockyer Street?" Edward Knight frowned.

"Yes. What is wrong? What have I said?"

"What has Lockyer Street got to do with it?"

"It is where she lived. Her family lived there."

"Never. Her family are in Brighton."

Fanny said, "Then I must have the name wrong. She said they moved around a great deal."

"Did she now?" His tone and expression were peculiar. "What else did she tell you? What is her version, for example, of her marriage to Sir George?" The tone sharpened. "I suppose she told you it was a perfect love match?"

"No." Fanny tossed the last bit of leaf away. "She

was more honest than that. She said she was introduced to Clarence and Sir George at a party in London. Sir George was lonely after his first wife's death and Clarence took him around—"

"That's what she told you?" Dark eyes gazed strongly into hers.

"Yes."

"That she met Clarence for the first time just before her marriage?"

"Yes." Fanny tried to hold his gaze.

"Your cousin knew Clarence for two years before he introduced her to his brother. She and Clarence lived in the same lodging house in Piccadilly."

The valley below was surprisingly tranquil, sheltered from the wind. A lodging house? Fanny watched a cart move on the road.

"She told me . . . I got the impression . . . she lived with her family," she said.

"Her family were never in London."

"If they lived in the same lodging house . . ." Fanny said, trying to come to terms with the facts, ". . . that doesn't mean to say they knew each other."

"It would be an odd sort of coincidence, don't you think, to live in the same house two years and not know each other?"

"It might be . . . unusual. But coincidences do happen."

"You don't believe in this one, though . . . do you?" He was taking hold of her shoulders, turning her. "Miss Milbanke—Fanny—you can't really believe it?"

She stared down across the woods, thinking that she really did want to believe it. Not to believe was an uncomfortable, frightening thing. She'd liked Caroline so much at first. They'd become friends so

easily. Fanny thought deliberately for the first time
about the alternative—suspicion—and in the process
found neither ease nor comfort. She said slowly,
"No. It would be too much to believe. But there
must be a reason for her telling me such falsehoods.
There will be a reason."

"Oh, yes . . ." His voice sounded soft. "There is
a reason."

"She would have been ashamed of having no re-
spectable home in London. A lodging house in Piccadilly is not an acceptable residence for a lady on
her own. Lady Austen would not approve of it."

"Fanny . . ."

She said, "Don't say it. Whatever it is, I don't
want to hear any more." Every word he said now
seemed to hurt. She wished he hadn't said anything
at all. Ignorance is sometimes a good thing . . .

"Just one more thing: have you ever seen this before?" He pulled a muddy square of white cambric
from his pocket and held it out to her. It was a
handkerchief, a man's pocket handkerchief. In one
corner the letter *B* was entwined with some kind of
snake.

"No. What is it?"

"It was found not far from Bob Steadman's body.
Down by Parson's Meadow."

"You think it belonged to . . . ?"

"To whoever killed him. Yes."

"It is very dirty. It may have been there for
months."

"It is only dirty where it was trodden in. The rest
is quite fresh. And quite fine work."

"Yes." Fanny turned it over. She gave it back to
him. "The snake . . . is it some kind of monogram?
Or emblem?"

"I imagine so. I'm still making inquiries. Does it mean anything to you at all?"

"No. No, it doesn't."

And yet there was something—somewhere—at the back of her mind. Some memory link that refused to be defined. Fanny shook her head. She couldn't help. She didn't know anything.

She wasn't even sure that she wanted to.

Chapter Eight

Sometime during the next few days, Fanny made some decisions. She walked around the house thinking, though outwardly she seemed calm.

She could go on staying here, talking to people, doing nothing. She examined the prospect: she'd be bound to feel a lot worse. No point in looking facts in the face if one didn't try to put them right in some way.

Fanny would need time to take in all the complexities of Caroline's character and, by watching her, to work out what, if anything, could be done in that direction. It needed time to observe and to listen, without giving away that she was watching and listening. What was supposed to emerge, she still wasn't sure.

There was one clear thing she could do, and that was to attempt to curtail Sir George's drinking.

It was not as easy as she first thought. There seemed to be so much of the stuff around, in every room of the house, almost. She wondered why she had not noticed it before. Decanters of brandy and glasses in the drawing room. Pink and white champagne, burgundy, and two sorts of claret in the dining room. Whiskey in the library. "It's no wonder he drinks so much," she said to herself. "It's staring him in the face everywhere he looks."

Fanny walked into the library looking for a book one wet morning. There had been two days of continuous gray rain blowing in across from the west, pounding across the conservatory roof, lashing into the long windows. She had turned her back on it and was fingering her way along one of the shelves, when the door opened and Sir George came in. He looked in a singular shambles, and she thought he would never stop coughing.

He stopped at last. "It's you, miss . . . ," he said when he saw her. "Thought you were one of the servants." His eyes were more bloodshot than normal, his collar awry. He kept trying to heave himself into his jacket sleeve.

"Here, let me help," said Fanny. It was pitiful to see him struggling.

"Blasted thing! Always crooked . . ." he said, short of breath.

"You've torn the seam," Fanny remarked as gently as she could.

"No great loss." He collapsed weakly into his chair. "Doesn't matter."

"Yes, it does," Fanny said. She didn't know whether to feel exasperation or pity. On an impulse, she knelt down by his chair. "Why don't you leave it off for a day or two?" she said quietly.

"Leave what off?" He glared at her.

"The wine. And the whiskey or the brandy? You really don't look well this morning."

"Think I'm tipsy, do you? Think I've taken more than my whack?" His eyes glowered. "Well, I haven't! Got a damned headache. And I'm bilious. So you can stop your blasted preaching."

"I'm not preaching. I just don't like to see you ill." Fanny tried a new tack. "Mr. Knight tells me you used not to touch it for weeks. A year or two back. When . . ." She was taking a risk here. ". . . when your first wife was alive."

"My first wife . . ." He looked at her. The words were scarcely recognizable, almost a whisper. "My only wife . . . ," he said, looking flushed.

Fanny, hopelessly awkward and embarrassed, took hold of his hand. "You mustn't . . ."

"I mustn't what?" Wheezing morosely, he shoved her hand away. "Mustn't what? Mustn't mention her?"

"No . . ." Fanny was floundering. "I didn't mean that. You know I didn't."

"You listen to me," he said. To her horror, all at once the tears started to roll down his face. He was crying, quite silently, his red fists kneading and unkneading while he did so. "She was my only wife . . . do you hear? Anne. My only wife . . ."

"I hear," Fanny said softly. She felt despairing, but it was necessary to sound cheering, to make him bear up. "But I wish you would not say such things. I am sure Caroline would hate to hear you . . ."

"You think so? You think so? Now wouldn't she laugh?"

"Sir George . . . please . . ."

"Have you ever happened to see her care anything about me? Have you? Have you? Eh?"

Fanny struggled for a convincing instance. "I saw her only yesterday. She said you shouldn't come down the steps so fast—you might fall."

"She wouldn't care . . ." His speech was agitated, his hands in a fit of the shakes. "Who would care?"

"We would care." It was like having to console a child, having to root around for comforting facts. "Caroline would care. You mustn't upset yourself so. You want to feel better, don't you?"

"Want to?" His head lifted, again like a defiant child's. With a sudden ferocity, he said, "No, I don't want to. It's not worth it. Nothing's worth it!" He still had enough force in his hands to lever himself up. "So you may stop all your damned little ways! And before you ask where I'm going, I'm off to find some beer. Some Bass or Calcutta to cool the heat in my throat. Does that suit?" he asked.

"No. It does not suit," Fanny said.

"Well, you may go to the devil if it does not. Because I'm going anyway."

Whenever she saw him after that, he was always in company, judging, she supposed, that if they were on their own, she would start on him again. So she tried to enlist Sherry's help. "Do you not think Sir George drinks too heavily?" she asked him. "I was thinking that if we all put our heads together, we might be able to help him in some way. He looks so . . . sanguine lately. Haven't you noticed? I think we should do something before it is too late."

"Sanguine?" said Sherry. He looked taken aback. "He's always carried a high color." Sherry thought the old man pretty much as usual. He wasn't sure it was a good thing to poke one's nose in, even with the best of intentions. Caro might think it a cheek—embarrassing to have to say so, but those who had to live there all the time and face the music ought to know best, and such.

Fanny said, "But if he didn't drink so much, there wouldn't be so much music to face."

"Shouldn't interfere, Fanny." Sherry's smile was a bit nervous. "Better things to do, aren't there?" Here he touched her under the chin and made her look at him.

Fanny blushed and hesitated, and in the end all she said was, "I suppose so," and forgot Sir George for five minutes.

She did take up the subject with Caroline, if only indirectly. Did not Sir George look peaky lately, she asked. She picked her way nearer and nearer the desired subject. Sometimes a diet could have a detrimental effect on one's health. A change of diet could work wonders. One could sometimes wield an influence. If one really decided to do something, one could usually accomplish it with a little perseverance.

Caroline stopped reading and looked at her. "Fanny, are you trying to say something?"

"I did not know the best way to say it." Fanny colored up. "Sherry thinks . . . That is to say, I don't want to sound interfering, but . . ."

"Fanny—"

"I think you should try to curtail Sir George's drinking." Fanny made a wild gesture with her hands. "Indeed I do!"

A little silence. "So I am in hot water, am I?" Caroline's voice was amused and as silky as a cat's coat. She looked at Fanny. She said, "Sherry warned me of something of the sort."

Fanny was mortified. She felt furious with him for having run to tell Caroline.

"My dearest Fanny, you really shouldn't fret yourself about Sir George's health."

"Shouldn't I?"

"There's no reason at all for you to fuss." Caroline shook her head slowly. "You are such a soft-hearted little thing. I watch you sometimes, you know. I see all the dangers of a nature such as yours. You are too feeling. And very young, if you do not mind my saying so. At nineteen, you see everything either black or white. It is not so simple as that, Fanny. Life rarely is." She gave Fanny a melting smile. "My dear, Sir George is too set in his ways to do what I would tell him."

"But . . ."

"Fanny . . ." Caroline's hand came out to touch her. "I know best. You must believe that. I don't want to upset you. But he has good weeks and . . . bad weeks. Mark my words, he will put himself right."

She made it sound so convincing. Like the story about Lockyer Street. Fanny thought, I wonder if Edward Knight could be wrong. After all, he lives miles from London; he could have gotten hold of the wrong facts in his inquiries. But he doesn't get things wrong. Though I disliked him intensely at first . . . I sense that he knows what he's doing.

And then Sir George called for his solicitor. Fanny was in the hall when the gentleman came. Unless it stopped raining soon, she was thinking, there would be a flood to cut them off from the village down on the lower ground. One could not help looking out of the windows at the roses all sodden on their stems and the cattle standing in wet grass and at the sky getting deeper and deeper by the minute.

The solicitor had gotten out of his carriage. He was reaching back deep into it for his papers. He looked like the kind of professional man who counted up things in his head, not on paper. Gray, lean, dried up. He wore a great, thick Wellington cloak and he looked hard across the rain-pocked gravel at the house before striding into the porch as fast as he could.

Clarence was watching for him. Yes, Clarence was back. He had arrived the night before very late and there had seemed an urgency about him at breakfast, saying little, baiting no one. Was he worried about the solicitor's visit? Fanny wondered. Had he known the man was coming? Was that why he was back? Fanny felt sure that it was, but it was only an instinct.

She paused in the window recess, almost unnoticed as Colman took Mr. Pickering's wet cloak and his hat. Clarence made it his business to come forward then, as if by some accident, to greet the newcomer.

"Mr. Pickering!" he said suavely. "How are things with you?" Clarence pumped at the solicitor's hand. Sounded bluff, charming, everything he had seemed at the very beginning. "Good of you to come at short notice. Caroline tells me he would not be put off! And you know what George is like when he gets something into his head . . . It had to be today, this very morning. I hope it has not inconvenienced you?"

"It is of no consequence." The solicitor's tone was dry and formal. "We had not much on. The river has burst its banks, I hear. Bad for the farmers."

"Indeed, indeed!"

The voices disappeared toward the library, where Sir George and Caroline were waiting. It was one of the few times she had ever seen them in there together, Fanny thought. Caroline had been pale this morning, strung up. Clarence didn't go in with them. He closed the door, stood there for a minute alone, his face considering, half impatient. A powerful amount of thinking seemed to be taking place and Fanny, pressed silently back behind the drapes, knew quite well that he wanted to be in there, but couldn't.

The house stood seemingly empty for almost half an hour, no one coming or going. The clocks ticked slowly.

One thing was odd. Fanny heard hard, strong footsteps about halfway through. She could not resist a look out through the gap in the curtains to see whom they belonged to. The footsteps stopped outside the library door on the polished tiles. Fanny's head moved and a voice—Céline's voice—said, "Go in."

Deacon, the new gamekeeper, went in, dressed in rough tweed, clutching his hat in his hand, following Céline. The door closed behind them. Céline did not come out, either, for another five minutes.

Fanny felt uneasy all morning. It was like being in the middle of a play. The house felt . . . theatrical. The solicitor—a small bit part in the drama—left at eleven. Caroline saw him out. There was no mistaking the relief in her voice. Fanny heard her apologizing again. "I do hope it has stopped raining, Mr. Pickering. We shall all be drowned soon, if it does not." She knew her part. Perfect poise, entire self-confidence. End of a scene.

Is Caroline theatrical? Fanny wondered. Yes, I think she is. She would have made a good actress. She tells engaging stories. I have heard her. Caroline was in high spirits at luncheon. She even chivvied Sir George—albeit playfully—about the amount of Madeira he took with his beef.

"Fanny has been nagging at me to lecture you, George. Did you know that?" Lightly, she tapped at his hand with her fork. "You are not to take any more wine for the rest of the afternoon, do you hear?"

Today he was worse than ever. Stumbling in tongue, fumbling all over the table for the salt. Yet he seemed extra active, feverish almost. "No need to go on . . ." he mumbled. "Call Colman . . . going for a nap." The word slurred off. "Damned long morning . . . Colman! Where is the blasted man?"

"That is the best thing you could do, George, dear. You will feel so much better after a nap. Colman will get you right into bed. This weather is so bad for the spirits. Colman, help Sir George up to his room. I will come up later, George, and see how you feel."

Fanny felt a little surprised at this show of concern, but didn't show it. Perhaps her remarks to Caroline had had some effect. Caroline might have fobbed her off on the surface, but perhaps something had sunk in. She hoped so, at any rate.

Sherry made a point of waiting for her after luncheon. "If anyone asked me," he told her, "I should say you were down." He tucked his hand into her arm, as if making it his business to cheer her. He had such a way about him. "Come and play at cards with me. It is fit for nothing else this afternoon." He was already leading her into the drawing room. "We can sit by the fire and toast ourselves."

"What about Caroline? She may want to play."

"Caroline has to see to Sir George."

"I am pleased about that, at any rate," Fanny said.

"I thought you would be." He smiled down at her.

Fanny thought of something else. "But you cheat."

"I won't cheat today. That's a promise."

She did not really feel like playing cards, but she couldn't be bothered to argue. And Sherry's eyes looked very blue and pleading and monstrously flirtish, and when he lounged into one corner of the sofa and drew her down with him, there was no defense at all against his smile and his teasing.

At the end of the first game, he said, "I've a mind to put away the cards. You beat me, Fanny."

"You let me win." The thought came across her that he was not playing seriously. "Why did you let me win?"

"Because I chose to," he said and touched at a loose strand of her hair.

"Well, you mustn't. I would rather lose than be allowed to win."

He took another, longer strand and said, "You are too pretty. That's why you win. It distracts me."

"Nonsense!" Fanny started shuffling the cards fast. "I have a bone to pick with you."

"What's that?"

"You should not have told Caroline what I said to you about Sir George."

"Did I?" he asked languidly.

"Yes. You did. And I felt a fool when she let me know it." The fire crackled. She looked at him. She weighed up the odds, was still half unsure, then made the decision. She had to talk to somebody about it. "I hear," she said in a rush, "that Caroline and Clarence knew each other when they both lived in Piccadilly. Long before Sir George came on the scene. Did you know that?"

"Piccadilly?" Apparently, he was startled.

"Yes. I thought you would be surprised." She half wished she hadn't said it, seeing the look on his face. Blank, uncomprehending. "I suppose that's why she does not find more fault with him?"

"Who told you they knew each other?" Sherry asked lightly.

"I . . . I just heard it." Fanny fiddled with the

cards. Instinct—pure instinct—told her not to mention Edward Knight. "One of the maids, I think."

"The maids?" said Sherry. "You don't listen to them, do you? They're a devilish gossipy bunch. They'd tell you anything."

"But is it not true?" Fanny persisted. "It is only curiosity. You see, Caroline never mentioned knowing him first. Indeed, she told me quite a different story . . ."

"You know what?"

"What?" Fanny said, much confused by his suddenly taking hold of her hand and holding it in both of his.

"If I were you, I should not inquire too deep about Caroline's history." His smile was almost awkward. "She's very sure of herself . . . very controlled in front of the servants—and in company—only"—he turned her hand over, looked at it as if reading his fortune in it—"it's all a bit of a blind, you know. She is not half so confident as she makes out. She puts on a bit of an act."

"But that is exactly what I've noticed myself," Fanny said.

"She is not half so poised as she likes to pretend."

"I know that," Fanny said.

"But she don't deserve to have us let on that we know. It wouldn't do. You see . . . Caro's been like a sister to me." He seemed to find it difficult to express his feelings. "I've never told this to anyone before. When my brother was being . . . well, such an old screw . . . when I was almost down and out, it was Caroline who picked me up and sorted me out. So don't be too hard on her," he added tautly. "If she don't like people to know of her hard times . . . about her living in some lodging house. What I mean is . . . Oh, never mind. I can't put it into words."

"I know what you mean." He looked so uncomfortable that Fanny was quite touched. "I wasn't criticizing her or prying or anything like that. I was just puzzled." She gave his fingers a squeeze. "Shall we have another game? I'll let you win this time."

He'd made her feel mean-spirited. And he wasn't just a flirt. He had a tender heart; that was commendable in a man. Don't judge Caroline, he had said, and he was quite right. It wasn't for anyone to judge. Uncharitable, she thought. That's what I've been and it's time I stopped.

Fanny was tolerably wide awake when she went to bed that evening. It took a long time to feel drowsy. She heard a clock strike, vaguely, somewhere a long way off. Absurd to lie there counting. Eleven. No, twelve. She had come upstairs early.

Too much wind on the roof outside, that was the trouble. The skies had cleared, but another gale was coming up. No need to worry about it. If the tiles came off, someone would be up there tomorrow to mend them. Not like at Wentworth Street, where the house was half falling to pieces and Mamma could not afford to make the necessary repairs.

Plenty of money here. Caroline must have found it a welcome change, at first. When she began to think about Caroline's branch of the family, little memories began to float to the surface. Things Fanny's father had dropped out, mostly in dry, pithy phrases, mostly derogatory. "Always flying his kite, that was Charley Milbanke . . . he'd stick at nothing . . . A regular cheat . . . a regular blackleg. Stacked cards and loaded dice, that's what Charley liked to live on."

Fanny just couldn't drop off. She was too hot now. She had gotten all twisted up in the sheets and she got out of bed to straighten it out. She was padding around the bed to the other side, when she heard a meaningless noise from outside. She froze. The wind? Not out there. There was nowhere it could get into the passage.

A vase flung over? One of the dogs wandering? I'll go and look, she thought . . . No, I won't. It might be Sir George again.

It didn't sound like Sir George. No thumping or mumbling. She went to the door. She would look—she had to. Otherwise, she'd just lie there imagining things all night.

Sounds have a way of carrying at night. Creaks, little bumps, especially in an old house. Fanny opened the door. No one. But it was farther down, around the corner. Silently, she slipped down to the end of the passage. In true cloak-and-dagger fashion, she stopped at the corner, flattened herself to the wall, and peeped around.

Clarence. Perhaps he had caught his foot on the oak chest in the semidarkness. He was not stumbling, merely standing bent over and holding on tight to his shin. He was dressed for bed, his dressing gown an exotic yellow brocade that ought to have graced a younger, fitter figure. He could not find the exact spot he had knocked, so he stood there rubbing the whole shin and cursing under his breath. Then he straightened up, tightened the sash of his dressing gown. He was going on down to his room.

No. Not his room. Fanny stiffened. His candle threw a long, flickering shadow over the carpet.

Not his room. Caroline's room.

As he opened Caroline's door and closed it again

behind him, Fanny was left standing there in the dark.

Well? What now?

He'll come out in a minute, she thought. There has to be some good reason for him going in there.

She stood there in the dark, waiting.

Nothing. No sound. Sir George was ill again, that would be it. Clarence had gone in to fetch her. Silence. Absolute stillness. She couldn't wait there all night. Between herself and Caroline's door there was a long expanse of darkness. Between reality and unreality, a long stretch of . . . what? Fear. Immeasurable shock.

He wasn't going to come out.

Ten minutes later, she went back to her own room, closed the door, stood behind it. Her knees had turned to water. That was it, she thought.

What do I do now?

There are some mornings best forgotten. Fanny hunched herself over a book for an hour after breakfast, reading words without comprehension, seeing only their shapes.

"You are a thorough bookworm this morning, Fanny," Caroline told her, coming in and seeing her half hidden in the window seat. "You are very quiet. Is it your head? You had better take some hartshorn."

Fanny replied quietly, "No. I . . . I read too late last night. I feel a little tired." She avoided Caroline's eyes.

"You remind me of when I was your age," Caroline said, sighing. "Always shut away with some novel or other. Did you ever see such a dreamer, Sherry?"

"Perhaps it is a copy of Lord Byron," Sherry said. "All the ladies are mad on him, they tell me."

"It is the life of Mr. Burke," Fanny said tautly.

"It is some novel with a fine little filly in love, I'll be bound!" That was Clarence, who had just come into the room with his mocking, patronizing laugh. "Prostrate bodies and officers and dukes and a duel or two."

"There is nothing wrong with a novel," Caroline told him.

"Better the real stuff, though . . . eh, miss?" Clarence went on persistently. "Brings more roses to your cheeks. I say, Sherry, how come the lady is reading all about it, instead of getting giddy with the real thing? Something wrong somewhere, don't you think?" He started to laugh again.

"I said it is the life of Mr. Burke," Fanny said in a low, tight voice. Something flickered in her eyes as she looked at Clarence. "It is not a novel."

"I never heard such a dull title," Caroline said, also looking at Clarence.

"It . . . it is not so dull as it sounds," Fanny said heavily.

"Are you sure you're all right?" Caroline asked her.

Fanny placed the book on the table and thought it was time to get out of the room for a while. "I have to write to Mamma," she said. "I'll go and do it now, before luncheon . . . or else I might forget."

Everything still felt unreal. With regard to Clarence, she thought, it makes very little difference. I disliked him so much anyway. I always did feel the poison seeping out of him. But Caroline . . . How can I carry on here? Go on seeing her day after day? Talking to her? While she plays her husband false?

Edward Knight said Caroline and Clarence were

old friends. Does he know they were . . . are . . . lovers? He might suspect it. It would explain his strong aversion to her. Perhaps I have badly misjudged him.

And I've been feeling sorry for her because she's married to an old man. Clarence is an old man, too. It is revolting!

She paced the room and finally stood looking out of the window.

Two grooms were shouting to each other down on the graveled drive about one of the horses, which had gone lame. The taller groom insisted it wasn't lame, that it was only walking gingerly because of a knock, but the other one said that was rubbish: you could see the fine hair crack on the hoof itself.

"Aren't I right?" the second one said.

"I can't see it." The big one scratched his head. "But then, I'm not so sharp as you. I'm as dumb as an adder—isn't that what you always say?"

There was a flash of something in Fanny's brain. Something came back: the answer to one of Edward Knight's questions. And suddenly she knew whom she must talk to.

I'll go this afternoon, she thought. And instantly she felt better.

Chapter Nine

There was no sweeter day after the rain and no better way to escape her thoughts than by galloping at full tilt out across the sodden park. Fanny had been most insistent. She needed no one to come out with her on her ride. She had taken the route before, she knew where she was going; she would not be long, she told them, and was relieved to find that no one was really interested in riding that afternoon. She assured them that they need not fuss. All she wanted was a jaunt in the air to clear her cold.

Everything still felt disjointed. Propelled by a barrowload of agitations, she went up the track to Leigh Wood at a faster rate than usual, and the horse was tiring a little when they came down to the arches of the ornamental bridge at the near end of the lake. Six days of rain had swollen all the banks.

She tried to draw up the horse as they approached a wash of mud and water, but he did not want to do as he was told. She scolded him hard to keep him away from the edge, yanked hard at the reins to turn his head away from the water.

No drainage underfoot meant all sorts of patches of quagmire that made the going tricky. The path, though, Fanny reckoned, should lead right away from the lake in a few more yards. As energetically, yet as casually as possible, she dug in her heels and pushed him on. The next deep puddle should see the end of the lakeside. After that, the path would go up and on.

But it didn't work out like that. There was deeper quagmire. Two frisky paces and the wind caught at her mantle, throwing her slightly off balance. The horse took instant advantage of it and veered to the right, went straight for the water, ducked its head, and waded in to drink. Fanny, though a skillful horsewoman, was not prepared for the sudden immersion in water. She went forward in the saddle much faster than she had intended.

"Whoa! You stupid . . . thing! Whoa, there! Come here . . . !"

A sudden thrashing underneath her and then she was over his head, in the deep water. When she came up, she took a great lungful of air.

The heavy cloak pulled her down again. Heavy with water. Help me, she thought. Somebody help me . . . !

She thrashed around with her arms and shoved the horse away. Her feet could feel nothing underneath. With a wild, kicking movement, she launched herself toward the bank. The chill of the water was only just beginning to strike and cling to her underneath her dragging skirts.

"Hold on!" a voice shouted.

Even then, she went under again. She swallowed half a gallon of the lake and came up choking. I don't want to drown, she remembered thinking. Then she saw the branch being flung into the water, heard the sharp bass voice—Edward Knight's voice —prevailing over her panic. "It's all right," he said. "Take the branch. I'll pull you in."

While he hauled her into the bank, his face was full of concern and concentration, but after that, she had a sneaking suspicion he was only just stopping himself from laughing. He propped her up on the grass, waiting for her to stop spluttering and coughing, and squeezed her hair dreadfully hard to get all the water out of it. He offered her his handkerchief to mop her face.

"It's not at all funny!" she told him when she could speak.

"Would I dare laugh?" Dark eyes with a fleck of hazel gazed right back at her.

"Yes, you would!"

"What did I say?" He went on looking.

"You didn't say anything. It's the way you look."

"Can I help how I look?" There was a small twitch at the corner of his mouth. "We do seem to have trouble with our horses, don't you think?"

"Yes." Fanny glared up at him.

"Couldn't you see he was heading straight for the lake?"

"How could I tell he was going to wade in? I didn't know what he was going to do. The stupid animal has a will of his own."

"You're very wet," was the next comment.

"That is an acute observation!" Fanny said, exasperated. Then her voice changed. "I want to talk to you."

"I thought we were talking."

"Oh . . . not here! Not like this." Her teeth suddenly started to chatter.

"Of course not." His voice was all at once full of compunction. He had hold of her arm, was helping her up. "What am I thinking of?"

Her legs felt like lead weights. She stood there leaning against the tree, a little wobbly. "Where's he gone?" she asked.

"Who?"

"Tranter. My horse."

"He's wandered off. We'll catch him later." He went over to where his own chestnut was tethered, brought him back to the bank.

"Are you going?" She felt a dart of panic.

"Don't be silly."

He mounted the chestnut and took in her woebegone condition. The huge green eyes and the fair hair in rats' tails. The slight body with too few curves. The slim, delicate fingers desperately hanging on to her sodden skirts. "Come on," he said, and, leaning down, lifted her easily onto the horse in front of him.

"Comfortable?" he said.

"No, but . . ."

"Well, just sit still. Don't wriggle . . . Louisa will find you some dry clothes."

She realized what he was saying. "But . . . but I can't arrive on your sister looking like this."

"You wanted to talk, didn't you?"

"Yes, but—"

"And you don't want to die of pneumonia?"

"No."

"Then just sit tight and wait till we get to Leigh Park. It won't take long."

Fanny sat tight. She did not dare do otherwise. Two or three times, she was jerked back against him, crossing the ditch out of the wood or dipping down into the lane that led at last into Home Meadow. But for the most part she sat still and stiff to stop herself from coming back into contact with his tall body. Once, he said, "Lean back or you'll overbalance. I won't bite." It wasn't the easiest or the most comfortable journey she had ever taken, and she was glad when it was over.

"Tom, get up to Leigh Wood and bring back Miss Milbanke's horse," he said to the groom in front of the house as he lifted Fanny down.

And to the housemaid who came running to the door as they went up the steps, "Jane, Miss Milbanke will need hot water, some things of

Louisa's, and one of the guest rooms. She has had a slight accident with her horse."

"My dear Fanny . . . !" Louisa Knight came out from the drawing room at that moment. She took one look. "What has happened? Are you hurt?"

"I'll tell you in a minute, Louisa," said Edward Knight. "Fanny, Jane will make sure you have everything you need. Get out of those wet things straight away."

Half an hour later, clothed from head to foot in Louisa Knight's clothes—fine linen, a gray sprigged gown and pale slippers—Fanny sat looking around the guest room. The maid had declared her hair almost dry.

"I will put up your topknot, miss, but leave it in a looser loop at the bottom. That way, the rest will dry out."

"Thank you, Jane." At present Fanny's eyes could only see the room through the mirror. The most beautiful patchwork coverlet and draperies hung over the bed. A mosaic of tiny block prints in pinks and browns and pale cream. The walls were papered in chintz, the bureau a pretty little inlaid piece.

"How lovely the patchwork is," she said.

"Miss Louisa made them," Jane replied.

A look of admiration crossed Fanny's face. "All of them? By herself?"

"Miss Louisa's cousins sometimes come to stay. They sit at it together."

"How clever! How long have you worked here, Jane?"

"Three years," said Jane. "It is a good place."

Fanny's gaze met the girl's. "Susan Steadman . . . how is she now? I believe she came here?"

"Susan." Jane's face clouded. "She is better than she was."

"She looked ill the last time I saw her."

"She was ill. We all felt bad. Bob . . . he was a great favorite here. Susan will not get over it for a long time. None of us will . . . But she is as settled as she can be, I suppose."

"Do you like her?"

"She is odd sometimes. But she is nice enough. I liked Bob better."

"What a lucky thing Edward found you," Louisa Knight said as Fanny came into the drawing room a half hour later. "My dear, you might have been drowned! Do my things fit you? Yes, they do. That gray looks better on you than it does on me. Now, sit down. You look pale. Are you recovered?"

"Quite recovered," Fanny said.

"I should have died of fright. It is a good thing you can swim."

"I don't swim," Fanny told her. "The cloak was like a sail. It kept bringing me up."

"It didn't seem to be bringing you up when I found you," said Edward Knight.

"I panicked," said Fanny. "That was birdwitted of me."

"It was quite natural, I should think." Louisa handed her a cup of scalding tea. "Edward and I have been talking. It is raining again outside. It will not be good for you to get another soaking. I could send you home in the carriage, but I think it wiser for you to stay the night. You mustn't argue. Dr. Baillie is coming to dine. He can take a look at you when he arrives and see there is no real harm done."

"But I am perfectly fit," Fanny protested.

"You may feel it now. Later, the shock may set in. Now, someone can ride over to Cranthorne and tell them what has happened. They can say you are to return in the morning, if that suits. Will you have a slice of fruitcake? Or a wafer? You must eat well to keep off any fever."

All these arguments were presented so swiftly and expertly that Fanny was prevailed upon to stay. To tell the truth, now that she was dry again and warm, her legs did feel oddly like stuffed rags. She had little desire to move from her comfortable chair, and little energy, either, to think of departing. She might even have dropped off to sleep if circumstances had allowed.

All the details of the accident were repeated to Dr. Baillie when he arrived and they increased in danger as they were told, so much so that Dr. Baillie, leaning across the table with a twinkle, actually said to Fanny, "Miss Milbanke, we shall have to have a report of this in the *Courier.* What do you think?" To which Fanny replied, "I don't think it would make lively reading, sir. It was not quite sensational enough. I did not quite drown."

Whether it was the result of the accident or Dr. Baillie's good conversation, she had the distinct feeling after dinner that she had drunk too much good wine. It did not only restore the roses to her cheeks, it made her head feel a little tipsy, too, and she was aware once or twice, toward the end, of getting her words somewhat muddled.

Edward Knight missed nothing. When Louisa had led off Dr. Baillie to examine some new book she had gotten, immediately after dining, he said with a look at Fanny's face, "We had better take some coffee before we talk."

"I . . . the wine does seem to have gone to my head," she said with as much dignity as she could muster. "Very like, it is the shock."

"Very like," he observed gravely. "You had better take my arm going into the other room."

"It is not so bad as that," she told him with some dignity.

She proved it by walking in state through the dividing doors and sitting down on the sofa. She took the coffee he poured her with a perfectly composed and stately smile, while Edward took the chair opposite and looked across at her.

"So you want to talk," he said. "Has the coffee steadied your head?"

"Quite, thank you." Fanny wondered if the lights were uncommonly bright tonight or if her eyes had gone queer, too. And extraordinary things seemed to be happening to the patterns on the carpet. They all shifted now and again, when she looked at them hard, as if there had been a small, under-floor earthquake. She pulled herself together. "I . . . I had rather a shock last night." She took a deep breath. "I don't know how to begin to tell you."

"Just tell me."

She looked at him. Was this a good idea after all? Perhaps not. "It . . . it's a little indelicate." She looked away again and went bright scarlet. "It's about Clarence Stanhope. And . . . and Caroline."

"What about them?" He was watching her closely now.

"I . . . I saw Mr. Stanhope last night," she said, getting agitated. "He . . . ." How could she say it? The whole thing was so terribly improper, and yet whom else could she turn to? "There are certain things I have seen at Cranthorne House," she began delicately, then hesitated.

"Yes?" he prompted. "What sort of things?"

Fanny could not bring herself to look at him. She

stared into the cup as she spoke. "I think my cousin has been deceiving us all."

Silence. She lifted her head. His face was expressionless, blank. His eyes were on her face, but still he said nothing. The silence grew unnerving. She said in a voice of entreaty, "Say something! Are you shocked? Yes, of course you are shocked. Who would not be?"

He shook his head. "No, my dear Fanny," he said at last. "Your cousin may have deceived you and Sir George, but she has never deceived me."

"You do not think I've made a mistake, do you? Please say something. Anything . . . You don't think I'm evil minded, do you?"

He got up from his chair and Fanny, with agitated eyes, watched him move to the hearth. He said, "I don't think you're evil minded."

"Tell me something: Is there a connection between this . . . between Caroline's behavior and Sir George's drinking? There is, isn't there?"

Edward Knight turned, shoved his hands deep into his pockets. From the way he frowned at the fireplace, she knew he found the question difficult to answer. "Yes, I think there is," he said at last.

"Sir George drinks because he knows about them? Knows what is going on? Is that it?"

A small hesitation. "Hard to tell," Edward said. "He's an old man." He was being cautious. "I'm not sure how much he knows about your cousin's . . . alliance. I have never questioned him."

"So did you know about it? You knew something was affecting him, or you would not have had Susan spy for you."

"I was worried about the effect they were having on him . . . yes." He walked away from the grate, turned, walked back again. He looked restless and a little grim.

"So what is to be done?" Her eyes, large and green and long-lashed, went up to his. "We must do something, must we not?"

Silence again. Why doesn't he look at me? Fanny thought. She did not think she liked it. It was like being examined under a microscope. "What do you suggest we do?" he asked slowly.

"I . . . I have no idea." It wasn't true. She had an idea, but it scared her. "Confront them, I suppose. Tell them we know. Tell them they must stop it all."

To her horror, he laughed. "And you think that will sort it all out?" he asked. His tone was at once soft and ironic.

"I don't know!" Fanny said. "How do I know how they will react?" She looked up straight into his gaze; she found his laughter unfair. "I thought . . . well, it will do no harm to try, will it?" she said with a twist of hurt pride in her voice.

"Fanny . . ." he said, suddenly coming right over to her.

"What?" she said. "And don't laugh at me again . . ."

"I wasn't laughing at you. I didn't mean to hurt your feelings." He dropped onto the sofa beside her. They looked at each other for a minute with a curious kind of intensity, he taking in the distress on her face, the fine arch of her brows.

"Look . . . Fanny . . ." he said finally. "You're very young. There's so much you don't understand."

"Everyone tells me that," Fanny said crossly. "I get very tired of it! I understand enough."

"Do you?"

"I think so."

"You think so . . . ?" A curious look on his face. Almost a softness, but there was still that hard line to his jaw. His eyes went down to her mouth.

"These people that you think you know . . . ," he said. "They live in a different world from yours."

"I know I haven't been out much in society—"

"I didn't mean that," Edward said impatiently.

"I . . . I do not think Caroline all bad," Fanny said. "I have tried to remember all her kindnesses to me."

"Tried?"

"It is difficult." Her face was coloring again. "It hasn't been easy."

"I don't suppose it has." He had leaned back as Fanny spoke to him, stretching his arm sideways along the back of the sofa, sure and decisive in relaxation as he was in action. He said, "What we are up against is greed."

"Greed?" Fanny said.

"And something else . . ."

"What?" She turned. She looked at him. He seemed very close. As Fanny fixed him with her green eyes, he didn't move. His arm was still stretched along the back of the flowery chintz, his long legs stretched on the Turkish carpet in front.

"Don't you know?" Was he teasing her? It was difficult to tell with men like him.

"No." There was no point in pretending.

"I thought you understood these things." The room was perfectly quiet. Still the same unexplained note in his voice. He lifted a hand, touched the still damp loop of her hair, and unexpectedly let his hand fall to her neck. "I meant"—his whole body moved nearer—"this." The next moment, he kissed her. His hand on the warm skin of her neck was cool, like his lips.

The kiss grew longer, more intense.

Fanny tried to free herself, but now his hands were one on each side of her head.

It lasted seconds only, then she was sitting back staring breathlessly at him. Her voice did not seem to belong to her, her hair was all loose at the back. "What did you do that for?" In her haste to get back away from him, she could not check the gauche question.

He hesitated, then touched her face with one finger. "Is that the first time you've been kissed?"

"No . . . No, it isn't!" stammered Fanny. "And it's extremely indelicate of you to ask, if you don't mind my saying so."

He said, "I don't mind."

"It was also extremely indelicate of you to . . . to . . ."

"To kiss you?"

"Yes."

"You are right. I apologize." There was a smile in his eyes.

"Thank you," said Fanny in a stifled voice. "I . . . I suppose you thought you were making a point." Her hands were still shaking as she tried to retrieve some of her dignity. She still didn't know why he'd done it. "About the nature of the relationship between my cousin and that man. If it was a practical demonstration, I don't think it very relevant . . . or necessary."

"You're right," Edward said, still looking at her.

Fanny got to her feet. She went over to the china shelves, stared at the plates a little. She had never realized how a man's touch could take hold and keep burning away minutes after the actual contact had ceased. It was necessary to change the subject, force the conversation back into safer channels. "What did you mean," she said, "when you said we were up against greed?"

"Think about it."

She wasn't sure she was capable of thinking about anything very logically. She said, "Sir George is a wealthy man. Is Clarence trying to get hold of some of his brother's money through Caroline? Do you think she would wheedle some funds out of her husband to help Clarence with his debts?"

Again that ironic smile. "Something like that," said Edward.

"She would have to work very hard. Sir George hates him. Perhaps she tells him the money is for other things." A sudden chill. She sat down again, in a chair well away from Edward. She said, "I think he must know. About Clarence and Caroline."

"What makes you think that?"

"Sir George's solicitor came to visit the other morning. I was thinking afterward, it was perhaps something to do with a will. They had servants come in to witness something . . . Deacon and Céline. Do you suppose he would cut them out of his will?" She thought some more. "No. That would not fit their behavior. Caroline was very cheerful afterward all afternoon. She would not have been cheerful if she had been cut out."

"Who was this solicitor?" Edward asked tensely.

"A Mr. Pickering. That was his name."

"James Pickering . . ." He simply sat there. He wasn't looking at her anymore. Elbows on knees, he was staring straight ahead at the paneling.

Fanny said, "There's one more thing. That handkerchief. The one you found by Bob's body. I remembered where I saw one like it."

"Tell me." His voice changed. He turned toward her and unclasped his hands.

"I saw Clarence use one like it when we were in the garden a week or two back. I was sketching. He was pretending to wipe Sherry's brow with it and making him feel small." She recounted the full story. "I am sure it is the same kind. The embroidery is very distinctive. Does that help in any way?"

"If we can identify it as belonging to him. Susan recognized it, too. She had seen it when dealing with Clarence's laundry."

"Then why does she not tell the magistrate?"

"It is not quite so simple. Her word, her honesty has been discredited, remember. Clarence, if accused, will say she is lying to get her own back. That she's a biased witness because she has a grudge against him."

Fanny said, "But Clarence wasn't here on the night of Bob's accident. He'd gone back to London."

"You mean he wasn't at Cranthorne. It doesn't mean he'd gone back to London."

"I suppose you're right." Fanny picked up the silver spoon from the saucer. She looked at Edward. Something had occurred to her. "Did Clarence . . . did they make up the story of the stolen ring in order to get Susan out of the house?"

"I'm sure of it."

"But why?" She made herself work it out. "Susan had seen what was going on between them," she said slowly. "And she threatened to tell Sir George."

She saw by his face that it was a correct guess.

"But it's so unjust . . . !" Fanny shook her head almost in disbelief. "How could they . . . ? How could Caroline . . . ? I would never have thought . . ." She gave him a slow glance. "Tell me

—I don't understand—why should Clarence be involved in Bob Steadman's accident?"

"In his murder." He spoke steadily, without any emotion.

"Murder?"

"That's what it was."

She looked at his increasingly familiar face, felt the full power and shock of the word, sat there for a second or two trying to regain her emotional balance. "Are you sure?" she said faintly.

"There was no poaching going on in Leigh Wood that night. Taff Jenkins knows all the local scoundrels. He went to see them all. He knows them all well enough to tell when they are lying. This is a small place. And they were as shocked by Bob's death as the rest of us. The Steadmans are well liked."

"Outsiders, then? Poachers from outside?"

"It doesn't happen. Poachers are like the birds— they stick to their own bit of territory. So . . ." He let out his breath. "Whoever was in the wood that night with his shotgun . . . he was not poaching."

"Then why . . . ?"

"Bob saw something. Something he shouldn't have seen that they didn't want him to blab about."

"But what?" Fanny felt bewildered.

Edward didn't answer directly. He said, "Will you do something for me?"

"Anything. If it will help."

"Will you watch Clarence for me? And your cousin. I know you will find it distasteful, but it's the only way the questions can be answered. And that new gamekeeper who seems to be in with them —Deacon. He is not a local man. He's a Londoner, by his accent. I want to know his connections with

Clarence, if any . . . Can you do that for me? Keep your eyes and ears skinned to what is going on?"

"I think so." Fanny looked around at the quietly furnished room. The real explosion of thoughts and feelings inside her was only just beginning. She said, "Why did they want me there? I should have thought they'd want as few people . . . witnesses . . . around as possible. Didn't it occur to them that I might see something? Notice what was going on?"

"I think you were their one great mistake." He looked at her for a moment with almost a smile. "Your appearance is deceptive, if you don't mind my saying so. You look very quiet and docile. Clarence wanted, I think, a young girl who would be manageable. That is how he saw you when he came visiting at Wentworth Street." There was speculation in the dark gaze. "No one would ever guess how much spirit and energy lie underneath that calm face of yours. No . . . Clarence thought you could be easily managed."

"Managed into doing what?" Fanny was mystified.

"I can't say at this stage." The words were strong, bass-voiced and cagey. He seemed to be struggling against some instinct or other, but in the end he said little. "I just want you to go on looking meek and mild, but stay alert. Watch them closely."

Fanny didn't reveal all her apprehensions, but the questions kept on multiplying inside her head. "The handkerchief," she said. "With the snake and the letter *B*. What do they signify? Have you any idea?"

"It is one of the more theatrical trappings of the Barbary Club."

"The Barbary Club? What is that?"

"It's a gaming club in Covent Garden frequented

by a crowd of degenerates who behave themselves, for the most part, worse than animals. Don't ask me to say more. Except that it's exactly Clarence Stanhope's sort of place."

His voice came quietly and steadily across the space between them. "I want you to be careful, Fanny. We are not playing games with amateurs. I would not choose to put you in this position if I weren't so worried about . . . worried that something might happen to Sir George."

"Happen to him?" Fanny said. "What might happen to him?"

Edward hesitated, but decided on frankness. "Greed and appetite and murder . . . put the three together and you have a pretty dangerous mixture. Clarence has killed once, I think, and would not hesitate to do so again. I won't beat around the bush. I have great fears for Sir George's safety—"

"You think Clarence would kill his own brother?" Fanny was aghast.

"It is what I've thought all along." He looked at her. "And if they've got him to alter his will . . . though we've no proof about that . . ."

"They?" She stared back. "You actually think Caroline might help him to kill Sir George? To get at his money?" Silence. His face had not changed. "Yes . . . you do." She felt sick suddenly.

"Fanny . . ." He clasped his hands under his chin and sat there leaning on them, looking at her. "I have no proof. It's just an instinct . . . But please be careful."

"I'll be careful," she said promptly. And wondered why she found his insistence so reassuring. She picked up her coffee cup and had to put it down again, her hands were shaking so much. Then she gazed for a moment at the patterns on the carpet, thinking that a shock this big was amazingly good for rendering a person stone-cold sober. The patterns didn't shift an inch.

Neither would the fear, she thought, for a very long time.

Chapter Ten

Before she went back to Cranthorne the following morning, Fanny and Edward sat talking out on the lawn. A low table held fruit cordial and glasses. Louisa had gone into the house to fetch a book. Edward sat there looking at her. It made Fanny feel uncomfortable.

He said, "Are you equal to going back?" She could not read the expression in his eyes.

"I think so."

"You must be sure."

"Otherwise . . . ?" She gazed back at him.

"Otherwise you stay here."

"And how would that look?" She took her eyes away, concentrated on the great copper beech at the bottom of the lawn.

"It doesn't matter how it looks. If you're not sure, you're not safe. And if you're not safe, then you stay with us."

What she liked about talking to him was that it gave her a rare feeling of honesty. Only the trouble was, honesty can sometimes be disturbing. That un-

flinching dark gaze did things to her . . . especially
after last night.

Everything this morning was washed bright green
with yesterday's rain. The grass stretched all the
way down to the lake and the woods beyond. Earlier, the sky had been a pale, pale gray, but now it
had turned a pearly blue and the sun had come out.
A wood pigeon called down in the trees.

She did not want to go back to Cranthorne, but
she would not tell him so. She wanted to stay here
in the peace and quiet where it felt safe; yet she
smoothed the fine spotted cambric of the gown she
had borrowed from Louisa and hid what she really
felt.

He said, "If you have anything to tell me, you can
always send over a message by one of the servants.
Annie Bates, the little parlor maid, is to be trusted.
Susan always said so."

"I'll remember that." Fanny saw Louisa come out
of the house and stop to talk to one of the gardeners.
The cambric went into even finer shapes under her
fingers.

"Fanny . . . you're not frightened, are you?"

"No." Her voice was high, yet restrained.

"I should not have told you any of it."

"I am glad you did."

"Are you?" He looked at her again. He believed it
no more than she believed it herself. His gaze was
long and deliberative.

Wood pigeons called again. The sun was warm on
her neck.

"Does Louisa know what . . . what you suspect?" Fanny asked quickly.

"No. Not exactly. She knows I am worried about
Sir George. She shares my worry about his state. But
as for the other—my fears about what Clarence and

your cousin are planning at Cranthorne—I've never quite been able to put it to her . . . find the right words. I didn't want to trouble her too much."

"I see." She liked his dark, straight gaze, the slow burn in his eyes. "But you told me?"

"In your case, there was not much choice." The slow burn turned into a slow smile. "You have this way of launching yourself into the arena . . . either by throwing yourself under my horse or into lakes and such."

"I didn't throw myself." But now he had made her smile, too.

"I was only teasing."

She knew it. She rather liked it, though being teased by Edward Knight was a novel experience. It offered quite another side of him, she found. It made her feel very peculiar and alive when his voice teased like that.

Edward said, "I don't want Louisa to know everything just yet."

"I understand." She studied her hands very properly for a moment, then said, "I shall not tell her. I hope very much that you might be mistaken . . . about Caroline, at least."

"I wish to God I were," he said in a low voice. "Fanny—" His voice was abrupt. "There's something else—"

But he was interrupted. Louisa was there behind them. She said, "Here we are . . . I wish I was not half so forgetful. It would ease my legs a good deal! Edward, that bit of garden by the stables is in a shocking state. I do not know what we are going to do with it. I caught a glimpse of it as I was coming out of the drawing room windows. Hoggett says he cannot get round to it and he mentioned that he met a young man in the public house in Stamford who was looking for work. I wondered if we might take him on. Hoggett says he seems an honest sort of a fellow . . . discharged from the army or some such thing. Which reminds me—I don't know how— when Sir George comes to dine tonight . . . it is Monday, is it not? . . . I must remind him that he left his riding gloves here last week when he came. The trouble is, Fanny, he gets himself embroiled in some argument or other with Edward and then he forgets half the stuff he brought with him. Last Monday it was some long-winded contention about voting in the election . . . do you remember, Edward? He got himself in such a state . . ."

Fanny saw Edward's amused yet slightly sad little smile. She did not know how she could have missed the sensitivity of his face when she first met him. Except that they had fed her a lot of prejudices against him, she thought abstractedly. So many half-truths and small insinuations, and she had swallowed the lot. Stupid, she said to herself. Very stupid. The wood pigeon flew out of the trees and winged its way down across the park. I shall know better from now on. I shall watch them and think for myself. It is the only way to go on. To find out what is really happening.

Fanny went back to Cranthorne prepared for a certain measure, not of hostility exactly, but criticism, perhaps, for having stayed a night in the enemy's camp.

The criticism was carefully rationed.

Falling off one's horse and into a lake was not a ladylike thing to do. It was not very sensible. Falling into the lake when Edward Knight was at hand to pull one out and carry one off to Leigh Park for the night was downright carelessness. No one exactly said so, but they did not need to. Not in so many words.

It was going on for luncheon time when Louisa's little chaise brought Fanny round the loop of the drive and stopped just past the steps and the porch. The terrace at the side of the house caught all the morning sun. Some of the house chairs had been carried outside, but it must have been too hot, for everyone seemed to have gone inside again.

Fanny climbed out of the chaise and crossed the loose gravel to where the long windows stood open into the drawing room. Magnolia leaves lay brittle and brown on the stone flags. The thin line of shade under the house was sharp and blue. She must have stepped on a leaf and snapped it, because there was a movement from the windows and Caroline came out, her dress catching in the breeze.

Her voice said lightly, "Fanny! It's you!"

Her hair was light and perfect, as usual. Her hand came up from the lace jabot and played with the two gleaming gold chains at her neck.

"You worried us to death," she said, again very lightly. "Not coming home . . ."

"I'm sorry." Fanny tried to sound normal.

"I thought you could handle Tranter, you silly girl!"

"So did I." Fanny gave a little laugh. "He wanted to prove me wrong, I suppose. He's an incredibly stubborn animal! I don't know why I didn't discover it earlier. They're bringing him back this afternoon for me."

"Well, you must not ride him again."

Fanny said, "He's really not a wild horse. I should know better next time."

"My dear Fanny, there won't be a next time! Don't you know when to take a warning?" Caroline gave her a mock stern look. "And having to have Edward Knight come to your rescue . . . ! My dear, how they must have enjoyed that! Well, it just serves you right." More smiling severity. "Perhaps you will learn a little lesson."

"I did feel very foolish." That was true enough, at any rate.

"I should hope you did!" Caroline pulled one of the chairs into the shade and sat down. Fanny gave her a guarded scrutiny. These last few weeks she had not supposed Caroline to be an angel. But a prospective murderess? Back here, it was hard to believe. She looked a little pale this morning, in spite of the sun. Or perhaps it was because of the sun.

"Aren't you feeling well?" Fanny asked.

"I'm quite well," Caroline replied quickly. "It's just too hot."

"Perhaps you should go in."

"And worrying about you did not help." Caroline summoned up a frown.

It sounded very convincing. Caroline's face was calm now, lightly smiling. Then Sherry came out from the drawing room. He said, "She made me ride all out to the turnpike to look for you." He reached down to the table for some cordial. Even in this heat, he wore an olive green coat with fine, long cuffs almost down to his knuckles and a cream embroidered waistcoat. "So did you have an exciting stay, Fanny?"

"Hardly exciting." Fanny remembered Edward's instructions and gave them her blandest smile. "It was comfortable enough. I felt very stiff first thing this morning. That is because I'm not used to swimming, I suppose. Louisa insisted I take it easy."

"Louisa would." Caroline leaned across and

picked up a glass, then put it down again and pushed it away. "She likes to make a fuss."

"Do tell me," Sherry said, giving Fanny a thoroughly heavy look with his bright blue eyes, "how you managed to survive a whole evening of Mr. Knight's conversation. Did he sit there all night and stare at the wall as he does here? Or . . ." He removed a biscuit from the plate and took an exploratory bite. ". . . or does he turn into Bluebeard at night, abandon all his restraints, and turn wild with passion?"

"Nothing so far-fetched," Fanny told him, smiling. She did not much like him making fun of Edward in such a tone, but she could not show it. She examined a scuff on the toe of her shoe. "Dr. Baillie dined with us. He kept the conversation rolling." Important to make it all seem very, very casual. "Or else it might have been very dull."

"They say Miss Knight has actually bought some donkeys from a pack train that passed through." Caroline laughed. "Is it true, Fanny? Can you imagine? Donkeys? They are cheaper than horses, she says, for running things around the place. What do you think they will do next? Isn't it a scream?"

"My dear Caro . . ." Clarence had come out of the house. He was puffier than ever, Fanny thought. So much weight crammed into those tight white trousers! So many chins over his high, starched neckcloth. ". . . What do you expect?" he said, pushing back his scant hair with a podgy hand and coming over to Fanny's chair. "It's like to like, don't you think? The Knights have an unerring sense of what suits them best. Donkeys for donkeys . . . eh?"

"I don't think that's very kind." It was out before Fanny could stop herself.

"Don't you?" Clarence said pleasantly.

"No, I don't." She sat there a little flushed. She told herself to take care, to preserve the meek and mild image. They hadn't guessed anything, had they? She didn't think so. She managed to find a smile from somewhere. "The Knights are . . . well, they were very civil to me last night, that's all."

"Quite the little volcano there for the moment," Clarence murmured. The podgy fist dropped on to Fanny's shoulder. "First time I've seen you bite back, my dear. Quite engaging . . . Who'd have thought it?"

Fanny drew her shoulder away.

"Don't needle her, Clarence," Caroline warned.

Clarence grinned and sat down in the chair next to Fanny. "I like needling people," he said. "The ladies especially. Bit of fun. Produces some interesting results. Little Fanny here was just getting stirred up." He laughed. "Get the ladies a bit steamed up and who knows what will follow? Don't you find it so, eh, Sherry? Don't look so coy, my boy. You know what I mean, don't you now?"

Fanny stood up and tipped back her chin. Her hands were trembling, but she hoped her voice was quite even. "I shall go and cool down before lunch."

"Perhaps we all ought to," Caroline said.

"What, and spoil the fun?" Clarence told her, and his laugh followed Fanny on into the cool house and up the stairs.

Luncheon was one of those ritualized affairs that felt like perfect torture, conversation coming on now and again but never quite bringing the whole table together. Caroline's manner was quite odd, remote and somewhat peevish. From her face, one would have guessed her calm and easy, but her body was strangely at odds with this impression. Stiff face muscles. She was very tight in her movements, refusing wine, picking at her food.

Fanny attempted a conversation with Sir George. "You go to Leigh Park this afternoon, I believe?" she said to him. "It's Monday. Mr. Knight expects you as usual, he says. You could have gone over there in Miss Knight's chaise instead of riding. I never thought of it. I should not have sent it right back."

"Carriages are for women," Sir George mumbled into his port. "Always go on Horatio."

"Are you sure you're fit enough?"

"Fit? Perfectly fit, miss!" He glared at her, blue eyes watering, and yet incredibly, behind all that fierceness, she felt somewhere the warmth of friendship.

"She's right, George, old boy." Clarence had wedged a piece of cheese on his fork and leaned over the table. "Ought to take more care of yourself. Stands to reason at your age—"

"Don't try any of your damned hypocrisy here!" Sir George bit back.

"All right, all right!" Clarence, fork in hand, was enjoying himself immensely. "Don't go off at half-cock. No need for that. Only looking out for your welfare, you know . . ."

"Only looking out to what you can get." Sir George shoved back his chair, his face looking like a thundercloud. Silence once again hung across the table, and he swayed for a moment as if pushed by a paroxysm of pain.

"I told you, George. You'll be all right as long as we're here to see to you. You'll have all the care that you need," Clarence said. "Isn't that so, Fanny? Can't say fairer than that."

That afternoon, Caroline suddenly decided upon a

drive to Lowton. In the end, all four of them went,
Fanny and Caroline in the barouche, Sherry and
Clarence riding ahead. As they rattled round the
corner by the Swan, Caroline wiped the nape of her
neck and patted at her forehead and cheeks, which
were shiny from the heat. She said, "I have one or
two things to do, Fanny. The dressmaker, for one
. . . Perhaps you would like to get your ounce of
darning cotton and poke around the place, and we
will meet in the linen drapers' in an hour?"

Fanny assented. She had little choice. When
Sherry joined them, Caroline said edgily, "Where is
Clarence?"

"He has gone over to Mallet's to ask the agent
about some note or other," Sherry told her.

"He is gone to the Swan, more like." She sounded
tetchy and sharp.

Sherry said, "I saw him go in the door at Mallet's."

"And out again in two minutes, I expect," the reply snapped.

Her temper was so variable lately, Fanny thought.
She would be glad to get out of the way of it. She
looked at Sherry. He must have read her thoughts,
for he made a droll face at her behind Caroline's
back, but Fanny did not dare laugh.

An hour seemed to go quickly. The shops were a
little old-fashioned in Lowton, but she enjoyed herself well enough. At the appointed time, Fanny
stood outside the linen draper's, altering the traveling dress in the window to suit her more modern
ideas. If the color was changed, she thought, to
something not so dark, and if the sleeves were a
little more puffed . . . and the neck lowered somewhat . . .

She turned her head and saw Sherry coming down

the street with Caroline on his arm. A carriage went by throwing up dust. Caroline at least looked more pleasant, less strained. That was a relief. Sherry had soft-talked her, perhaps, in that special way he had.

Fanny suddenly remembered the darning cotton and decided she had better run in and buy it as she was meant to do, or else Caroline might turn funny again. As she went up the steps into the shop, a large lumbering wagon backed out of the livery stables, and Sherry and Caroline had to cross the street to get out of the way of it. They almost bumped into Clarence, and she noticed how expansive Clarence's greeting was when he first saw them.

Inside, the long window faced the street. Fanny picked up one or two of the cotton skeins and was relieved to see, when she took a surreptitious peep, that it was Sherry who was coming up the steps into the shop first. He was actually just inside, in the shade, when the rumpus all began.

A dark-headed girl—no, woman—came straight out from an alley across the street and forced her way into Caroline's path.

As Caroline tried to step aside, the woman said, "Oh, no you don't!"

Suddenly Clarence moved in. "Go inside," he said quickly to Caroline. For once, even his blandness seemed to be disturbed.

Caroline looked coldly at the woman, which appeared to infuriate her even more. "You think you've got everything, don't you?" she spat out at Caroline. She had savage eyes and a haggard face.

"I beg your pardon?" Caroline again attempted to get past.

The woman said, "Don't pretend you don't know about me. Don't ask me to believe that." Eyes flashed. "And if he didn't tell you, then it's about time somebody else did. He tried to pay me off. Did you know that?" A dig at Caroline's arm. "Thought he could get rid of me once I'd told him about the child—"

"Teresa—" Clarence had moved. He had hold of the woman's arm.

"A child?" Caroline's manner had not changed. She just stared blankly. "What are you talking about?" She had gone white, though.

Sherry turned for the first time. He had been half hidden from the doorway by a pile of linens almost as tall as himself. But now the raised voices had reached him. He turned and he looked. He said under his breath, "Oh, God . . ."

The woman's voice grew higher. "I don't want any of your damned money. I suppose you're quite cool and comfortable up there while I'm shut up all day in a stifling pigsty?"

"Teresa!" Clarence was trying to push her away. The woman resisted him furiously.

"I am not good enough to be seen in the daylight! Oh, no!" Something flew through the air and landed at Caroline's feet. Something gold and gleaming. Fanny leaned forward to see. A gold necklace.

"Didn't you know he had given it to me?" Teresa saw the look on Caroline's face. "Stole it, did he, because he hadn't got anything else to pay me off with? My God, you're a fool! Don't you know anything about his little ways . . . ?"

"Fanny . . ." That was Sherry's voice. He had come up behind her. He was evidently appalled that she should be witnessing such a scene. "Come on." He already had hold of her. "You must not stay here."

"What is it?" Fanny asked him. "What's happening?"

"Nothing that need concern you." He began to draw her away from the window.

Fanny said, "But she expects to meet me here."

"It doesn't matter. She will not want to meet you just at this moment." Sherry's voice was grim. He found the back entrance, thrust her out of it, paused as if to go back, changed his mind, and then walked her briskly down the alley toward the Assembly Rooms. When they got there, Fanny found that she was trembling, and she leaned against one of the Doric columns for a minute, feeling as if her legs had just gone.

She said, "Who was that woman? Is she . . ." She glanced at Sherry. She had better be careful what she said. She had better not let on for the moment that she knew of Clarence's affair with Caroline. Not for the moment. It would only complicate matters. Besides, she wanted to hear how Sherry would reply. "Is she a former mistress of Clarence? He . . . he knew her, did he not?"

"What do you know of Clarence's mistresses?" Sherry's voice had a peculiar note.

"I . . . know of his reputation. I know he has had a string of mistresses in London. I know . . ." She stopped. "I know he is licentious. I take it that one of his cast-off women has caught up with him?" A little silence. "But . . . but what has it to do with Caroline?" Go carefully, Fanny, she thought. Even if Sherry knows about the affair, he will not want to tell you. Try coming in at an angle and you may find out if he knows. "Is this woman a little . . . crazy? Does she think that because Clarence stays at Cranthorne, and Caroline is beautiful, there must be something going on between them?"

"Very probably." Sherry's gaze moved along the line of playbills on the wall. There was in his voice an odd kind of relief that he would not have to explain too much. He paused before saying anything else. "So you know about Clarence?" he said. He, too, looked shaken.

"Oh, yes. I know about Clarence." She looked at him. "How long do you think this woman . . . Teresa . . . has been in Lowton? Do you think she followed him down here?"

"Long enough," Sherry said.

"What will Caroline say, do you think, when we get home?"

"Enough." Just for a second, a long shaft of sunlight shimmered on some expression in his eyes that Fanny did not quite understand. Then he looked away. Nothing in his voice, either. It was quite empty. "There is a ball here the week after next. You will enjoy that. Shall we have a look around inside?"

You don't say anything, Fanny thought, but you know. You know about them. You are more loyal to her than I thought. I shall have to be extra careful what I say from now on.

Chapter Eleven

Caroline did not come down to dinner that evening. Fanny, on her way downstairs, had heard raised voices and then broken sobs from behind the closed doors of Caroline's room, and saw Céline hurrying down later with a disconcerted air that suggested that she, at least, among the servants was in Caroline's confidence. But on the surface of things, the evening went on without any obvious storms.

Clarence came down in a foul mood and drank silently and heavily. Almost to match his brother, Fanny thought. She felt relieved that Sir George was not there, that he was dining at Leigh Park with Edward.

Edward. She would have to tell him what had happened this afternoon, she thought, picking half-heartedly at a piece of potato on her plate. He might be able to make something of it. Sherry came down late. Fanny guessed that he had been trying to console Caroline, help put things right, but with Clarence in the dining room, there was no chance for Sherry to confide in her or for her to ask any more questions. The meal passed slowly, interminably. Fanny had never seen Sherry look so silent and mopey, distracted, almost, as if the furor had at last gotten through to him as well.

"Do you want some more wine?" he asked her. He spoke in a subdued voice, as if Clarence might hear him and start an argument.

"No. Thank you," said Fanny, pushing the potato to one side of her plate. Then she poked it back again.

"The pork was very good."

"Yes."

Clarence reached out and grabbed the wine bottle. She saw him aim a foul look at Sherry, but nothing more lethal, to her great relief. They went on eating for a while in silence. Colman came and took the plates away. Fanny thought, from a glance at Clarence's face, that it would have given him the greatest pleasure to reach out and knock both their heads off, but he just glowered instead.

"Mrs. Hurst says the weather will break tomorrow," Fanny ventured, longing to push back her chair.

"Really?" Sherry cast another surreptitious glance in Clarence's direction. His light tongue seemed to have entirely forsaken him for the moment. He was more nervous than she had ever seen him. Clarence poured more wine into his glass. She almost wished he would explode at them. It would be better than this awful waiting.

The custards were cleared and fruit laid in their place. Then Colman went out of the room and shut the door behind him. Sherry finished his wine as if his life depended on it. Fanny gazed steadily at her plate.

"I . . . I think I shall go upstairs now. Perhaps Caroline will need some company," Sherry said. She glanced up and saw Clarence looking at him. He replied sarcastically, "I shouldn't think so. Shouldn't think so at all. Company's probably the last thing she needs. Said she had a splitting head." A drunken sort of laugh. "Can't think what that's caused by, can you?"

"The heat, I expect," Sherry replied. His voice was quick.

"The heat . . . Ah, yes . . ." Clarence's bleary gaze went to Fanny. She did not look back at him. She was afraid he would see how much she knew. She scraped back her chair, ready to make her escape.

"Dear little Fanny . . ." Clarence drawled. "The eye always goes down." His tone was a mixture of menace and curiosity. "Such a self-contained little miss. I wonder what she is thinking? Sometimes you could almost be persuaded she sees right into you."

"I shall not bother Caroline tonight, then," Fanny said, her color high. There was nothing for it but to brazen her way out of the room. At the door, she looked at Sherry only. "Good night," she said.

"Good night, Fanny." And he gave her a sympathetic, brief little smile.

Caroline looked brittle when Fanny came into the breakfast parlor the next morning. They were the only two there. Caroline sat at the table drinking bitter green tea.

"Is your headache quite gone?" Fanny asked gingerly.

"Entirely, thank you." Her eyes had dark rings about them, though. A piece of buttered bread was on her plate, but she did not bite into it. She took the conversation a stage further with a brief, overzealous smile. "I suppose you are wondering about that little affair in Lowton yesterday?"

"What was that?" Fanny asked casually.

"That wretched woman who accosted me in the street." A tiny bite out of one corner of the bread. "Sherry says you heard something of it in the shop."

"Only a little . . ." Careful, Fanny thought. "I did wonder what was happening, it is true."

"I gather . . . Sherry says . . . you have surmised what sort of females my . . . Clarence . . . associates with at times." The words had cost her some effort. Caroline frowned at the cloth on the table, then at her cup, and finally at the trees outside the window.

"I . . . I had heard something of it in London, before I came here." Safe enough. And honest.

"Then you will know what kind of . . . woman it was that set upon me yesterday." The dreadful agitation in her eyes was beginning to show itself in other ways. She picked up a spare knife and began to turn it round and round in her fingers. "She was quite deranged, you know." A light laugh, none too steady. "I told him, if he has got himself into some scrape or other with some . . . slut . . . he must just get himself out of it again." Little breaths, coming fast, lifted the light stuff of Caroline's bodice. "I will not have them accosting me in the street because they think I can get him to pass on money for them. It is a blessing no one else was about. What in heaven's name would someone like Lady Austen have thought?"

"Lady Austen would probably have seen through her at once . . . as you did," Fanny added as a soothing measure.

"You think so?"

"I am sure of it," Fanny said pleasantly.

"Then you are probably right," Caroline said, giving Fanny a sideways glance through subtle brown eyes. "I still feel you must think it odd." She was using that small, rather childlike voice she sometimes assumed.

Fanny said, "Knowing Clarence, I would think nothing odd."

That relaxed her. It seemed to be the answer Caroline required. And she hadn't sensed Fanny's real reactions at all. "Did I tell you we are to go on Lady Austen's picnic tomorrow?" She changed the subject with obvious relief. "It is her annual do. It is a bit of a bore, but we are obliged to go. Everyone will." The voice was high, Caroline's policy plain. Back to normality. Back to the social whirl. She looked up. There was nothing in the brown eyes. No suggestion of pain or panic or jealousy or any other burning emotion. But Fanny knew they were all there.

Somewhere. Very well hidden. But undoubtedly there.

* * *

The picnic was at Lark Hill, on the edge of the Austen estate at Stamford Magna. It was a fine day with small cauliflower-shaped clouds as they drove up the gentle slope of Lark Hill. At the top was a view that looked out over three counties. All the guests were very civil about the weather this year and the state of the hedges. Then rugs were spread and a picnic luncheon of chicken and salads and pork pie and sausage was served, followed by apple pie and strawberries in wine and biscuits and plum-cakes, with six or seven bottles of wine and punch as well.

The hills across the valley were wide and green. Under the trees there was shade and no wind, and the party of twenty-five or so were scattered around in little groups. Fanny sat with Caroline and Sherry and the Misses Rushworth at one end of the little clearing. Close against her feet was a sharp blaze of sunshine. It was very hot and even the horses, tied up to graze in the field beyond, seemed to feel it. They stood around quietly and swished at the flies.

"Who is that with Lady Austen?" Fanny asked. She had tipped her bonnet farther over her eyes to keep off the glare.

"That?" Caroline said. "That is Miss Austen."

"I did not know there was a Miss Austen."

"Oh, yes. She has been away, staying in Derbyshire with her aunt." Caroline shut her eyes again.

"She does not look like Lady Austen."

"That is a blessing, then," Sherry drawled lazily. He was stretched on the grass beside them.

"That is not a kind remark," Fanny said, laughing.

"And Lady Austen is not very handsome. In fact, she is remarkably ugly," said Sherry. "Would you wish to look like her if she were your Mamma?"

"Not exactly, but . . ."

"Then the case is settled." His eyes were laughing. He leaned on one elbow and began to play idly with the pale green ribbon falling from Caroline's sash.

Fanny said, "She has beautiful hair. Miss Austen, I mean."

Miss Austen stood up as Fanny spoke and began to brush specks of grass from her skirt. Even with twenty yards or so separating them, Fanny could see the rich glints in Miss Austen's luxurious auburn hair. She had to admire the fine French cambric under the pelisse of amber shot with sarcenet, elegantly edged with cream satin ribbon. The same cream ribbon tied her flower-trimmed bonnet. Her morocco shoes were fine light kid.

"True." Sherry's eyes lingered on the lady's red hair.

"Her jaw is too large," Caroline said with a sharp turn of her head.

He did not say anything, but gazed at the branches of the trees above their heads. There was a laze in his voice. "It is a sign of breeding."

"In a horse, perhaps," Caroline said. "Still, I suppose she does look somewhat like a horse."

It was as well, Fanny thought, that Miss Rushworth had gone over to talk to the rectory people, though she supposed Caroline would not have been so openly cutting if Miss Rushworth had been around.

"You are only put out because she picked you up on your bad French," Sherry said.

"It is as good as hers," Caroline replied. "She merely wanted to put me down." She was wearing a small turquoise ring, and she started to twist it round and round on her finger, as if unscrewing some bottled-up emotion.

"You shouldn't have started it all by correcting her about Lady Oxford's furniture." Sherry plucked at a blade of grass and put it between his teeth.

"She has no more been inside Lady Oxford's place than I have. She only pretends she has."

"But Miss Austen is not the kind to be contradicted," said Sherry.

"Neither am I," Caroline said shortly. "You might take my side now and again instead of always picking at what I say."

"I do take your side."

"When it suits you. When you feel like it." Caroline went on twisting the ring. "You men are all the same. You say one thing and you mean another. You think you deceive us, but you do not at all." The ring turned and caught the sun. Fanny thought it all most uncalled for. She threw Sherry a glance, but he said nothing more.

Miss Rushworth came back with her sketching book and her drawing box. She smiled brightly at Sherry. "There is a dear little clump of trees over by that rock," she told him. "Can you see it? I mean to capture it with my pens."

"You could capture anything, Miss Rushworth." He sat up and gave her his most melting smile. He reached over and took her box. "Let me help you to get settled."

"I . . . I think I shall have to sit over there, to the right." Miss Rushworth was all of a flutter. She had gone bright scarlet.

"By this sapling," Sherry said. He got himself up from where he had been lying. He made a disproportionate fuss about getting her settled. Miss Rushworth could not take her eyes off him.

Fanny followed this little scene with her eyes and could not help being amused. "She will never be able to draw a single line now," she said. "He has got her in such a state."

"She can't draw anyway," Caroline said idly. She didn't sound spiteful anymore. Just cold and calm.

"He's a dreadful flirt."

"He always was," Caroline said. "It's the thing he's best at in all the world."

A warning? Fanny wondered. She found a light laugh from somewhere. "I think he could do other things just as well. He could do more, much more with himself, I think, if he put himself out."

Caroline turned her head. "You're very knowledgeable, for someone who has only just met him," she said.

"I've known him quite a time now. Almost six weeks."

"Six weeks!" Caroline sounded amused now, sardonic.

"It's long enough!" Why did she have to sound so scathing?

"Oh, yes . . . long enough." An odd note. What did that mean? Caroline's mouth twitched. "Men can do it quite easily in six weeks. All that they want to do. And by then, it's a little late, isn't it?" She started to laugh. "My God—six weeks! You are a scream, Fanny . . ."

Fanny had definitely expected Edward and Louisa to be there that afternoon, and she found herself vaguely surprised that they were not. A closer look at her reactions revealed an almost childish sense of disappointment mixed with all sorts of other emotions: a faint anxiety, restlessness, annoyance even. If everyone else was here, surely they should have come, too?

Sketching and reading took up a whole hour. Extraordinary how it dragged out, even in company. Fanny almost wished she had stayed home.

And then at three o'clock, they arrived. Louisa had been delayed by a trifling domestic disturbance. A bird had come down one of the chimneys and they could not get it out of the dining room no matter how they had tried. And then, of course, there had been soot everywhere and the small matter of some broken china and Mrs. Manning, the housekeeper, carrying on as if Vesuvius had gone up . . . All this was told with such a comic drollery that even Lady Austen was forced into a smile.

Edward wore a dark gray coat and a paler waistcoat. He leaned back against the side of the chaise, folded his arms, and waited patiently for Louisa to get to the end of her protracted story. When it was all told, he went over and stood talking to Colonel Long. Fanny looked across at him and his dark, almost expressionless face, his thick hair, his strong jaw and that little movement, now and again, at the corners of his mouth. There was a great part of him that she did not know, a great part of him she thought she wanted to know, but what had that to do with her immense agitation at the sight of him? Would her feelings toward him ever make sense? He was the safe, careful voice of reason to whom she had listened last night, believed in as a child would. So why did he still unnerve her so much? Why didn't he seem at all real this afternoon?

Louisa came over and spoke to them all, to Fanny especially, but Edward did not. He was ignoring her, she supposed, because he did not want Caroline to suspect anything, but she still felt childishly hurt and she wanted to make him come over, make him look at her. She remembered the evening she had spent with him at Leigh Park. All their conversa-

tions, and that kiss. Had she imagined it? She ought
to forget it as he apparently had, and push it right
out of her head.

"There's some chicken left," Lady Austen said,
coming over to them. "Miss Knight, you have had
nothing at all. Can we make something up for you?"

"Thank you, no. We dined at home." Louisa
laughed. "In the breakfast parlor. Mrs. Manning
made a great fuss of wiping soot off all the plates.
What a pretty sketch, Miss Rushworth! What is it, a
waterfall? I do hope those boys playing at shuttlecock won't disappear over the edge."

Sherry said, "Come and have a game with me,
Fanny. There are some spare racquets." His voice
was light and persuasive. He's doing it because Caroline's being all moody, Fanny thought. He's being
especially sweet-tempered because he does not want
her to spoil our afternoon, and he knows she makes
me feel uncomfortable.

She forgot Edward and Caroline and everyone else
for a while, but the game was a short one. The wind
kept whisking the shuttlecock high up into the trees.
Finally, it lodged there, out of reach on a green
branch. Fanny flopped down on the grass, breathless. She gazed across at Sherry, sitting with his
hands clasped around one knee beside her. He was
watching Clarence, who had arrived quite suddenly
just after the Knights and had gone over to talk to
Caroline at the other side of the clearing.

"Caroline is bored," Fanny observed. "Or else she
is still cross."

"She'll get over it."

Fanny nodded. She examined his blue eyes.
"Sherry . . . ?"

"Yes?"

"I wish . . ." She stopped. "You're quite close to Caroline . . ."

"Am I?" A slightly mocking grin.

"Well . . . usually you are. I know she's . . . crusty today."

"You can say that again . . ." He was gazing into the distance.

"Don't you think someone should . . ."

"What?"

"Oh . . ." She plucked at the grass. Her nerve failed her. "Nothing. I just thought . . ." How would he react if she came straight out with it? If she said Caroline was playing her husband false. She'd thought at first that she could say it, exactly like that, only now she knew that was foolish. She couldn't. She slightly lifted her head and looked right into his eyes. She said, "You have not heard what happened about the woman in Lowton? I . . . I half hoped it might mean that Clarence would leave. That it might have put an end to the . . . the friendship between him and Caroline."

Sherry seemed not to be listening and watched a boy run past with a hoop.

"But everything goes on just as usual," she said. "It is odd, is it not? Did you not think there would be more of an explosion?"

"Hard to say." He reached out and put the two racquets together. But he knows, she thought suddenly. In his eyes for a fraction of a second, there had been an expression—something guarded—that in no way matched his easy smile.

"Do you think he got Caroline to give the woman money? Is that why it has all blown over? It puzzles me. I wish you would say what you are thinking."

Suddenly, quite athletically, Sherry got up, leaned down to take her hands, drew her to her feet as well.

"I think," he said with an amazingly warm smile, "that you should stop asking questions or you will give yourself a headache. I never knew a woman who did not want to ask questions! It spoils the complexion and always leads to trouble. Did you know that?" The smile lingered and teased. "Are you any good at climbing trees? Because if not, we shall have to ask one of these boys to go up there for us. I get vertigo even climbing the stairs. Which one shall we pick? The boy with the hoop?"

Miss Austen believed herself the finest of the younger ladies present that afternoon. The fact was made obvious by her behavior. She did not mind trampling all over other people's feelings. Hardly a minute went by without her putting down someone else's opinions on the view, or mentioning the superior vistas to be found in Derbyshire, or arriving at her own conclusions at the expense of her mamma's.

There was another thing: she could not keep away from Edward. On the least opportunity, she was there at his side to smile at his every word.

Fanny was standing by the carriages still watching the children at play when Edward finally came across, almost as if by accident, to exchange a few words. There was a movement behind her and he was standing there looking down at her. He seemed extraordinarily tall. "You look fatigued," he said.

"Yes." Fanny flushed. "It is from too much running around in the sun."

"But you were enjoying yourself?"

"Yes." So he had been observing her, she thought. She suddenly remembered the incident in Lowton. "I have something to tell you," she said in a low voice. "Is there somewhere quiet where we can talk?"

A child tore past, slithering down over the grass. Edward said, "It's difficult here."

"I realize that. Only—"

"Ah . . . Mr. Knight!" Miss Austen's voice, husky yet penetrating. She had come up behind them. "I was going to ask you . . ." She stopped and looked at Fanny. "I'm not interrupting, I hope? You were not having a private conversation?"

"No," Fanny responded almost defensively. "No, of course not."

"Good." Miss Austen breathed out a smile. After that, she proceeded to ignore Fanny altogether and concentrated on Edward. "Do you know, Edward . . ." Her hand slipped possessively through Edward's arm. ". . . it is so strange to be back here in Stamford! To switch from one place to another is a very odd thing for a day or two. I do believe you are grown taller than ever! You must tell me all that has been going on. I'm dying to hear . . ."

"Are you?" Edward smiled. "What was it you wanted to ask, Annabella?"

"Oh . . . it will wait." A swift, sidelong glance in Fanny's direction. "Until later. Until . . . we are just the two of us. Actually, Papa wished to talk to you. He is over there at the other side. Do come now. I'm sure Miss . . ." She looked inquiringly at Fanny.

"Milbanke," Fanny said.

"Miss Milbanke will not mind, will you, Miss Milbanke? What a sweet brooch! You have lost one of the pearls in it, did you know? I only mentioned it, in case it is somewhere about."

She knows as well as I do that the pearl has been missing for years, Fanny thought, watching Miss Austen tow Edward away. She knows it is an old brooch, though very pretty, and that by pointing it out, it makes me feel poor and dowdy in front of Edward. He didn't try to stop her taking him off. But then, he wouldn't, would he? He could scarcely take his eyes off her. I suppose there is something or other between them. They come from the same sort of families. Rich, assured.

Fanny looked at them crossing the top of the slope still arm in arm and she thought how handsome Edward looked suddenly, more handsome than Sherry, taller, more striking. And all at once he did not seem like a friend anymore. He looked sure of himself and very strong. Yet something inside her whispered, I hate Miss Austen. She is as hard as nails; she is the last person I would want to know. And I hate him for letting her lead him away like that.

Fanny went back and sketched for a while. It was clouding over and they all began watching the sky. Lady Austen grew concerned about the bad effects of the evening dew. She was getting restless, making moves to go, to get the carriages harnessed up. "You cannot imagine, Miss Knight, what harm the dew can do," she told Louisa. "It is bad for the nerves. It makes you out of sorts. My feet are like bits of ice— even Miss Milbanke is shivering."

Fanny said she would walk down and fetch Sir George, who was down over the slope of the hill viewing the boys chasing their hoops. And, if Caroline approved, they could set off for home. She was really a little chilly now with the wind getting up and the sun gone.

"As you wish," Caroline said. "But George will not come unless he wants to. He is very stubborn, you know."

Fanny went down the slope and came up behind Sir George before he had noticed. She felt affected, suddenly, by the look on his face. Pensive, silent, almost nostalgic. A look most unlike his usual sanguine temper. She reached out and touched him on the arm. "The children are enjoying themselves greatly," she said to him.

"What?" He gave a visible start. "Oh, it's you, miss. Following me around! Can't get a minute's peace!"

He always said this. It did not mean anything, Fanny thought. "Someone has to follow you around," she said. They went on standing there, gazing out at all the fun. "Should you like to bowl a hoop again?" she asked softly. "I think I should."

"More skill in my time." His hands clasped and unclasped behind his back. "Could show those young monkeys a thing or two."

"I expect you could." Time seemed to run on. She smiled after a while. "That little boy is the quickest. The one with the reddish hair."

Sir George waited a moment, while he followed the boy with his eyes. "He is the wildest. I suppose it is the same thing." And he went on looking at the boy with a terrible lost look about his face.

"I suppose so." Had he heard her? She wasn't sure. She did not know whether to stay or not. "Are you coming back up? Everyone is going. The carriages are being hitched up." Oddly, she was loath to leave him there. He looked so absent, suddenly.

"In a minute," he said.

She looked at him, at his queer, expressionless eyes. Should she take hold of him, make him come?

"You know . . . it is a funny thing . . . we did not have any children." He held his hands together now, pressed the fist of one into the palm of the other. Pressing, turning. "All those years . . . all those months. I cannot tell why we had none. Can you?"

Fanny felt her heart shrink with pain. She did not know what to say to him. Below them the children went on screaming and running. Above them, unseen, above the brow of the hill, people scurried around and horses clanked into harness.

"If we had, it would all have been different. Would it not?" he asked gruffly.

A silence.

"Anne . . . would it not?"

His voice was harsh and questioning. He's in his own world, Fanny thought, horrified. He thinks I'm her, his wife. His first wife. Anne, his real wife. Oh, God, what do I do? Why didn't I see what sort of state he was in? What do I say?

She half took a breath, then put out a tentative hand. "Sir George . . . ," she said. "It's getting cool. It's time we went back up."

She moved. She tightened her grip on his arm. "There's such a black sky coming," she said.

Sir George turned his head, saw her, stared at her blankly.

She turned him half around, put her hand right into the crook of his, holding on so that he could not resist or push her away. The grass was a little slippery, but her shoes held on it. She had just started to get him to move when it happened.

She heard someone cry out suddenly, "Watch out! Move out of the way—quick!" Turning, she saw the wheels of a carriage slithering, skidding at a slant, coming straight for them over the brow of the hill. The horses could not stop it. They were being dragged along, too. Fanny acted in a flash. She put out both hands and shoved Sir George hard, saw him lurch sideways, felt him pull her with him . . .

The great crash was the carriage turning over onto its side and tipping down the rest of the hill past them. The neighing and the trampling was the horses being taken with it.

Fanny crawled out of a small ditch, shaking all over.

Sir George was winded but safe beside her.

"Fanny!" She heard Edward's voice shouting as he came down the slope.

Heard, but did not quite register.

Stupid. Quite stupid, she thought. There's nothing wrong with me, but my legs won't hold me.

The carriage plowed into a pile of bushes and stopped in its tracks only a yard or two from where a small band of children stood mesmerized.

Chapter Twelve

She was aware of being taken back to Sealham, the Austens' place. Aware of being made to lie down on a sofa in a huge, empty sitting room. The sofa was hard, blue, and shiny. They fetched her smelling salts and tea. She knew she did not want either, nor did she want all those people around. At last they all went away.

Except one. Edward. He stayed after all the others had gone into a room across the hall.

"Fanny, are you feeling better?"

"I don't know. I don't think so," she said. She stared at the glass in her hand. "I can't tell you."

"You are not hurt?"

"No."

"Then what is it? You are still shocked?" He bent down very close to her.

"No. I feel . . . nothing."

"You must feel something?" He didn't go. He was on one knee there beside her. She could almost smell the vitality in him, all that power from his hand on her arm.

"I'm frightened." It helped to have said it. She wondered, for no real reason, where Annabella Austen was. She half expected her to walk in through the door at any moment.

A silence. "What are you frightened of?"

"I'm not sure. I wish I knew. I'm frightened of Clarence . . . and of Caroline, I suppose." She looked up. "Do you suppose it was him—Clarence —the accident with the carriage?"

"I don't know." His voice was a mixture of taut-ness and regret. "It might just have been an acci-dent."

"Do you believe that?"

"I wish I did."

"Then you suspect something?"

"Yes." Another pause. "I'm sorry you are fright-ened. You have every reason to be, of course. It was not a pleasant experience."

"No." She attempted to make a small joke of it. "I suppose you will say next that I was throwing my-self under other people's horses again?" She ex-amined a deep grass stain down the front of her skirt. And the long, raw graze on her elbow.

"Not this time." He sounded gentle. His finger touched the grazed skin. "You must have that seen to or it will fester."

"I will have it seen to when I get home." Cranthorne. The thought now made her shudder.

"Did I hurt you?"

"No. No, it was not that." His touch had burned more than the graze, she thought. "How is Sir George? Is he pretty well?"

"He is sitting with a glass of brandy in the library." Edward sounded ironic.

"He was in such a strange state," Fanny said. "When I was talking to him, I mean, before it all happened. I wanted to tell you, but I didn't have time."

Edward's hand dropped to the blue damask of the sofa. He was still wearing the dark coat, though he had loosened the white neckcloth. "What sort of a state?" he asked.

"Abstracted. Not quite here. And he thought I was Lady Anne. Edward, there is something else. I did not have a chance to tell you; Miss Austen dragged you off." She told him of the incident in Lowton. "It was dreadful. She was left quite floored. I think she still is, underneath." She glanced at the closed door. "Where is Caroline?" she asked nervously.

"She is in the drawing room pretending to have hysterics about the accident." His eyes looked grim.

"It may be true hysteria. She is like that, though she tries to hide it. You have to be very careful what you say to her. Once or twice I have seen such near violence in her eyes. But then, perhaps it is not surprising when Clarence has been keeping this woman concealed in Lowton for weeks and weeks . . ."

"What did Clarence actually say to this woman?" Edward asked.

"Not very much. He had not much chance. She kept going for Caroline."

"And Mr. Crawley?"

"Sherry? He was not near enough to say anything. He was too much concerned, in any case, on getting me out of the way before I heard it all." She looked at him. "That must prove that he knows more than he lets on," she said slowly. "I suspected as much. What frightens me now is that this woman, Teresa, might come up to the Hall and cause another scene. Every day I expect it, even though it has gone so quiet."

She waited for him to reply. He did not.

Fanny said, "Do you think you will be able to find out who she is? What has happened to her and if she is still in Lowton? She . . . talked about a child. That was what shocked Caroline the most, I think. She went like a ghost."

"I will find out what I can." Edward sounded quite distant.

"I shall feel better if you do. Edward . . ."

"Yes?"

"Should I talk to Sherry, do you think? Perhaps he could help us. He knows Caroline has her faults, but it concerns me that he does not know the full sum of what we suspect . . ."

"No. Don't talk to him." His tone was harsh. He looked at her, softened his tone somewhat. "Or to anyone," he added quietly. "We cannot risk it. It must not get back to her."

"Perhaps you are right." She still looked troubled. "He does tell her things. Very well, I shan't tell Sherry." Yet, she thought. But if there are any more tight moments . . . then I shall make up my own mind.

"Good girl." She thought he was going to touch her again, but he did not.

"This afternoon . . . ," she said, suddenly.

"Clarence was near the carriages talking to the grooms. I saw him when I went down to find Sir George."

Edward said, "A good many people were near the carriages. Did you see any action of his in particular? Anything suspicious?"

"No."

"And I was talking to Annabella." A simple statement.

"So you . . . you did not see anything, either?" Fanny said stiffly.

"No. I was too absorbed." He answered absently, as if he saw no cause for hiding his preoccupation with Annabella Austen. "Lady Austen blames it on her new stable lad. He is clumsy, she says. Not worth keeping on, except that his father was a good servant. She has given the lad a good dressing-down for not turning the carriage more carefully."

"That is all very well, but I think you ought to get Sir George away." Her voice was low and in a rush. Suddenly, all the fear, the panic, was coming back. "I don't think he should stay at Cranthorne . . . Oh, Edward . . . can you not do something for him?" Her eyes came up to his. They were full of tears all at once. "Someone has to . . . that poor old man!" Her voice started to break. "I don't mean I am frightened for myself. It is for him . . . Can you help him? Please . . . ?" The tears started to roll down her cheeks. She did not even bother to stop them anymore.

"Don't—Fanny . . ." The two words, spoken in a low voice, sounded husky. At the same time his arms came out to reach for her. "I'll help him. I promise. You mustn't cry . . . Oh, God, come here . . ."

The kiss, over in a few seconds, shook her so

much that it might have been of an hour's duration. Her lips, soft as petals, moved away from his at long last as she let out a long breath and let her wet face fall once more against his. Still shaking, she could only say, "I am not usually like this."

"I know you are not." His hand ran gently down over the nape of her neck, moving over the loose, soft strands of her hair. His voice in her ear seemed to be smiling. "You are usually . . ."

She never found out what she usually was, for a second or so later the door behind them opened and a voice—Lady Austen's voice—boomed out, "Is she feeling better?" She strode into the room just as Edward let Fanny go. "Doesn't look much better," was her next remark. "Edward, I thought you were supposed to be calming the girl down. That is what Louisa said. Seems to me she is more flushed than ever! Been crying, have you? Got a fever?"

"No." Fanny threw a helpless glance toward Edward, but he was no use. He was right over there standing by the fireplace.

"You men are all alike," Lady Austen said, her sharp eyes on Fanny's face. "Not a bit of use in an emergency. Go and get her a glass of brandy, Edward. It is much more use than your soft words."

"I don't care for brandy," Fanny protested.

"How do you know? I daresay you haven't ever tried it." Lady Austen's gaze held a certain intensity, so that Fanny was forced to look away. "Thought so," she said briskly. "Well, go along, Edward! What are you waiting for?"

Fanny knew who Annabella took after. Bossy. A little overpowering. But there was a difference. She liked old Lady Austen. Annabella she did not like at all, and never would.

* * *

Fanny scarcely slept at all that night. Rather, she went off now and again into light, disturbing dreams that seemed more like reality than sleep. Annabella Austen, with her insolent voice, was calling to her in one of them, but Fanny was in a room where the door was locked and all the windows tight shut, so it did not matter if you did not answer her.

Then the room changed, became an unpleasant, hot kind of road with a tall, heavy tree at the end of it. And Edward was waiting by the tree, but the road was melting down in front of her and sticking to the bottoms of her shoes, and then Caroline was there telling her not to be such a slowcoach. Caroline was dressed in a yellow dressing gown, and there was something very wrong with her arms, because they were all stiff, and she was getting smaller and smaller until you got used to her being that small and you discovered that she was really a doll. A small, stiff, golden dolly that someone had thrown into the ditch.

Only when you picked her up, her face was not her own at all, but the shiny, aristocratic, pots-of-money face of Annabella Austen . . .

"We all had such a shock," Caroline said the following morning. "Of course, George should not have been down there. Heaven knows what he was doing wandering off all by himself! But there, that is what he is like these days. I certainly did not know that you were down there, too, Fanny. Nor did Lady Austen, she said. Still, it is a mercy you were."

"Yes," said Fanny.

"He would have been pinned down like . . ." Caroline disposed of her feelings with a little shudder. "But we will not talk about that. Mr. Knight seemed very concerned about you." Her voice went up a tone. "Really, my dear Fanny, I suppose you should be flattered. What was he saying to you all that time you were shut up with him?"

"I was not shut up with him," said Fanny.

"I should have called it so," said Caroline.

Fanny picked up her writing things, stacked them together, and became bland. "He was not in there with me the whole time," she lied. "He went through to the back quarters to fetch some brandy. He was a long time gone."

"But what did he say to you? What did you talk about while he was there?"

"He just wanted to know what had happened. If I saw anything . . ."

"Saw anything?" Caroline looked sharp. "Why should you have seen anything? What was there to see?"

Wrong move, Fanny thought. She said, "I did not mean that exactly. I meant he wanted to know if I had had any warning. I told him I had not. It was just luck that I turned my head at the right time . . ."

"Luck, indeed! That was what I told George." Caroline's face relaxed. The suspicion had gone. "I suppose you will not ride this morning? I suppose you will stay in?"

"Yes," Fanny said. "I have some letters to write."

Midmorning, she went to find some more writing paper. The library was empty. No paper in the drawers. Céline told her that milady had some upstairs. Fanny went up. The door to Caroline's bedroom was ajar, neither open nor closed. Was she in there? Fanny tapped. No reply. She pushed at the door with her hand. Caroline's maplewood workbox, the one with the silver clasp, lay on the table,

the bed was rumpled a little, but no one was there.
She had gone down again, then.

No sound from the billiard room along the passage.

No one around. No voices.

Back in her own room, where Fanny went next,
Mrs. Hurst was bending herself down, bit by stout
bit, to clear out the bottom drawer of the chest.

"You caught me at it," she said, stuffing a handful
of old newspapers and receipts into the basket that
stood by the window. "Clearing out rubbish. This
house is the devil, if you do not mind me saying so,
miss. I told Sir George I could not stand it many
weeks longer. Nothing was cleared out in the spring
because of my nasty turn, but it will be done now,
room by room, whether he likes it or not. You need
not tell him you saw me at it."

"I won't tell him," said Fanny with a smile. "In
any case, I do not think he would notice. He scarcely
spoke to anyone this morning. Have you seen Lady
Caroline? She is not in her room. She does not seem
to be anywhere."

"Not since breakfast," was all Mrs. Hurst had to
say. She ferreted some more. "Doctor's bills!" she
said, pulling out another handful of stuff. "From
Lady Anne's time! Now what does he want to keep
those for?"

Fanny thought of Sir George's face yesterday,
heard his voice as he talked to his first wife. She
said, "How did Lady Anne die? Was it sudden?"

"An illness of the head," Mrs. Hurst said,
straightening up for a minute. Sadness touched her
red face. "One minute she was sitting in the chair
with a cup in her hand . . . her sister was here. She
tried to get up and was suddenly taken with a strong
convulsion that stopped her from moving. We lifted

her, placed her on the sofa, and Colman ran for the doctor, but it was no use. She was unable to speak, poor thing . . . kept her senses for a few seconds, but after that she was unconscious. They tried purgatives and strong medicines, but she was dead within twenty-four hours."

"How dreadful!"

"Yes, dreadful," Mrs. Hurst said with a twist of her mouth.

Fanny moved to the window. Clarence was crossing the drive at the back, going down the graveled path that led from the stables.

"Everyone speaks well of Lady Anne," Fanny said.

"You can be sure of that." Mrs. Hurst tightened her lips. There was a little pause.

Fanny hesitated. Was she going to say more?

"I'd better go," said Mrs. Hurst. You could see her thinking more, but there was a difference, now, in her tone. Whatever it was, she was keeping it to herself. "There's some letters on your bed. One for you and one for Lady Caroline. Perhaps you would see that she gets hers when she is to be found? It would save my legs."

Fanny's letter was from her mother. It had been written in a warm humor, as usual.

My dear Fanny,

I hope you are making the most of your stay at Cranthorne. Of your prospects, I mean. I hope you are not sitting there deaf and dumb in a corner as usual. I declare, I envy you: being in such a beau milieu *would be like living in the lap of luxury. We, alas, go on the same as ever.*

I am very much obliged to you, dear Fanny, for

*inquiring about my health, but I am sorry to say it has
not been what it might. This is not surprising, considering what I have had to suffer lately. I have not been at all
well. It is my old complaint. I was scarcely able to get
down the stairs yesterday. We have got your aunt Lloyd
with us, which is some comfort. She does not get so impatient with my little distresses.*

*I am broiled like a sausage, it is so hot. For five days
we have had nothing but this dry heat. The dust comes in
everywhere. Of course, you will not know about that,
being in the country. It upsets my sister. She complained
about the leg of mutton last night. By bad luck, it happened to have gone off. Whatever gossip my sister knows,
it is always stale by the time she brings it. Pray do not
worry about us, Fanny. We shall get by, I suppose. I am
glad you are enjoying <u>la belle campagne</u> at Cranthorne.
My health need be of no concern to you. My convulsive,
catarrhal attacks are only a little more violent. There is
nothing to fret yourself about, no matter what Dr. Cook
says* . . .

Fanny sighed and dropped the letter. She picked
up a comb and poked at her hair. When she heard a
horse down in the drive, her heart leapt, but it was
only one of the grooms with a stain of sweat down
the back of his waistcoat. Why had she thought it
might have been Edward? She could stop thinking
about him if she tried. She would have to try harder,
that was all.

Presently, she remembered the letter that was ad-
dressed to Caroline. Fanny picked it up almost feeling it might bite her hand. She looked at it for a long
time, all the while knowing what she was going to
do. There was no real alternative. She had to know
more about what Caroline was planning. Curiosity
no longer had anything to do with it. It was a matter

of self-preservation, or rather, the preservation of
Sir George.

She broke the seal, unfolded it, and read it.

It was dated eight o'clock, 5 AUG, 1814, from an
address at No. 23, Half Moon Street, Piccadilly.

Dear Milady,

*Having received yours of Friday, the matter being
urgent as you instructed, I hope this will suffice, being
sent smartish within two days. The rooms you requested
are now taken, but in any case I do not think it advisable
to be here. There will be another room, in my opinion as
favorable a one, only smaller, in a place at William
Street at the time you mention. As for the other thing, I
flatter myself I have been reliable in the past. I hope you
may still think so; the woman you remember, a Mrs.
Bridges, would require the usual fee and will undertake to
do all the offices afterwards. I hope that Mr. Clarence is
well. If this arrangement does not suit, I suppose you will
let me know.*

Yours v. Truly, J. Palmer.

Fanny did not understand the letter at all. Why
was Caroline trying to rent a room in London? What
was the woman, Mrs. Bridges, to be engaged for?
And "the offices afterwards" . . . After what? Had
it anything to do with what Edward deemed them to
be planning for Sir George? Surely a flight to London after they had gotten rid of him would only
appear suspicious? Or perhaps they intended luring
him up to London again . . .

She put the letter down, then picked it up again
and hid it under the mattress. She would have to get
some wax and seal it again later before she delivered
it to Caroline.

Urgent, she thought. The word *urgent* had been

used . . . What did urgent mean? Three or four days? A week? Two weeks? She had to see Edward again. She sat there for half an hour trying to work out how it might be done. Then she wrote three lines to give to Annie Bates and went down to luncheon.

Edward must have been busy, because he did not answer at once. He was always busy, she supposed, with all that timber and three tenanted farms to see to. But before she had time to worry about it, the Assembly Ball was upon them and stirring the whole neighborhood. Caroline came into Fanny's room the following afternoon and started to drift about with small, even steps. Then she came over to the table and carefully tidied all the glass jars in front of her.

"Do you want anything?" she asked Fanny. "Anything to wear for the ball?"

"Thank you," Fanny said. "But I have my cream muslin."

Caroline went over to it and poked at it as it hung there on the cupboard.

"It will do, I suppose."

"Yes. It will do," Fanny said.

"Then that is settled." Caroline swung the gown a little as she let it go and made as if to leave, showing far more reluctance than usual and stopping by the door as though to examine herself in the mirror.

"Is anything wrong?" Fanny asked.

Caroline said, "No. Nothing. This room is getting horribly shabby. I only wondered if you had everything you needed."

Fanny sat there after she had gone wondering what that was all about. She thought of the letter from Half Moon Street. The new seal had been as

good as she could make it. She had not sounded
guilty or anything when she had delivered it to Caroline. There had been no questions since. No. No
point in worrying now. Whatever it was that Caroline had had on her mind would come out sooner or
later. Forget it, she told herself.

She would dearly have liked to beg or borrow a
new gown for the Assembly Ball, but had been too
proud to say so. She wore the boring old cream muslin. It left her honey-colored shoulders almost bare,
and she had tucked a creamy yellow rose into the
neck to try and buck it up, but it still drooped like a
very pale moth, she thought as she walked into the
Assembly Rooms in Lowton.

And it was no match for Annabella Austen's diamonds. She positively dripped with them as she
took the floor for the first dance on Edward Knight's
arm. Miss Rushworth was all agog.

"He seems quite captivated, does he not?" she
twittered in Fanny's ear.

Fanny did not answer. Why had he not answered
her note? All the liveliness had gone from her face as
she watched them. He should have replied, she
thought. Sent a note in return, something. Annabella
was dazzling tonight. Fanny hated her.

Then later, as Miss Austen leaned over to throw
some laughing remark toward Edward as he turned
her, Miss Rushworth said, "She is an excellent
dancer."

"I find her a little on the heavy side," Fanny per-
mitted herself to say.

"But so vivacious!" The abominable Miss Rushworth would not give up. Fanny felt she was doing
it on purpose to rile her.

Edward led Miss Austen off the floor at last. Caroline, standing next to her between the two pillars, suddenly looked thin and pinched by comparison. Fanny did not approve at all of the way Caroline looked tonight. Rouged up to the eyes and loaded with trinkets. Once again, she was overdone. And she need not have bothered. The occasion was not half so grand as Fanny had expected. The ladies were for the most part ill dressed. The dances were country dances rather than anything of the more cultured kind. After each dance the ladies fanned themselves vigorously from all their exertions. At one end of the room, the harpsichord held a long line of thick candles. The talk was of market prices and cows and corn.

Miss Rushworth, however, was not so discriminating. As she came out of the column of the fifth dance, Fanny heard her ask Annabella Austen how they did such things in Derbyshire. Was an assembly there the same as this or not so grand?

"Oh . . . much more grand, my dear Miss Rushworth," Miss Austen assured her with a laugh. "You can have no idea . . ."

"I daresay that is true . . ." Miss Rushworth looked suitably pink. "But what do they do that is more grand? Do they have more people? Or a greater number of candles? Or more fiddlers . . . ?"

"My dear Miss Rushworth . . ." Annabella spoke with piercing candor. "It is just a great deal less provincial." Then came a laugh. "You will have to go and see for yourself some day, will you not? You will have a great shock."

Over in the corner behind them, Louisa Knight heard her and said something to Edward. He did not reply, but went on looking at Annabella as she crossed the floor. Fanny did not know how to describe that look. It was intense, yet it had no expression. Perhaps he had not heard his sister, Fanny thought. Perhaps he was deaf to everything around him except the vision of Annabella. His face had the blankness of a wall. Then he turned his head slightly and saw Fanny looking at him, and for one peculiar moment Fanny felt a part of the blankness, too. It was hard to know whether it was contact or not, or whether one felt anything or not. She did not want him to stare at her like that, but she could not bear to look away. There was this taut string between them.

"Well, Fanny . . ." Dr. Baillie's voice, coming from behind her, breaking the knot. "It is my turn, I think. I may step on your toes." His pleasant, ugly face beamed right down at her. Already he was steering her to the top of the column. "I feel I should warn you about that, but if you do not mind dancing with an old man, I think I can promise you a spot of exercise."

After that, supper was served and Fanny found Miss Rushworth somewhat recovered from her skirmish with Annabella Austen; she was slightly wounded, a little defiant. "Well, I think this a very fine occasion," she told Fanny, "no matter what Miss Austen says." She helped herself to the chicken and fixed herself at Fanny's elbow. "I think she is a sly thing, pretending to be pleasant one minute and then showing off her knowledge the next! Mamma says there is no need for them to live as big as they do. It is all show, you know. Mamma says one should show some concern for thrift. And tea is so expensive now, Mamma says it is quite scandalous and we are determined not to drink so much of it . . ."

A half hour later, Fanny was glad to be rescued by Sherry, who came out of the corner by the refreshment table to whisk her onto the floor. "Had to get away from Lady Austen," he said. "Got me in a corner with all her gardening chat. No wonder Sir William's frisking about up at the other end with Mrs. Wyndham. Don't blame him in the least. You look very delicious tonight, Fanny. Did anyone tell you?"

"No. They didn't!" Fanny smiled back at him, but decided it was an empty compliment. "I wish you would tell the truth," she said. "And I can't agree with you about Sir William either. I'm afraid I do blame him for frisking, as you put it. At his age, he ought to know better. How do you think his poor wife feels?"

"Lady Austen? Oh, she's quite used to it, I imagine. Why should she care?" He whirled her around so that she was facing the musicians' end. "See that girl in yellow? The short one with the eyebrows and the flounced petticoats?"

"Yes."

"Well, that is Annabella's half sister. Her name is Eliza Wyndham. She is twenty-one years old and she was born six months after Annabella."

"Eliza Wyndham?" Fanny stared. "You mean . . . ? But how . . . ?"

"In the usual way, I imagine." Sherry used his droll face. He said, "Eliza is more like her mother than Sir William, wouldn't you say?"

"Sir William is Eliza's father?"

"Everyone knows about it," Sherry said. "Except Mr. Wyndham. I daresay he knows, too, in his heart of hearts, but he finds it more convenient to pretend otherwise. Eliza made her appearance between three brothers and two sisters, all of the more regular Wyndham stock, so one odd one here or there will make very little difference in the long run . . . don't you think?"

Fanny was visibly shocked. She almost stopped dancing. "But that is abominable! No wonder Lady Austen looks so down sometimes!"

"Dearest Fanny, it is common enough." He bent forward to try and coax a smile. "Provided all the social rules are observed."

"Well, I think it is abominable. I feel sorry for Lady Austen. Indeed, I do!"

"Why?"

"Because she is kind and she is getting old and . . . and I could not live with a man who served me so."

"Ah, but he probably would not serve you so," Sherry said with a laugh. "There is a difference, you see."

"What difference?"

"You are lively and beautiful. A man would not need to frisk if he had you."

"That is no argument." Fanny looked severely at him. "You mean I should altogether be thrown on the dust-heap once I got past forty? In any case, it does not explain why Mrs. Wyndham should be deceiving her husband. He is a handsome man! He talked to me about the roast fowl at supper."

Sherry laughed. "He is a dull fellow, then, if that is all he can talk to a pretty girl about! Perhaps that explains it."

Before she knew what was happening, he had whisked her out through an archway and around the corner into a deserted conservatory where, by day, one could take the waters and examine the marble busts. Fanny had been alone with him a good many times, but tonight, for some reason, it was different. She didn't mean that she was scared of him, but he was—as he seemed to want to be—in a new mood. His arms were on both sides of her, trapping her, almost, against a pillar. His eyes were bright; his voice had become smooth and satisfied.

"You're the prettiest girl in the room tonight, Fanny." His body came closer. "Do you know that? You've grown up a lot since you came to Cranthorne."

"You mean I was not pretty before?" Heart thumping, she quickly turned it into a joke to head him off.

"You know I didn't mean that." She felt his touch on her bare shoulder. His hand strayed sideways. All those weeks ago, she found herself thinking, she had wanted him to touch her. Now that it was happening again, she was startled to find herself flinching.

"I must go back," she said breathlessly. "I promised Mr. Rushworth—"

"Oh, come on, Fanny . . ." Now he had hold of her properly and was pulling her toward him. "You aren't shy, are you?" Was his speech a little slurred?

"No . . ."

"You are shy . . ." Then he could not repress himself any longer and his mouth came down on hers. The more she struggled, the bolder he got. If she panicked, it would only make things worse . . .

"So here you are." Edward's voice, sounding terse.

Fanny freed herself with some force. She felt she could face no one, let alone Edward Knight. He came out from behind the tall palms and moved finally to a spot in front of them.

Edward. Looking grim.

"Mr. Rushworth is looking for you," he said evenly to Fanny. "He could not find you anywhere."

Fanny, scarlet-cheeked, looked at him.

"I . . . I'll go back to the ballroom."

He inclined his head. "I think you should . . ."

"It . . . it was hot in there," she said wildly. "That's why we came out."

She made her escape at once, threw one savage look at Sherry, and made for the door. He might have said something to help. He might at least have joined in her attempt at conversation and removed that bemused look from his face. The upsurge of acute embarrassment took her out of the conservatory and into the thick of the dancers; it only evaporated into dumb misery when she had located Mr. Rushworth, who was waiting down by the musicians' platform.

Chapter Thirteen

The dance ended. Mr. Rushworth escorted Fanny back to her place. His daughter came over almost at once. Not to chatter, but to pass on a message. She looked like a hare with her big, curious eyes.

"Someone is asking for you at the door," she said.

"Asking for me?"

"Yes. I believe it's the Steadman girl. The one who used to work at Cranthorne. I cannot imagine what she wants. She would not tell me and she did not wish to be seen."

Odd. Fanny went to the door Miss Rushworth had indicated and pushed it open. Out in the passageway—a dim one at the back—the air was cooler. It smelled of dank stone. Susan Steadman was standing in one of the corners, watching the doors.

She stepped out of the shadows, tugging at her shawl, and came forward to take Fanny by the arm.

"Over here," she said. She led the way down to an alcove that led to the kitchens.

"What is it?" Fanny asked. "Is anything wrong?"

"Mr. Knight said you wanted to know about a woman here in Lowton. A woman called Teresa Harley." Some of the pallor and anxiety of Susan's face had gone. She looked better. More stable.

"Teresa Harley. Is that her name?" Fanny said. "The woman who attacked Caroline—do you know her?"

"Yes. I know her."

Fanny said, "Have you come with the Knights?"

"No. I didn't stay at Leigh Park. They were good to me, but I had to get away." Susan said, "Didn't he tell you?"

"I . . . No." Fanny looked away. "I have not had a chance to talk to Mr. Knight tonight." Gloomily, she thought of Annabella Austen. "He is otherwise occupied. When did you leave Leigh Park?"

Susan said, "I started going to Lowton a week or two ago because I felt better there. Less lonely. The people there didn't know me. And they never mentioned Bob, which was a relief. I knew I had to go on and make the best of things, but it was hard at Leigh Park—anywhere in the village. So I got employment at the Swan here in Lowton."

Fanny said in a low voice, "Don't tell me if you don't want to. If it hurts you to tell."

"No. I'll tell you. You ought to know." Susan was more talkative than Fanny had ever known her; the young woman looked at her squarely for the first time. She went on, "I was coming out of the Swan late one night, going down the street toward the livery stables when I spotted him. Clarence Stanhope."

Her voice changed, grew bitter. "He was going down a back alley. His stealth made such an impression on me that I started to follow him. Nothing definite came of it that first evening. He went into a house by the corn stores. But I followed him again the next night, and sat down in a doorway opposite in the dark until he came out and had gone. I went into the house and asked some questions until I found out. I went upstairs and knocked and I found Teresa Harley in a garret at the top of the house. She was not so hard to deal with. She wanted someone to talk to. She would have talked to anyone. I knew she would tell me a lot of things I wanted to know."

Fanny said, "You talked to her?"

"Yes."

"Does Mr. Knight know?"

"Yes. He was going to tell you."

Fanny said, "He has told me nothing. He did not even answer my note."

"He has been away," Susan told her. "He has been in London to make certain inquiries. He only got back this afternoon."

"Oh." At least it was an explanation. Fanny said, "This woman . . . Teresa . . . She seemed in a bad state. Is she likely to cause more trouble? Is she desperate enough to come up to the Hall?"

"I don't think she will do that." Susan looked at her. "But she will not go away, either. Not without trying to squeeze them."

"How can she squeeze them?" Fanny stared back. "Does she know things?" A faint feeling of excitement rose inside her. "Is she likely to know anything . . . ?" She paused. "What I mean is . . . does she know of their plans? Does she have any facts about the death of your brother? Anything that could incriminate them?"

"She knows a great deal. Things dropped out to her in moments of laxitude. When they were drinking and whoring . . ." A quick glance at Fanny. "You will excuse the word, miss. It is the only one that is suitable. All the secrets she has picked up . . . they hold the key to her future. They are trying to make her leave, but she is determined to use her knowledge as a lever. It is her only hope." Susan folded her arms. "There is something I wanted to ask. Your cousin . . . how is she? Is she ill or well?"

"Ill? Caroline?" Fanny considered this question. "Now that you ask, she does not seem exactly well. She suffers from the heat this week. And she is snappy with everyone. But that might not signify. She is very volatile."

"Has she made any visits to London?"

"Not that I am aware of." Fanny said, "She gets letters from London."

A door opened behind them. A servant scuttled out with a great pile of dishes. Fanny moved out of the way to let her pass.

Fanny thought of something else. "You heard about the accident with the carriage the other day? Does Teresa know anything of that? Is there any evidence she could give?"

"She could not give evidence." A faint smile touched Susan's face. "Or if she did, they would not believe a common prostitute."

"Is that what she is?" Fanny looked down at her feet. She did not know what to say.

"She once plied her trade in London."

"I . . . I suppose she was starving," Fanny said, her cheeks scarlet.

"Starving?" Susan laughed. "Teresa has never starved in her life and does not mean to begin now."

Her face softened as she looked at Fanny. "You do not know much, do you?"

"Perhaps not." A silence. "But I have learned a lot lately."

"We all have."

Fanny looked up at last. "How long has it been going on? How long has she—Teresa—been in Lowton?"

"Months," Susan said. "Long before the other man came on the scene."

"The other man? What other man?"

"The sarcastic fellow. The one with the sharp tongue, only he is not half so clever as he sounds."

All Fanny could do was stand there and sound bewildered. "She has another lover as well?"

"Not lover, no. At least, I don't think so. He's always around there, hanging about . . . putting her up to things."

"What does he look like?"

"He is thickset and dark. Around thirty. Always poking about trying to get at the servant girls, they tell me."

"And what is his name?"

Susan said, "That I don't know. I only glimpsed him once or twice. The rest I got from the old woman in the rooms below."

"But where does this man live? Does he live around here?"

"It can't be far away. The old woman says he comes crashing in at night, throwing his weight around and hardly ever paying for the drink she takes up."

"Does he know Clarence?"

"I'm not sure. I never saw them here together. He knows Mr. Crawley, though."

"Sherry?"

"Yes . . ."

A door opened behind them again as Fanny tried to assimilate this new piece of information, her shock and her surprise. She almost failed to register the new voice behind: Clarence's voice from the sharp wedge of light.

"Well, well, well! What have we here?" Clarence wiping his shining forehead with a pocket handkerchief and moving slowly toward them. Fanny could smell that mixture of scent and sweat that she associated with him. Her mouth went dry.

He was only a yard away now. His eyes were smiling, yet shrewd. "Well, Susan!" he said. "It is Susan, isn't it? How are you, my dear? I did not expect to find you here."

"You mean you would not wish to find me here." Susan's gaze did not waver. She did not seem afraid of him at all.

"Did I say that?" His voice had gone soft, but his eyes were still sharp.

"You did not need to. It is obvious."

"In tip-top condition, that is quite clear," Clarence murmured, as if half to himself. "And what are you doing with yourself, Susan, now? May one ask? Or will that be taken the wrong way, too?"

Fanny thought it time to break in. "Susan is working at the Swan next door," she said quickly. "And she is helping in the kitchens here tonight." The invention came to her on the spur of the moment. "I . . . I walked right out into her and I was asking her how she was."

Clarence looked across at Fanny, then back at Susan. His voice was gently cutting, loaded with irony. "Working at the Swan, are you, Susan? And helping in the kitchens here tonight." An infinitesimal pause. "Then we shall have to watch our valuables, shan't we, my dear? Yes, indeed . . . Perhaps we had better warn everyone. Can't be too careful. Eh, Fanny . . . ?"

"I'll see you in hell before I'm finished!" Susan's face was white; her voice came out in a low whisper.

"Hot-headed as ever!" Clarence stood there shaking his head. "You will have to watch that temper, Susan. It may get you into trouble. Does it go with the hair, I wonder?" Another pregnant pause. Then, "Your brother was hot-headed, I hear. See where it got him . . ."

Fanny had no intention of letting that one go by. She said, "I do not think you ought to say a thing like that, Mr. Stanhope! It is unkind and uncalled for." She felt the anger burning inside her.

"Is it, indeed?" Clarence stood there with a sly smile on his face. "Little Fanny is giving me a lecture on etiquette! Do you hear that, Susan?" His tone changed. His head turned. Fanny felt his eyes going up and down her. "Does Caro know you are out here hobnobbing with Susan?" he asked suddenly. "Mmm? Do you know, I do not think Caro would quite approve, if she knew. Do you think so, Fanny? Shall we ask her?"

"I . . . I only came out for some air. That is not forbidden, is it?" Fanny's eyes met his straight on. She was determined not to be intimidated.

"It may not be forbidden," Clarence told her softly, "but I should cut back in there straightaway, if I were you. You know what Caro's temper is like . . . you can imagine how . . . savage . . . she may get if she gets wind of it."

Was that a threat? Fanny decided that it was. Her head went up. "I think I may ask after someone's health without being savaged by Caroline," she told him, standing her ground.

"All the same, cut along," Clarence said. His voice was hard and a trifle frightening, but Fanny still hesitated to leave Susan there all alone with him in the passage.

"They will need me back in the kitchens." As Susan said it, she gave Fanny a taut nod. That was her way of saying don't make a fuss.

"I am sorry to say Fanny is not half so . . . pliable as she was when she arrived," Clarence said to no one in particular.

Fanny stood still. She thought hard. It was no use stretching it out for the sake of a principle. Anyway, she ought to use her head and exercise restraint.

"I was going back in anyway," she said. "It was pleasant to see you, Susan. I'm glad to hear you are feeling better."

Very sensible, she thought, as she went back in through the door. No fuss. No big scene. The heat of the crowd came out to meet her and she felt relieved, in a way, to be out of danger, but there was more to it than that. Because I walked away, she told herself, I'll beat him yet. He won't win. That is certain. Not in the end, he won't—for Susan's sake.

Caroline was talking in a listless sort of way to Lady Austen in the corner. There was no sign of Sherry. The livelier sort of skirmish had just finished and the musicians were striking up one of the new waltzes. Fanny had never performed any such thing before, so she pressed back into one of the pillars, hoping not to be asked, but luck was against her. She saw Dr. Baillie approaching and inwardly groaned. He had not been mistaken about his clumsy feet. Her toes were still bruised from the last turn she had taken with him.

"Ah, Fanny!" he said. "Now what would you say to standing up with me again?"

It was not to be, however. Just at that moment, Edward Knight came up beside them. He said, "I'm afraid you are out of luck, Dr. Baillie. Fanny promised this one to me before supper." He already had hold of Fanny's arm and was drawing her onto the floor before Dr. Baillie could utter another word.

"What did you say that for?" she demanded at once. Perhaps it was embarrassment about the scene in the conservatory earlier that made her more truculent. Attack was a subtle means of defense. "You know it is not true."

"I wanted to talk to you."

"Oh?" Not dance, she thought. Talk. Irrationally, her prickles went up even further.

"You were out there a long time," Edward said, steering her expertly toward the center. "What were you doing?"

"Out there?" For a moment, she stared up at him, startled. "Out where? In the passage?"

"I did not mean in the conservatory." Dark eyes gazed at her steadily. "I am aware of what you were doing in there."

Immediately she turned bright red and stopped looking at him. She said with as much dignity as she could muster, "I did not invite Mr. Crawley's behavior."

"I am sure you did not. Mr. Crawley would need no such invitation." He gave her a straight, assessing look and there was a subtle shift somewhere in his eyes. "How many times has it happened before?" he asked. "Does it happen very often?"

"No! It does not." She looked at him and her face was still flooded with color. A thought struck her and she felt very startled. Was that how he thought

she conducted herself? Was that why he himself had
. . . taken liberties? Kissed her? Floundering in a
quagmire of doubts and bewilderment, she wanted
to hit out at him suddenly for suggesting such a
thing, but the crowd of dancers at that moment
threatened to engulf her and he gripped her more
tightly, drew her into him for a moment so that his
body seemed to fuse into hers and she was incapable
of saying anything. When he suddenly loosened his
hold, however, and the crowd thinned again, she
found her wits once more. She reached out and
caught hold of one clear, clean fact that pierced
through all the emotions like a sharp knife.

"I thought you ought to know," she said, holding
herself very stiffly now, "that I read a letter to Caroline that someone sent her from London. I found it
and opened it. It was from a woman in Half Moon
Street in Piccadilly and I think she must once have
been Caroline's landlady."

She looked up at his face, saw his expression
change. Not much movement beyond the deepening
of two lines at the corner of his mouth, but when his
face grew taut, it became a mask. "Half Moon
Street?" His hand moved on her back and he was
staring down at her.

"She seemed to be trying to rent a room," Fanny
said haughtily. "And a woman to assist in some way
after the room had been let. The matter seemed to
be urgent."

"You read this in a letter?"

"Yes. I made a copy of it before I sealed it up
again. You may see it if you wish."

"That was a dangerous thing to do. What if your
cousin should find the copy?"

"She will not find it."

"Where have you put it?" He sounded almost harsh.

"It is in a locked drawer in my room." Her heart was thumping.

"You must get it to me at Leigh Park. As soon as possible."

"I would have done," Fanny told him, "only you did not answer my letter, did you?"

"I was in London. I did not see it until this afternoon."

Fanny said, "You might have told me you were going. What if something had happened? What if I had needed help?"

"I could not tell you. I had to go in a hurry to meet an appointment. I did not think anything would happen for a couple of days. It was a risk I had to take."

"You told Susan Steadman you were going." She enjoyed scoring this point over him. "So why could you not tell me?"

"Susan?" He stopped almost still in the center of the floor. "Where the devil have you seen Susan?"

"In the passage. Out there. You asked me what I was doing: I was talking to Susan." She enjoyed, too, seeing the surprise in his eyes. "She asked me if I thought Caroline was ill. Do you suppose it could be the reason for her renting a room in London? Do you suppose she is to see a doctor?"

"Where is Susan now?" The question was abrupt.

"I left her in the passage with Clarence. I would not have done . . . he was foul to her . . . but he practically ordered me to come in."

"Clarence?" She saw him turn his head at once to scrutinize the room, looking for Clarence, and felt him relax simultaneously as he spotted the gentleman bluffly making conversation with Colonel Park over by the door.

"Did you tell Miss Austen you were going to London?"

"Miss Austen? Why should I tell her?"

"I don't know." She smiled at him with such a big-eyed, melting smile that he viewed her almost with suspicion. "You seem to have told everyone else. And Miss Austen seems scarcely to move without knowing your opinions."

He looked down at her and for a moment his hand gripped her back so tightly that she thought he was going to shake her. But instead, he let out a long, weary sigh. "Fanny, are you setting out deliberately to provoke me for some reason?"

"No." Their eyes met and held. "Why should I do that?"

"I don't know."

"I had no thought at all of provoking you," Fanny said. "I would not dare do such a thing. I do not know anyone else who would, either. All things considered, it would be the worst thing in the world for them to do."

"You are trying to provoke me." The music was slowing. His hand moved from her slim, erect back up to her shoulder. His eyes were dark and dangerous as he held her there, almost motionless, on the very edge of the floor. Something soft yet daring sprang up that moment between them. So daring that Caroline's voice behind them came sharply from another part of the world.

"Why, Fanny, there you are! I did not know where you had gone to. I have scarcely seen you all evening . . ."

For a second or two, Edward did not relax his grip on Fanny's shoulder. Then, apparently, he changed his mind, gave her a single look and Caroline a brief bow, then went off across the room, pushing his way through the thickest of the crowd.

"I wonder if you would fetch me some iced water, Fanny," Caroline went on. "The gentleman's manners do not improve much, do they?" Her eyes were sharp with curiosity and some other emotion. "You seemed to be having a very intense conversation. I was watching you for quite two minutes. Pray what was it about?"

"It . . . it was nothing. It was about London. He . . . he has just been up there on a visit."

"Really? You quite looked as if you were arguing."

"Argue with Mr. Knight?" Fanny found the resources from somewhere to give a light laugh. "I would not do that! There is Sherry. He has been outside, by the look of him. I think he is coming over."

"He can please himself," Caroline said shortly. "He has not been near me for hours either. I suppose he will pretend to spare me a minute before prancing off again to keep some foolish girl in spirits? For God's sake, stop fidgeting around and fetch me the water, Fanny! I cannot stand a fidget and I am dying of thirst."

Fanny went and was glad to go.

They set off for home at a quarter to one, Fanny and Caroline in the carriage, the other three—Clarence and Sherry and Sir George—riding behind with a servant. Soon Fanny could not see any lights at all. They were right out of town. The carriage hit a rut now and again and she thought of the coach going in the ditch that very first day. Her mind ticked on steadily. How long ago it seemed! Another time, another age. She thought of Edward coming across her in Leigh Wood when she had tipped him off his horse. Her feelings for him were such a queer mixture. Few men had made her smart so much, excited her so much or made her so furious. Few men! She almost laughed. How many men had she known? None. Well, perhaps that one little romance—if one could term it a romance—in London last year.

A boy who had looked at her at one of Aunt Lloyd's evenings and had smiled and brought her a pretty book and called with some frequency until he had gone off to Ireland for some unspecified reason.

What had a small episode like that to do with real passion? And she thought of Edward again and how he had held her while they were dancing. Strong and sure, without that tendency to limpness that Mr. Rushworth had, and without any self-consciousness. His hair thick and dark. The very clean, clear tan on his skin . . .

Then she saw him standing there in the conservatory, staring across at them with that long, strong stare of his. More muscular than Sherry, she found herself thinking. Tight jaw, strength of movement. He would not ever slur his words, as Sherry had done, or say things he did not mean.

And now she did not know at all where she stood with him. It all felt so inconclusive. She needed him to help with all the goings-on at Cranthorne. She depended on him and respected him . . . there was no one else. She had thought, until tonight, that perhaps Sherry could be depended on . . . But after that scene in the conservatory, that dreadful scene that made her go hot all over to think about and that Edward had witnessed, after that, she did not know what to make of Sherry's behavior. He had not

proved himself a gentleman, and besides, he had
been more than a little drunk.

She had seen the disgust in Edward's eyes, and
because of her stupid embarrassment and discomfort
and because of her jealousy of Annabella Austen,
she had goaded him, later, into a ridiculous argument . . .

Stop it, Fanny, she told herself. Stop thinking
about him—there's no point.

She shifted in her seat and watched Caroline turn
over. She had fallen asleep ten minutes ago. It was
getting darker and darker by the minute. The land-
scape entirely blotted out. The coach rattled along. It
was like being in a great, rattling box. Fanny could
just see, in the flicker of the lamp, Caroline's face.
Her eyes closed, her mouth flopped a little open. Her
scent drifted across now and then, filling the darkness with musk or amber or something oriental. All
her schemes and plans and complaints gone for the
minute . . . Fanny was aware of a feeling of acute
dislike, almost of disgust, toward her cousin. She
was like a limp doll. She would come to life in the
morning and start at it all over again: the maneuver-
ing, the scolding, and the schemes . . .

If I had had more experience of life, Fanny
thought, if I had been out more, had met more people, I might have seen through her at once. But I was
raw and green.

Sherry was right about one thing: I have changed.
I've grown up.

Too late, probably, for Edward. For Sir George?

There were still servants up when they reached
the house. It was half past one in the morning. Caroline led the way into the small drawing room, where
one of the maids had put hot chocolate and biscuits.
Though Caroline had slept most of the way home,

she would not go to bed. She seemed wide awake now as she crossed the plum-colored carpet. Her restlessness had returned. She almost seemed to think that it was morning and that conversation was in order; therefore Fanny, though weary, felt obliged to stay up and keep her company until the men came in.

"I suppose that will be the end of the summer things now." Caroline sat on the edge of her chair and spoke to fill the silence. "I suppose that autumn will set in and we shall be shut up here in the gloom for hours and hours on end."

Fanny said, "Will you not go up to London for a change? Most people do." She held her breath and waited to see what the answer would be.

"London?" Caroline said, picking up her cup. "George hates London."

"But you could go?"

It was the silence that lingered, not Caroline's gaze.

"I suppose I could. If I wanted to." The clock ticked. "But I don't think I can be bothered."

Nothing more. Just the casual statement. After a while, the silence fell again. After almost half an hour, Fanny plucked up the courage to say, "They are a little late, are they not?"

Caroline got up and started to pace the carpet. She said, "It's a fair ride."

A latch clicked open and shut outside in the hall and seemed to startle her. She swung around with her large, lustrous eyes on the door. The little parlor maid came in and smiled apologetically. "James . . . locking the back passage, milady." Tiredness lay in blue smudges under the girl's eyes. She looked fit to drop, too, Fanny thought. Poor thing. I wish that they would come so that she can get to bed. She will have to be up again at practically dawn, I suppose.

"Take the cups away," Caroline said, without getting rid of that odd, restless look.

"Why don't you go to bed?" Fanny suggested.

"Because I don't care to," Caroline snapped tensely. What was she so tense about?

Fanny gave up and sat there dumbly in the chair tapping her fingers for another half hour. The clock struck three. They can't be long now, she thought. I would go to bed myself, only I cannot very well unless she suggests it. The wind moved the windows. Waiting. More waiting.

Oh, God, won't they ever come? Three-twenty. Caroline, all her rouge rubbed off, her eyes glinting, said, "I have hit upon it. I believe the horse must have gone lame. It was not right yesterday."

"Whose horse?" Fanny looked at her.

"Why, George's, of course!" The tawny eyes were huge and watchful. "I hope nothing has happened. I hope it has not thrown him. Or . . . anything."

Or anything? Fanny felt a wild, sudden lurch of fear.

What did that mean?

Was the remark an attempt to prepare her for . . . something? She got up and walked quickly round the room. Is this it, she thought. Is it to be tonight that they do it? Why didn't I think of it before? Why did I allow Sir George to ride home alone with Clarence, on horseback, in the pitch black? What could be easier—quicker—than a sudden blow in the dark?

The servant is with them. They could soon lose him, a voice in her head told her. But then, Sherry is there. Sherry is drunk. He would not notice. They could easily outpace him in that state. And besides . . .

Besides, what? Sherry has some sort of connection with the other man who visits Teresa Harley. He could not be in with them, could he? The thought chilled.

Clarence will call it an accident, of course. The horse shied. Nothing anyone could do. She could imagine him saying it . . .

At three-forty, there was a noise outside. Several noises. Voices and horses and the crunch of gravel. Then a pause. Then Colman's voice, loud in exclamation from the front door. Fanny froze in her chair, then moved. Caroline was right behind her.

A voice said, "Let it alone, man! It will do in the morning." Sir George's voice. Fanny almost dropped down with relief. He came in first, big and bluff, dropping off his cloak on the chest by the door. "Here at last," he boomed roughly. "Damned near exhausted! Thought I'd never see my bed tonight!"

"But . . . what kept you?" A white glaze had come over Caroline's face. A shine of perspiration when she caught sight of Clarence coming in behind her husband.

"Damned bit of trouble at the back of the livery stables." Sir George threw down his crop and walked with unsteady gait toward the foot of the stairs.

"What kind of trouble?" Caroline said.

Sir George inclined his head toward Clarence and, without looking at him directly, said, "Ask him. He's the one that found her."

"Her . . ."

No strength in Caroline's words. No hesitation about asking, either.

"Woman in the alley behind the Swan. Cut her wrists. Suicide. Nasty business . . ." Sir George ended his account and made the first three stairs.

"What was her name?" Caroline moved suddenly across the parquet. Four or five yards so that she was nearer the lamp.

Fanny looked down at the floor. Jelly in her legs. Susan, she thought. Not Susan Steadman. I left her out there at the back . . .

"Harley. Teresa Harley," Sherry said. No one had heard him come in. His voice sounded a long way away.

For several seconds there was complete silence, then the sound of a small, sighing moan. Caroline had slipped to the floor in a heap. "See to her," Clarence told the maid. "She's fainted. What a night! What a damned night it's been!"

Chapter Fourteen

The sun shone on the next morning. When Caroline finally made her appearance, her voice was quite careful. High, delicately pitched, unnatural as a false chime.

"As for this woman in Lowton," she told Sir George, "she was in the town once before, it seems. She was well known among the lowlife. Of her background they know nothing . . . indeed, she probably has none. But her story seems to be a familiar one. The wretched woman was desperate with drink. She got into some sort of brawl with her landlady and then went out and slashed her wrists . . ."

"How dreadful!" Fanny felt sick, though she did not believe a word of Caroline's story.

"Dreadful indeed! But these things happen all the time among that sort. It is no good to think about them." Caroline watched Fanny all the time, her eyes narrowed and uneasy. She went on immediately. Once into the prepared subject, she needed to finish. "They will bury her tomorrow, Mrs. Hurst says. I suppose as a suicide. I wish the servants would not talk so much of it. It quite makes the house feel dismal. They parade the details around all over the place. I have had to stop them already this morning. Colman, this milk is curdled. Take it away and bring fresh. It is not fit to be drunk."

There was less asperity in her voice when she spoke next to Fanny. "We shall sit out in the shade later. The house is so stuffy. Do you not feel it? My dear Fanny, you look washed out."

"I did not sleep well," Fanny said in a low voice.

"My dear, which of us did?" Again the false voice. "Even Clarence is not himself. He knew the woman . . . I daresay you know that." A sideways glance. "Clarence mixes with all sorts. I told him perhaps it will teach him a lesson. Make him more choosy whom he runs after in the future." There was a long silence. Then Caroline said, "You must not let it get to you, Fanny. In a day or so it will all be forgotten."

"I find that sad." Fanny kept her eyes down.

"I daresay, but life is like that." She changed the subject abruptly. "Sherry is gone over to see his friend, Brandon, who is leaving the area, I gather, next week."

His friend, Brandon. Fanny felt her stomach cramp up. It could not be . . . could it? The acquaintance of Sherry's who had visited Teresa Harley? And if so, what did Sherry know about it? Why had he gone straight over there this morning?

"The ball was rather dull, was it not?" More conversation on Caroline's part. "I never saw Miss Austen dressed in such finery. It was all for Mr. Knight's benefit. They deserve one another, I should think. They are both of them mighty taken with themselves."

What was different about Caroline's attitude this morning? Fanny wondered. There was something. Among all the careful lines, there was a kind of lightness in her voice. More ease with the world. Was it relief? Could you call it that? Relief that an obstacle—Teresa Harley—had gone?

She listened for another half hour while Caroline went on about the ball. She had not chattered so much in weeks. And yet last night she had had to be carried up to her room in shock.

Fanny always went upstairs just before luncheon, which was without variation on the stroke of one. That day, she went up early, the blue-and-cream gown she was wearing sticking to her back with the heat.

Caroline had grown more lethargic as the morning had gone on and had stayed out under the tree in the garden when Fanny told her she was going in. The men were all out. The house seemed silent, in consequence.

When she had sponged away some of the stickiness that clung to her, Fanny changed the blue dress for a white one and took out the copy of the letter from Half Moon Street that she had locked away in the drawer. She sat there reading it again.

"The matter being urgent as you requested . . .
the woman you remember, a Mrs. Bridges, would
require the usual fee . . ."

What fee, Fanny thought. What for? "I hope Mr.
Clarence is well," the letter went on. "If this arrangement does not suit, perhaps you will let me
know . . ."

Had Caroline let her know? Had anything been
sent in reply? Or anything more come from London?
Fanny did not know. Couldn't know. All she knew
was that Clarence was quite well . . . well enough,
she suspected, to have murdered Teresa Harley last
night because she was trying to blackmail him, and
to come home afterward quite calm and controlled
. . . He had even had the nerve to pretend to find
her in the alleyway behind the Swan.

It was not suicide. Teresa Harley was not the type
to commit suicide. There had been too much of the
vixen about her. Especially not about some trivial
matter like a quarrel with her landlady about
money. That was what Caroline had said. But Teresa
had never starved in her life or worried about
money. She remembered Susan's insistence. Teresa
had intended to squeeze them and she had died for
her mistake.

But how to prove it? Other papers . . . other letters. Fanny looked at the paper in her hand.

She had to find more. More evidence. It is the
only thing that will nail them.

Where? In Caroline's room. In her bureau. Three
quarters of an hour, yet, to go before luncheon, and
she is asleep in the garden, and there is no one else
around.

She took two steps toward the door. Hesitated.
Went back to look out of the window. Yes, Caroline

was still down there, asleep in the chair. Worn out, no doubt, after such a long, hectic night . . .

Funny, she thought. I don't feel at all guilty about the idea. Should I feel guilty? No. Guilt could only come from doing something against her moral principles. Defeating someone's plan to commit murder was not against her moral principles. Defeating those who had murdered already and got away with it.

She was shaking, though. It made her knees turn to jelly.

That is because she feared she might get caught, she decided. But she couldn't get caught if there was no one around. It was impossible. So she made herself get on with it while the situation still lasted. It might not, for long. Now was the time.

Fanny slipped into Caroline's bedroom like a shadow, knowing that if there was even so much as a creak, her nerve would fail.

A pair of Caroline's shoes had been kicked off over by the bed. Two clean, folded towels beside the washstand. The delphiniums stood stiffly in a jug in the window. Careful. She mustn't go near the window. She might be seen from the garden.

Trying to keep her breathing even and make no sound on the carpet, Fanny very cautiously moved over to the bureau and reached out a hand for the smallest drawer where she had once seen Caroline put the key.

She found it. Took it out. Inserted it in the locked drawer. It turned.

She slid the drawer out. It made a slight sound. Fanny stopped dead with it two inches out. Waited a second or two. It seemed to be stuck now in its groove.

She stood there trying not to force it too much. Then she nearly leapt out of her senses. Footsteps. She heard quick, light footsteps outside, around the corner, a voice at the top of the stairs and another voice behind.

A dart of panic shot right through her. Fingers frozen stiff with tension. Dry mouth. Sweat breaking out all over her. She shoved at the drawer so hard that it shut with a snap. The key—quick! Lock it again. Push the key back in the small drawer. Where to hide? Too late to get out. The steps were coming nearer. She could see only one place and that was the closet.

Trying to get the door closed behind her without actually fastening herself in totally, she held on to the knob with shaking fingers and hid there among the rails of Caroline's clothes, trying not to breathe, not to move, not to do anything that would signal her presence.

The door opened, then closed again. Someone came in. No, two people. Clarence, sounding sulky. He must have gone and woken her up, Fanny thought, just when it all seemed clear. Clarence saying, "What's wrong with that? Nothing wrong with that, as far as I can see."

Caroline said, "I don't want anything else going wrong." She moved across the room. Her voice sounded nearer. "You've bungled too much already."

"Oh, come on, Caro!" Clarence came nearer, too. Fanny could almost feel his great weight on the boards. "What's all the fuss about, for God's sake?"

"I don't want any more complications." Caroline's tone was very sharp and cutting.

"Complications? Where's the complications?"

"You know!" Low and vicious. "You know what I mean."

"Caro . . . !" A comically guilty, ingenuous sigh. Like a naughty child caught with his fingers in the pie. A naughty child who knew his powers to cajole. "I really don't know why I'm in such hot water. Why you're so damned fearful . . . Can you recollect a time when I didn't get us out of these little scrapes?"

"It is not a little scrape!" Caroline had turned on him. "You cannot call two deaths a little scrape! That woman's, particularly . . . It could have made real trouble."

"*She* could have made real trouble," Clarence said. "What does it matter?" He was smooth and persuasive now. "One little whore the less . . . I should have thought you'd be more grateful, my dear. You found her superfluous enough in life."

"I did not tell you to . . . I did not tell you to do that."

"My only reason for doing it was to preserve our position here. She was much more persistent than I expected. I had planned to buy her off, but she wanted too much. Much more than we could afford . . . and she would not wait. She was going to be a nuisance. Hanging around waiting to drop hints about us all over the place . . ."

"You're so cool!" The swish of a skirt as Caroline moved again. "My God, you're cool! I would not have thought it possible. I knew you were hard, but I didn't think you'd be as ruthless as that."

"Do you know . . ." Clarence was smiling. Fanny could hear it in his voice as he moved closer to the closet. "I've never yet met a woman who would face doing the dirty work herself. They are prepared to take their share of the loot, of course, but never to do any of the real dirty stuff. I did think at one time that you would be different, Caro . . . I really did." That oily tone. He must be touching her. Fanny cringed back into the soft stuff of the gowns. But a sharp movement took Caroline's voice to the other end of the room.

"I did not plan on all this," she said.

"Then you should have taken on a different partner, my dear," Clarence suggested. "It's no good moaning now. You knew the score . . ."

"I knew you could not keep away from trouble . . ."

"Then you should not complain when it gets a bit squally," Clarence told her softly. "And I wonder how on earth you committed that other little faux pas? I wonder how the devil you got with child?" A little scrape of a ring on the bedpost. "Was that all my fault, too?"

With child? Fanny caught her breath. Caroline . . . with child?

"My God, you're a pig!" Caroline spat it out.

"My dear, it takes one to know one. We will not say any more about that, seeing as I have clearly won my point. All we can do now is hope to get the rest of it over quickly. I will concede one thing: matters have changed since last night. My brother's . . . departure must be accomplished slightly earlier than we had planned. Your . . . condition demands it as well. What a pretty thing it would be if George found out about your being *enceinte* with nothing having, shall we say, existed between you since the wedding night. What a thunderstroke that would be, to be sure . . ." Clarence started to laugh. "The shock of it might even carry him off for us. Did you never think about that? But I daresay you are right about the other thing, too. I daresay it would be better . . . accelerated . . . now, before anyone attempts to put two and two together. Also, my funds are almost out again and my creditors are getting somewhat hot on my heels."

A pause. A muffled movement. Caroline had moved again. Abruptly, she said, "There is something else, too. I think Fanny suspects something."

Fanny froze. Her fists clenched.

"Fanny?" Clarence's voice changed. "What do you mean?"

"I think she suspects us. Something. Have you seen the way she looks at us?"

"My dear, the girl always shied off."

"And you did nothing to cause it, I suppose?" Caroline shot at him. "But I don't mean just you. She looks at me oddly now."

"I did find her a touch belligerent last night . . . it is true." His tone was thoughtful. "But you are probably exaggerating. It is your condition, I expect. Women in your state often imagine things. Get these fits. Little Fanny is safe enough. Not enough spark there to pick up anything."

"I think you are wrong."

"You always think me wrong."

"She is jumpy. She watches us, I tell you."

"Women always watch everything," Clarence said with a laugh. "What else is there for them to do, except breed? Fanny is probably saving it all up to tell that hag of a mother of hers when she gets home." There came a tapping sound, as if his fingers were drumming on the top of the bureau. "But we will speed things up anyway. I think we can wait no longer. On Monday, I think. And the original plan."

"The original plan?" Caroline, for once, sounded frightened. "Is that wise? After the affair with the Steadman boy?"

"He died in the woods at the hand of a poacher,"
Clarence reminded her. "It is almost forgotten now.
If some other little . . . accident happens up there,
who will put the two together? You must stop being
so jumpy yourself, my dear Caro. You are a bag of
nerves. In only a few days it will be all over and
then you will feel better." A grin. Fanny could hear
it. "And you may put all your acting talents into
mourning the tragic death of your husband, the father of your unborn child. The father who never
knew what it was that he did not see . . . And
then, perhaps, you will leave me alone and stop nagging my head off all the time. I should like that. I
should like to spend half of George's money, too.
That was what we agreed, was it not?"

"Not a half. We did not agree that." Caroline's
voice was sullen. "You have not had to live with him
all the time. You have not had the half of it."

"We will argue about that after he is gone," Clarence said. "It will pass the long winter evenings.
Now, are you getting ready for luncheon or not? It
always takes you a devilish long time."

Fanny did not go down to luncheon. After she had
heard Caroline go down, after she had crept out of
the closet and back to her own room, she sent down
a message pleading a tired headache. Then, thinking
only of what she had heard in Caroline's bedroom,
she paced slowly up and down the floor in a room
heated by long slats of sunshine that came in
through the long windows.

She thought about Clarence's voice, about the
child of his that Caroline was carrying, about the
sickening plans they had to end Sir George's life.
Whatever happens, she thought, they must not see

me or try to talk to me until I've got some sort of
hold over my reactions.

She thought of Edward. She had to see Edward at
once. It was imperative now. She needed his calmness, his sense of reason. She needed him to tell her
what to do. That most of all.

And yet there was this odd change in her now:
she was no longer frightened of them. She had
somehow gone past that barrier. Doubts and fears
went hand in hand, and when one had been gotten
rid of, the other went, too.

She knew now without any doubt that they intended to kill Sir George. She knew when and
where. Edward could go on from there, once she had
apprised him of the facts. All she had to do was to
see Edward. Today was Saturday. She would send
him a note. Yes, that was the best way. Find Annie
Bates, the parlor maid, and get her to deliver a note.
He was not away from home this time. Last night, at
the Assembly Rooms, she had heard Louisa telling
someone they were to dine at the rectory as they
had rather neglected the Elthams lately.

If Annie could take the message over to Leigh
Park by this evening, then tomorrow she would see
Edward at church. Nothing would happen before
then. Sir George was quite safe for the moment.

Fanny wrote the note and went down the back
stairs at three o'clock, taking the most roundabout
route to get to the kitchen passage without being
seen. She could hear the servants talking, coming to
and fro from the kitchen into the scullery and pan-
try. There was a delicious smell of cooking meat,
and suddenly she regretted not going down for a
substantial luncheon.

She went around the corner into the bottom turn
of the passage by the scullery door. Fortunately, she

had been down there once or twice before, carrying messages for Mrs. Hurst from Caroline. It would not look so very odd. One of the dogs was sniffing around the flagstones. Fanny skirted around him, almost bumping into the little kitchen maid, Martha Dean, as she did so.

"Oh, miss—you gave me a fright!" Martha Dean had little, piggy black eyes in a round face.

"I'm sorry, Martha. I didn't mean to do that," said Fanny. "I was looking for Annie Bates."

"Annie?" The girl looked at her without curiosity. "She's not here today. Her mother's bad. She went home to see her."

"Oh." The fierce disappointment was followed by a streak of anxiety. "When will Annie be back? Do you know?"

"Not until tomorrow, miss. Mrs. Hurst told her to take the night off." Fanny's anxiety must have transmitted itself to Martha. She said, "Is there anything I can do, miss?" Fleetingly, the piggy eyes looked curious.

"No. No, it's nothing urgent." She could not risk sending Martha. The girl might talk all over the place. "Thank you, Martha. I'll . . . I'll see Annie tomorrow."

"Right you are, miss."

So she could not contact him tonight. It would have to be tomorrow at church . . . The fear began to trickle back, but she forced herself to control it.

Chapter Fifteen

It was a strange ride to church next morning. Fanny sat in the barouche, her back propped against the solid upholstery. She could see Sherry passing a hand over the back of his brown curls. He had not apologized for his behavior the other night. He would not now, she believed. He had gone to some pains not to be alone with her at breakfast this morning.

Clarence began to hum, tapping the tips of his fat fingers on the grotesque rounds of his thighs as the barouche passed into the village and began to ease its way around the narrow corner by the inn. Caroline was the only one staring out at the cottages; there were few green gardens now, and most of those had been seared to some extent by this August heat wave.

"We shall have thunder before long," said Caroline. "It is impossible it should go on much longer."

"Don't think it will," said Sherry. "Wind's getting up. Fare thee well, summer . . . eh, Fanny?"

"Yes." Fanny kept her eyes down, but managed to find a fleeting smile. It was difficult to be natural with any of them this morning.

Sherry lifted his watch ribbon. "We're late," he said.

"Never mind, dear boy," Clarence said. "They will see you all the better as you walk in. Isn't that how you like it? I mean, just look at the picture you make . . . covered in all that velvet and embroidery. No good if you can't make a decent entrance, is it? Turn all the ladies quite giddy at the mere sight of you—"

"That's enough, Clarence," Caroline said shortly.

"Only lightening the gloom, my dear," Clarence told her.

"There is a great art in knowing where to leave off," Caroline said.

"If you say so, dear Caro. Only making polite conversation." Clarence turned his head. "Better try Fanny then, if Mr. Crawley is to be out of bounds. I never heard you say, Fanny, whether or not you are enjoying your summer at Cranthorne?"

"I have enjoyed it a great deal." Fanny could not stop herself coloring slightly as she said it. It gave her a creepy feeling to be sitting there with Clarence's knee almost touching her own this morning. And she could not bear feeling the warmth of Caroline's body right next to her own. Caroline, with the beginnings of Clarence's child inside her. Fanny almost shivered at the thought, in spite of the heat.

"You do not sound so very enthusiastic," said Clarence.

"I do not know why you say that." It was necessary to meet his eyes. "I am not in the habit of using superlatives, that is all. It has been an interesting stay. A beautiful summer." That much was true, at any rate. The park shimmering in the sun all those weeks. The weather going on and on.

"But you use the past tense," Clarence mused, his voice as oily as his smile.

"Only because Mr. Crawley said summer was almost over," Fanny said.

"Mr. Crawley . . . eh?" Clarence's eyes flicked from Fanny to Sherry. "We are very formal all at once. Haven't done anything to offend little Fanny, have you, dear boy?"

In the ensuing small silence, Fanny looked away. Did Clarence know about the night of the ball? The thing about Clarence was that he had that deadly way of insinuating himself into your thoughts. "No one has offended me," she said quickly. "I suppose Sir George has gone right on ahead? He seems to have left us behind."

"Can't keep him off that damned horse of his," Clarence said.

Caroline added, "He always rides to church." It sounded like an automatic response, but she moved restlessly and there was a shade of distraction in her large, tawny eyes. "So you have enjoyed your summer, Fanny?"

"Yes." Fanny looked at her hands for a while and then into the distance. Then she said, more out of exploration than anything else, "But I must think about going home soon."

"Home?" That got Caroline's full attention. A quick glance at Sherry and then at Clarence. "You are not thinking of going home, Fanny, are you?" Her voice was light but her brown eyes sharp.

"I . . . I ought to think of it. Mamma has not been well. She keeps hinting."

"You did not say." Caroline's eyes kept up their scrutiny.

"She . . . she wrote to me last week again." Hard to get that out without thinking of that other letter. The one to Caroline from Half Moon Street. Fanny thought she had an inkling what that was all about now: the child. The unborn child. Caroline had, perhaps, been providing a bolt-hole for herself in case things went wrong. Making contingency plans for its birth. Her heart was thumping, but she kept her voice level. "Her symptoms do not seem very favorable. I think I must go soon."

"But you must not think of going yet!" Caroline said in her throaty voice. "We need you here, Fanny."

"You have a great deal of company," Fanny said. "I . . . I do not think you would miss me too much."

Another small pause. Then Caroline said, "I should miss you a very great deal!" She suddenly reached out a hand and pressed Fanny's fingers. "You are a silly goose, Fanny! I shall not allow you to go. Your mamma exaggerates everything. You told me so yourself, did you not? So, we will have no more talk of your leaving just yet. Do you hear?"

It was absolutely necessary to let her hand stay there underneath Caroline's, not to let any of her distaste show, but it took all Fanny's self-control not to snatch her fingers right away.

The barouche jerked to a halt beside the lych-gate. It was such a relief to get out. Fanny held a calm smile on her face as she walked up the church path, but though outwardly she showed nothing, her tumult of mind was no less strong. She could not stand Caroline's slyness or Clarence's destructive talents for many more days. No longer than Monday. By tomorrow it must all be resolved one way or the other. She would tell Edward so. There was a vast relief in thinking that inside an hour, she would be able to get the message across to him.

But Edward was not in church. Neither was Louisa. As the congregation launched into the first psalm, Fanny stood there desperately searching for him in case he was, for some reason, in a different pew today. She found it difficult to comprehend that, for the first time since she had come to Cranthorne, he was not there at all. Yet he was not. Not at all. As soon as she felt certain of it, her stomach cramped and she felt sick and faint.

Dr. Baillie, Lady Austen, and Miss Austen were all

outside the church porch after service. Dr. Baillie came up first. He said, "Well, Fanny. Here we are again! And how are you this fine morning?"

"Thank you, sir, I am quite well." She was still searching for Edward with her eyes.

"Not been falling off your horse into any more lakes or throwing yourself at any carriages?"

"No." She smiled vaguely.

"You look blooming," he remarked. "That is because you are young and your system springs back. But pray make sure you do not get into any of these wild scrapes when you are forty," he added cheerfully, "or I would not be responsible for the outcome."

"I will try not to."

"There was a lady of fifty I was reading about in the *Courier.* She went off to Italy and took to riding there at the hottest part of the day and paid for it by coming down with a fatal cough and dying within three days."

Fanny could not work out the connection between the riding and the cough, but she did not say so.

She focused on the little group down by the gate. She had this mild hope still that Edward might suddenly appear there between Sir George, who was taking his horse from the groom, and the Rushworths, who were passing the time while they waited for their carriage by wondering at the length of the grass on either side of the path.

Caroline had just come out. She had put her hand into that of the curate. Fanny could hear her light, girlish voice going on about an inspection of the church roof. In a moment, Clarence joined in, promising a fine sum toward putting the slates back in order. All the practiced hypocrites going through their routines, doing the rounds expertly, taking their time about it.

And Sherry came out behind them. A handsome young man. All the ladies smiled at him.

Fanny watched him. Some sense of unease stirred inside her. She did not think it possible he knew of Caroline's affair with Clarence, that he was acquainted with their true natures . . . and yet . . . ? How could someone have any spark of intelligence and stay here all summer and not see it? she wondered. Even if he had noticed a tenth portion of what was going on and had turned a blind eye to it, what did that say about Mr. Crawley's moral principles?

A great deal, she thought. And the other night at the ball, he had not shown himself in a good light by his behavior toward her.

Then there was some connection, even if tenuous, between him and the dark young man who had also kept company with Teresa Harley. I will try to keep an open mind about him, she thought to herself. But today it was not so easy.

"Well, Miss Milbanke?" Lady Austen's voice. Gruff, authoritative. "A bit lost, by the look of you? Out of it all?"

Fanny started and attempted a laugh. "No, not exactly," she said.

"Thought so." Lady Austen was not deceived. She leaned over and said succinctly, "You shouldn't let them get you down."

"Them?" said Fanny.

"People."

"Shouldn't I?" Fanny was startled. The old lady was either slightly daft or amazingly acute.

"No. Take my advice and stick to dogs." The

words were accompanied by a light tap on Fanny's arm.

"Dogs?"

"Yes, dogs," Lady Austen boomed. "Faithful creatures. More faithful than humans. Good for a last resort."

"A last resort?" Fanny said, parrotlike.

"I knew you wouldn't understand." Lady Austen's old, hawklike eyes met Fanny's. "But then, how could you? Far too young. You won't see for years yet."

"Won't I?"

"With a bit of luck you won't see at all." Lady Austen's gaze was in the distance, following her husband, who was making a beeline for the younger, prettier Miss Rushworth. "Never mind." The voice came closer to Fanny's ear. "You stay at Cranthorne for a bit. Stay as long as you can. You're doing George good."

Fanny did not know what to say to this. She felt distressed that the old lady was not half so thick-skinned as Sherry had suggested, and she wanted to offer some sympathy, but thought she'd better not. So all she said was, "I . . . I don't suppose you know why the Knights are not here this morning?"

"Edward is not always at liberty to parade up and down to church." That was Miss Austen's voice behind them. Fanny turned to be confronted with her very superior gaze. "He has inherited property to the value of almost a hundred thousand pounds, you know. You could not conceive, Miss Milbanke, what a responsibility such a concern can be."

"I know him to be always involved with something or other," Fanny said. "I did not think his business would keep him away from church."

"You probably do not comprehend the calls on his

time," Miss Austen remarked in a supercilious tone. She was dressed this morning in a very handsome gown with broad green straps over a white bodice. "My father would tell you. Our estate joins on to Leigh Park. They have similar preoccupations."

You mean similar fortunes, Fanny thought. I know exactly what you mean. She lifted her chin and said, "I only asked about the Knights because I feared some sort of illness."

"There is no illness," Annabella Austen said crisply. "If there were, we should have been the first to hear, take my word for it, Miss Milbanke. There is a great closeness between our two families." Her glossy auburn hair moved in the light breeze. Her eyes were as brilliant and as hard as the diamonds in her ears. "You need not concern yourself about Edward. I have no doubt he will be over to see us this afternoon to explain his absence from church. Mamma, it is time we were leaving. Come along. The carriage has come."

Lady Austen took her leave of Fanny, but Annabella did not. Fanny was not sorry. It would scarcely drive her distracted, she thought, if she did not have Miss Austen's friendship. In fact, she could very easily do without it, so there was very little to add on that score.

That afternoon, in her room, Fanny fidgeted around, walked up and down a few times, sat down, got up, wandered around some more, then came to a decision. She would walk over to Leigh Park this very moment, under the pretense of taking a Sunday stroll.

She had to see Edward. Even if he had gone over to Sealham, as the odious Annabella had suggested, Louisa would probably be at home, or the servants.

She could leave an urgent message. He had to come to her this time.

She walked around some more, wedged on her bonnet, went downstairs. But before she had crossed the hall, she remembered the copy of Caroline's letter that Edward had told her to bring, and she went back upstairs at some speed in order to fetch it.

She opened her bedroom door. Céline was in there. She had the closet door open and was in the process of taking out one of Fanny's gowns.

"Why, Miss Fanny! You give me the shock!" It was true, it seemed. Céline looked very flustered. "I was . . . I was taking out that blue thing to put it right. You told me there was red wine on it."

"But that is not the one," Fanny said quietly, looking first at Céline's face, then at the yellow gown she was holding.

"Is it not?" Céline found a trickling laugh. "I did not notice. I thought I had the blue one. Is too much sun, don't you think? It gets to your head, milady says."

"Perhaps it does." Fanny went across to the closet, took out the blue gown, gave it to Céline, and hung the other one back inside. She closed the door. They stood there looking at each other.

"You . . . are going out?" Céline said.

"Yes." And you thought I had gone already!

"For a walk?"

"Yes." Would Céline never take the hint and go? What was she doing in here, anyway?

"You like to walk. It is the English all over."

"Is it?" Fanny said coolly. A pause. Then, "You may take the dress now, Céline, and bring it back tomorrow."

"Mais oui." Céline's sallow face went into action. "There is nothing else I can do for you?"

"No. Nothing. Thank you." She waited until Céline had gone, then crossed to the drawer. The copy of Caroline's letter was still locked inside, seemingly untouched. She took it out, stuffed it deep into her pocket, relocked the drawer, went downstairs again.

I am more suspicious now, Fanny thought, but that is to the good. Her thoughts remained quite steady as she walked out the front door. Céline should not have been going through that closet. She had not been looking for the blue dress. She had been all of a dither when someone walked in and found her there. Caroline had sent her to look for something. For what? No way of telling. No time to worry about it now. More important to get right away from the house before anyone asked where she was going or asked if they could come, too.

Fanny crossed the park and went up into Leigh Wood with admirable calmness. Caroline had been lying down; Clarence was nowhere to be found. It was a great comfort to find it all so easy. Sir George had been the only person she had encountered on the way out. Hard to disentangle all the emotions she felt when in the presence of that flushed, unsteady old gentleman. Hard not to entreat him, then and there, to walk out with her and get away from the place while he was still safe and in one piece.

"Well, miss . . . ?" He had stood there looking at her, caught between the dining parlor and the library. "Going out?"

"Yes. For a half hour."

"Like the park, do you?"

"Yes. Yes, very much."

"Used to walk when I was young." He stabbed at the floor with his stick. "Slept more then. Different," he mumbled. "Thought nothing of sleeping all night . . ." He gave her a fierce, bleary-eyed look, and said, "Almost never now . . ." He stopped, seemed lost for a minute. "If you see him, tell him . . ."

"What?" Fanny said, gently.

"Tell him I heard a good account of . . ." He had forgotten the end of the sentence. Saw Fanny looking at him, waiting, uncomprehending. Turned on his heel, said, "Well, get along, then! Get along with you!" Abandoned her there in the middle of the floor, made it to the library, and slammed the door behind him.

He is not fit to be left here, she thought. He does not make sense. But I could not make him come with me if I tried, and it will be better to let Edward take charge of it all. In the long run, it will be better. He will not have to suffer like this much longer . . .

The wood was quite cool, even though the sun poured down upon the village in the valley. Fanny took the higher track that led straight across to Leigh Park. The trees had a sort of blue glaze upon them, a stillness deep in the center that is only found in the mellowest part of summer. When the path began to turn downward again, at a spot where she could see the whole lake stretched out below, she knew that she was only five minutes' walk away from Leigh Park. She could see the chimneys as she came down through the thinner part of the wood. There was a man down by the boathouse about as small as a dot, but when she came out of the trees to the spot where the track met the lane, she could not see him anymore; the ground was too low.

She crossed the lane. Almost there. She quickened her pace. The edge of a meadow lay in front. To the left, the wood. On her right, the long, twisting lane that looped out toward the coach road and the village. Two steps more and she was making for the grass. It was then that she clearly heard the sound of horses and voices. Her heart lurched. Her pulse began to race once more, as when she had found Céline in her room. Her brain told her to stand quite still for a moment, to look as if she were merely waiting for whoever it was to pass. Not to panic, whatever happened, or look guilty.

One of the voices she knew. She recognized its familiar tones. The laugh. Sherry. He came around the bend on a dark horse she had never seen before.

"Fanny!" he said.

"I did not expect to see you here." She recovered from her surprise as soon as she could.

He reined in the horse, looked around to tell the other rider something. "Nor I you," he said. "Where are you headed?"

"Oh . . . nowhere in particular. I came out through the park. It was such a fine afternoon, I think I have walked too far."

"Introduce us, Sherry, old fellow." The new voice struck Fanny as being very self-possessed. It belonged to the dark, stocky young man on the other horse. He was all muscle and dark eyebrows. "Always the same," Sherry's companion went on blithely. "Keep the pretty girls to yourself." Dark, slightly insolent black eyes smiled down at Fanny. "Think I might filch her from you, is that it?" he demanded of Sherry.

"Fanny, this is Brandon. Henry Brandon." Sherry's tone suddenly struck Fanny as being restrained. Constricted. Or was it unwilling? "Brandon, this is Miss Milbanke."

"Not dear, sweet little Fanny?" The words came

out accompanied by a grin. "I've heard all about Fanny," Henry Brandon said, eyeing her up.

"Miss Milbanke is staying the summer at Cranthorne," Sherry said stiffly.

"Lucky old Cranthorne!" Brandon brought his horse unnecessarily close and sat there still looking at her. "You didn't tell me she was such a delightful creature, old man. No wonder you wanted to keep me away from the house. Wouldn't let me anywhere near, Fanny—did you know that?"

"I . . . I think I must be getting on." Fanny liked nothing about Henry Brandon. Neither his overfamiliar tone of address nor his ogling gaze.

"God bless us, I'm scaring her off!" Brandon said.

"Which way are you going back?" Sherry asked her abruptly, having dealt Brandon an emphatic look.

"I . . . I had not thought." She was forced to prevaricate. "Through the wood, I suppose. The other way is ten times as long."

"Then I'll come that way with you." The answer was instantaneous.

"Oh, but there's no need. Really!" Fanny stammered all sorts of excuses. "You did not intend . . . I mean, I would not dream of taking you out of your way. I shall probably walk too slow . . . You should carry on with your ride . . ."

"Our ride is finished," Sherry said. "Brandon is going back the Chewton way, so it will suit me to separate here."

"Getting rid of me all of a sudden, are you?" Brandon laughed. "Can't say I blame you. Shouldn't mind a stroll back through the woods with Miss Milbanke myself. Suppose I'm going to be shrugged off though, old chap. Ditched for a lady without even so much as a last farewell or an apology! But there: such is life!" He leaned right down toward Fanny. "I should watch my dear friend, Mr. Crawley, though. He is a delinquent of the very worst kind. That is what I tell all the ladies. Not that they listen, of course! Not that they ever listen . . ."

He went off still laughing.

Fanny had no choice, of course, but to turn around with Sherry and to make the long trek back again toward Cranthorne through Leigh Wood. It was vexing. Her temper raged inwardly. She felt so desperate, she did not speak to him for a full five minutes. But there was nothing she could do about it. She had no excuse at all for calling at Leigh Park, and she could not now do so. It seemed as if everything was combining to frustrate her plans. They would walk home, talk nonsense when she could bear to bring herself to do so, go back into the Hall, dine together . . . and there would be another evening gone.

Monday: tomorrow. How was she to see Edward? She went on asking herself all the way up the track, but no answer came. It was that kind of day.

Chapter Sixteen

Sherry walked behind, leading the horse all the way. At last, at the top of the track, he said, "You must not mind that fool, Brandon. He was always the same. A fool, but harmless enough."

"I did not mind him," Fanny said stiffly. "I only saw the gentleman for two minutes. Why should I take any notice of a complete stranger?"

"Nevertheless, he did upset you."

"I did not think you would choose to spend your time with such as he." It was said with a light little toss of her head.

"I told you. He is a stupid dog. A man's man."

"He is no gentleman; that is for sure!"

"His father was a clergyman in the next county."

"A clergyman?" Fanny was shocked. "Then he ought to know better, should he not? Few gentlemen would treat a lady with such . . . such familiarity." She looked at Sherry and decided to say it. "Did Mr. Brandon have any connection with that poor woman who killed . . . who died? With Teresa Harley?" She could believe it now, once having met him.

"Brandon?" Sherry's face went completely blank. Then he said with more emphasis, "Brandon?"

"Yes."

"What made you think that?"

Take care, Fanny. Be careful what you say. "I believe I heard one of the servants gossiping."

"The servants . . . !" he said explosively.

"Well . . . is there any connection?"

"Not that I know of." He said with some conviction, "The Harley woman has . . . had no connection with any of my acquaintances."

"Except Clarence."

"Except Clarence," he agreed. His eyes changed in the soft, green light, became half apologetic, half exasperated, the long lashes ridiculously thick and curly, boyish-looking. "Look . . . Fanny . . . do we have to talk about things like this? They can have no connection with us, with you and me . . ." His face was open and candid. No anxiety or inner stress. "Can't we talk about something more pleasant? You are not going to leave us, are you, as you hinted at this morning?"

"I did not exactly say I was leaving. In any case, Caroline was very much against it." She looked at him. "I would not wish to offend her." She had only the haziest idea of testing him out, beyond leading into a subject that might give her some leads. "She has been . . . well . . . not very easy of late."

"Oh, Caro has her blacks," Sherry said with a laugh. "You should not take any notice of that."

"Her what?"

"Her blacks. Her black humors." He made an imitative face. "Sometimes there's no pleasing her, so you just have to get out of her way. It should not make you wish to go back to London. She always recovers, given time."

Fanny said, "I was merely giving it some thought, that is all."

"Oh, Fanny . . ." He shook his head.

"What is the matter?"

"Isn't it plain?" His voice was soft.

"No. Isn't what plain?" She stared at him.

"I would miss you." He wore a crooked little smile. "Did you not think about that?"

Fanny began to walk faster. She wished he would not say such things. She did not now want him to—

and there was a good way yet before they got safely back to the Hall.

"Could you not guess it?" he said. He dropped the reins suddenly over the branch of a tree and caught her up. A hand came around her waist. "If I'm not much mistaken, you did not find my attentions unwelcome a few weeks back?"

"That was a few weeks ago." Fanny colored up.

"So what has changed?"

"Nothing."

"Nothing?" He stopped her walking by drawing her toward him. "What's the matter, Fanny? What did I do wrong?" A pause. "If it was that business the other night at the ball . . . I had had too much wine. I . . . I found you too tempting, that is all." Another silence. "So how can I make amends? Put things right between us . . . Fanny?" His lips were already reaching for her own, one hand was in her hair.

"No!"

"Fanny . . ."

"I said, No!" She pushed him away so hard that his face registered surprise.

"Now who's in a black?" he said, trying to look amused.

"I do not have black humors like Caroline!"

A silence. "That was heartfelt." Sherry's tone had changed. "You really don't like Caroline's moods, do you?"

"No, I do not." Now it was necessary to soften the statement. "Look, Sherry, I do not mean to quarrel. Truthfully, I don't. It is the last thing on my mind. There are other things much more important to think of."

"Other things? What other things?"

"Oh . . . nothing. It does not matter." She had not meant to say that.

"Fanny, won't you tell me?" His eyes were soft and brown and pleading. She looked at him, torn, hesitated, then decided against it.

"No," she said. "It does not matter."

"It must matter if you are so . . . desperate about it."

"I am not desperate."

"No?" He had hold of her arm, but gently this time. "You look desperate. It's all right," he said. "I shan't begin again. Yet." There was that catching gleam of laughter in his eyes.

"You won't begin at all," she said severely.

"Understood," he said. "As long as you guarantee to keep ten feet away from me."

Impossible not to smile back at him. He knew how to coax, she thought half crossly.

"So what if we were to wander around a mile or two more and take the long route back?" he said. "Will that help my cause?"

"No, it will not."

He stole a little glance at her as they strolled on. "If what I am thinking is true," he said lightly, ". . . if you do not find me downright repulsive . . . then something has changed lately. You are different. I have noticed that."

"You have noticed?" Now she felt . . . trapped.

"I was thinking," he said, ". . . perhaps it is something Caro has said." Another sidelong glance. "Is that what is upsetting you?"

"No. It is nothing she has said."

"Something she has done, then?" Inexorably, he was getting nearer the truth.

Fanny did not know what to say. She walked on faster than ever, a frown on her face.

"Fanny, stop!" He caught her up, stopped her himself. "I wish you would tell me. You seem so strange. Perhaps I could help."

"Help?" She did look at him then. She looked at him with unsure and unhappy eyes and saw the solicitude it put into his face.

"Yes. Fanny, perhaps I can help."

"I . . . don't know." She kept on looking at him.

"Well, try . . ."

After a long pause, she looked away, took a long breath, and made up her mind. "Very well, then. I wish . . . I wish to know how much you have noticed about Clarence and Caroline. About their relationship."

"Their relationship?"

"Yes." The blankness in his tone was comforting. It encouraged her to go on. "You do not know, then? I am relieved about that."

"Know what?" Sherry said.

"This is so difficult to say, but I have proof, incontrovertible evidence, that Clarence and Caroline are . . . are having an illicit relationship."

"Clarence? And Caro?" His face was a picture.

"Yes." Fanny hurried on. "I know it does not seem likely. I know they have kept it very well hidden. But she is now . . . I do not know how to tell you this . . . she is going to have Clarence's child."

"His child?"

Fanny almost felt sorry for him, he looked so amazed. "You do not believe it. I knew you would not. I wish I had not been forced to tell you, but you said you wanted to know what was wrong and you wanted to help, so there is no alternative. Can you see that?" She became emboldened by his silence. "There is more. I fear they are planning to

harm Sir George, too. Oh, I know . . . I know . . .
I can see by your face you find that hard to swallow,
but can you not see that by the very nature of
things, they cannot afford to go on long as they are?
I overheard them talking yesterday in Caroline's
bedroom. If they . . . if anything were to happen
to Sir George, they would inherit all his fortune between them. You say nothing. Sherry, you must not
run straight to Caroline and tell her what I have
said. Promise me you will not. It is not some light
kind of tittle-tattle. It is all too important. It is—I
fear—life and death for Sir George."

More silence. Sherry's face was as white as a
sheet. She said quietly, "You look just as I felt when
I first found out. I did not believe a word of it, either, at first. Sherry . . . say something . . .
please."

"I . . . can't believe you." There was sweat on
his forehead and he appeared to be struggling for
words. "I . . . I have noticed nothing. What made
you suspect anything?"

"I saw Clarence go into her room very late one
night. And he did not come out."

That was even worse. He looked across at her
with something like desperation in his eyes. "Clarence . . . in Caro's room?"

"Yes. It gave me a considerable shock, but I saw it
with my own eyes. And now she is going to have
Clarence's child. That is what I overheard them dis-
cussing yesterday." She redoubled her efforts to
convince him. "Sherry, would I tell lies to you?
What reason would I have? I am not mad; I am quite
sane. These are facts that I tell you . . . nothing
more, nothing less."

"And she is going to have Clarence's child?" He

said it woodenly, automatically, shoving his hands in his pockets.

"Yes. Are you going to believe me?"

"I have . . . no choice."

She had told him the facts perhaps more through desperation than from any real hope that he could help her. She had been prepared to have him argue with her, defend Caroline with all the loyalty that friendship could muster, put up some fight before caving in to the facts.

What she had not expected was the devastating effect it would have on him. She saw him, in that moment, look blankly across to the chimneys of the house, quite close now, his face a frightening white, his whole body rigid and his eyes all glassy like a sheet of water. If she ever felt sorry for him, it was now, but she had only one thought and that was to pull him out of this enormous state of shock.

"Sherry, don't look like that." She even put out a hand to touch his arm. "I had to tell you. Someone has to help me, be with me . . . for Sir George's sake. Can you not see that?" Slowly, his eyes, his consciousness came back to her. "The matter is so pressing."

"Yes . . ." He came to what appeared in his mind to be a decision, walked over to his horse, then back again and stood there just looking at her.

"You will help?" Fanny said. "There is not much time."

"Yes." It seemed to strike him for the first time that she was physically present. "Yes, I will help. But you must give me an hour or two to think about it. To let it soak in. I . . ." His color was coming back a little. "I ask you for just a little time."

"Of course," Fanny said with some sympathy.

"Perhaps we can talk about it again later. There is

more I need to know." He shook his head. "I still feel confused . . . it is so unexpected."

"I know." Fanny squeezed his arm. "I had no intention of telling you when we set off together. It has all been too hurried and I have done it badly." The worst of the great thumping of her emotions was beginning to die down, but she still felt shaky as she asked, "Shall we walk on together?"

"No. No, if you do not mind, Fanny, I will go off and ride for a while. I . . . I need to think."

"I can understand that."

"And to go back over it all. All that you have said . . . all that has happened here this summer."

She almost felt relieved that he would not be coming back into the house with her. It was not that she had any thought now that he would go running straight to Caroline. The strength of his reaction had convinced her with some certainty that he would not. But she needed some time, too, a quiet space in which to gather together her powers of reason before they discussed the matter further. So she said, "Go and ride. I will walk the rest of it on my own."

"You do not mind?"

"I do not mind."

"Thank you." An echo of the old, teasing Sherry came back; a pale gleam of the eye, a twist of the mouth. "We'll talk after dinner, then. Will that suit? I may need something inside me to sustain me. You do not know how odd I feel."

"I do," Fanny said, considering him with a grave smile. "Believe me, I do. But that will suit me perfectly. I will meet you after dinner. Where?"

That almost floored him. He had to think hard for a moment, his eyes in the distance. "In the billiard room," he said.

"The billiard room? But I never go there!"

"Exactly," Sherry said. "So no one will expect to find you there. We shall be undisturbed."

Fanny raised her face to his. "Yes. That is a good idea."

"Seven o'clock, then?"

"Seven o'clock."

"Then I'll leave you," he said.

The walk home seemed unreal, though there was nothing different about the park or the gardens or the house itself. There was a heavy silence in the hall, all dead, all quite still, and Fanny almost felt she should take off her shoes and walk in on stockinged feet. She half heard the murmur of voices and sensed that Caroline and Clarence were perhaps in the drawing room. She could only hope that the door was not too much open or that they would not look out and see her pass. The door was almost closed. She slipped past it and up the stairs. No quizzing from Caroline as yet as to where she had been. No need to be gently upbraided for not letting them know that she had intended going out.

The bedroom was all tidy, all cool and well ordered, and she distracted herself for a quarter of an hour or so with freshening herself up and putting away her dusty shoes. She concealed the copied letter again under the heavy mattress: no point in risking the locked drawer again, with Céline around to find the key. She could not help standing by the window for a few minutes and looking wistfully out in the direction of Leigh Park; she had no idea why. It was of no practical use, and with a very severe reprimand to herself, at last she turned away.

Two or three things still whirled around and around in her head. Doubts about confiding in Sherry? No. She supposed this feeling of unease proceeded from having to adjust to this new situation. Sherry was an ally now. She need no longer keep everything all to herself. Suppose he changed his mind, though? Suppose he had second thoughts about helping her and came home and had it out with Caroline and managed to let the cat out of the bag completely?

So . . . she would have to deal with that if it happened, make some contingency plans of her own. She tried to imagine what she would say to Caroline if it all came out. This effort of the imagination lasted only a very short time. She did not think she would discuss the situation with Caroline at all. She would attempt to get out, rather. At once, without waiting for her cousin's reaction. And this time it would not be a brisk walk, but more of a swift run.

There was a sharp tap at the door, then another more urgent.

Fanny moved swiftly to open it, her reactions faster than usual.

"Oh, you're there, miss," Annie Bates said. "They said you'd gone out, but I thought I'd try."

"Annie!" For no logical reason, she was delighted to see the girl. "Come in." Quickly, she shut the door behind them both.

Annie said, "They told me you wanted me."

"Yes. Yes, I did. I wished you to take a letter to Leigh Park for me. I was in a great hurry. How is your mother?"

"She is better now." Annie Bates looked at her. "Do you want me to go this evening?"

"Could you?" A rush of relief went through her.

"I suppose I could try." The girl looked doubtful. "I had last night off, you see. But I know Mrs. Hurst wants a basket of poultry fetched from Leigh Park. Normally James would do it . . ."

"I should be so grateful if you could manage it," Fanny said. "Only . . . Annie . . . please tell no one. Mr. Knight said I could trust you."

"Everybody can trust me, it seems." The girl was dark, with a cheerful air and a swift, spontaneous smile. "Susan Steadman gave me a letter for you. I saw her in Lowton when I went home." She fished into her pocket for a crumpled piece of paper. "It seems I am turning into a regular post run . . ."

When Annie Bates was gone, Fanny tore open Susan Steadman's note. It did not take much reading. Less trouble, Fanny thought, than the girl had had writing it, to judge from the painstakingly drawn letters and the abysmal spelling. The grubby piece of paper had a butcher's account on the back. Fanny ironed out the creases and wondered what had been so urgent as to make Susan attempt such an unfamiliar form of communication, construct such very awkward-looking sentences.

She soon found out. The letter read:

> *Mr. Clarence was so vile that we could not talk moor—it was not untill I had time to think and talk to Mr. Edward agane that I relised—I had no idea you did not know—he shold have told you I think but he says not it prayed on my mind after that pore womans end—you must relise—it is not Clarence your cosin is intimat with —not his child she carries but Mr. Crawleys—I tell you for yr own safety—yrs Susan Steadman.*

The sunshine continued to pour in and Fanny still sat there, motionless.

Time grew dislocated. Someone walked past the windows down below and a dog barked.

It cannot be true, she thought. Never. I will not believe it.

There were people downstairs, a small banging around of doors. Clarence and Caroline . . . not lovers.

Not Clarence's child, but Sherry's. Winning, handsome, teasing Sherry. Yet what proof was there?

Hope tried to rekindle and she said to herself, He was as shocked as I was an hour ago, out there . . . He went ashen when I told him about Clarence. But another voice in her head offered another explanation. He went ashen because I had knowledge of the plot against Sir George. The other affair is only secondary in importance.

And Sherry is a great flirt. A lady-killer. Everyone says so.

She screwed up the letter, thinking of him with a terrible discomposure.

A man with a certain vanity. Who always dressed finely, and knew his effect on women.

What else? His long stay here. The oddly close . . . yes, almost intimate relationship he had with Caroline. Clarence always needling him about one thing . . . his way with women . . . as if he had some secret knowledge, that gave him excellent sport.

There was one thing more. One thing more desperately important than anything else. "Oh, God," Fanny said aloud, and thought how stupid she had been. "I poured everything out to him. Every smooth, pat, naive little thought in my head. And I expect he will be much obliged when he has got himself together and comes back to the house."

She got up from the chair, not knowing whether such stupidity was good because it had made her

aware that she would have to get out of the house
right away, right now, before dinner, or whether it
was bad because she had planted herself in such obvious danger. With a mind half distracted, she
pushed the screwed-up letter in her pocket, took her
bonnet and a light shawl and, as a kind of frenzied
afterthought, the copy of Caroline's letter from under the mattress, and with her fingers beginning to
shake, she opened the bedroom door and took a
quick look outside.

No one. All clear. She slipped out into the passage, closed the door quietly behind her, and then
with a heart thumping at ten times the normal
speed, rapidly made her way toward the turn at the
end and the back staircase.

It was Clarence's cough more than the opening of
his door that made her start and turn around. She
looked at him thinking that he had just come casually out to make his way to the billiard room before
dinner, but she saw at once that she was wrong.

Clarence was smiling expansively. Clarence's
cough was well timed in order to stop her in her
tracks. He found it a pleasure to think that he had
surprised her, and he took increased delight in moving swiftly into the corridor to block her way so that
she could not go farther.

Fanny's gaze traveled past him into the room he
had just left. Caroline was there in her yellow china
crepe and, just behind her, Sherry. Discomfort,
unease, and an almost admirable attempt at nonchalance crossed his face in smart succession.

Clarence said, "Well, my dear Fanny, I hear you
have been finding out all sorts of unpleasant things
about us?"

"I . . . I was just going down to see Mrs. Hurst,"
Fanny said, trying to keep all her wits about her.

"Were you? Were you indeed?" His eyes, always gleaming, held a fond expression of regret. "I'm afraid we don't think that's a very good idea, do we, Caro? Not a good idea at all. In fact, we were rather hoping you would favor us with your company for a short space of time. There are . . . things we should very much like to discuss. Perhaps you would just like to step inside, my dear? I think we might all find it quite interesting."

Chapter Seventeen

Six-thirty. Sunday afternoon.

Clarence, still smiling in that unpleasant fashion, led Fanny across the room. Stood her against the chest of drawers, looked at her, went on smiling. "So you thought it was I who was sporting with our Caro?" he said. "Well . . . well . . ."

"I know now that it was not," Fanny replied. She turned her head and looked at Sherry. "I have learned the truth . . . a little too late." She kept on gazing at Sherry's handsome face. "I was such a fool," she said slowly.

"You know?" Sherry spoke for the first time. He sounded shifty.

"Yes, I know."

Clarence's voice, breaking in, was sharp. "Indeed? And who has been filling you in, may one ask?"

"Susan Steadman. I received a note from her not half an hour back."

"Susan Steadman . . ." There was a knife edge, now, in Clarence's tone. "We should have dealt with her, too. She has caused us a great deal of trouble. So . . . you have found out the truth, have you? That is why you were about to slip down the back way so fast?" He came nearer. "In a way, I am disappointed," he murmured. "I was immensely flattered, my dear Fanny, when you suspected me of carrying on with Caro. It quite polished up my image. I felt twenty years younger, I declare . . ." His eye went over to Sherry, who stood by the window. "To be thought of on a par with the fancy Mr. Crawley."

Fanny looked at Sherry, too. His face was familiar, the thick-lashed blue eyes, the curly hair, the rather boyish mouth, but his expression was no longer recognizable.

Fanny said to him, "How could you?" Her voice, very low, was shaking. "You and Caroline . . . I would never have believed it."

Clarence was laughing. "What you did not know, my dear, is how great a store of—shall we say—animal spirits the gentleman has. Yes . . . a very healthy flow of . . . spirits."

"It is disgusting!" Fanny said. She had the satisfaction of seeing Sherry turn away.

"My dear, it is no use getting snappy about these little attachments." Clarence was enjoying both Sherry's discomfiture and Fanny's anger. "Everyone does it these days. It is the modern thing. Even Nelson and Lady Hamilton . . . Did you not read their letters in the *Morning Herald?* It is everywhere. Why, then, should you feel so . . . superior?"

"I would have expected it of you," Fanny told him with a flash of anger. "With you it would be the normal thing. But I did not think he . . . !" She could not even bring herself to say Sherry's name now. "I did not think him so degenerate. I do not know how he could have done it!"

"How?" Clarence's enjoyment sharpened. "Why, are you so very ignorant, my dear Fanny? Perhaps you are . . ." He came right over to her, so close that she immediately backed against the chest. "Perhaps we should teach you. Perhaps you would like to learn a little in the ways of the world from one or the other of us? I suppose you would prefer Mr. Crawley . . . he is, after all, the younger and has had rather more experience numerically speaking. I, on the other hand, could suggest a few little variations—"

"Clarence, enough!" That was Caroline. She glared at Clarence and looked right past Fanny. Her voice, her movements, seemed disjointed and jerky. "Get on with it," she told him. "And stick to the point."

"Very well, my dear. If you say so." He grinned. "So, Fanny, you are not half so dull as you look. You have found us out?"

"Is that why you kept coming to Wentworth Street?" Fanny asked him. "Because you thought I looked dull? Simple?"

Clarence said, "What we wanted, dear Fanny, was a little pigeon. A dear little, plump little pigeon to coo away for us as a witness when the time came. To witness on our side and tell them all what a clumsy drunkard my brother was." Thick veins stood out at the sides of his temples. His hand came out and gave her a long, lingering pat on the cheek. "Made a mistake there, didn't we, Caro? Made one devil of a mistake!" The hand moved down, caressed the downy skin at the side of her neck. Fanny tried to twist away. "Who would have thought the little pigeon would be so sharp?" His voice grew softer. He started to laugh. "But damn it all, you made mistakes, too, didn't you, Fanny? You never guessed what Sherry was. Really, one must use the word foolish. Whatever made you assume I was Caro's lover and he the boyish innocent? Mmm?" A fat finger touched the ribbon on the curve of her breast.

"I saw you go into her room late one night." Fanny held herself quite stiff. His touch made her flesh creep.

"Only to talk, my dear. To make plans. Nothing else, I assure you. Caro has other tastes." That grin again. "So have I." A pause. "And I thought you quite blind to it all! You know, it is rather like being sold a bad horse," he said, looking at her reflectively. "You expect one thing and get another. Now that is not quite fair, would you agree?"

"I am not a horse," Fanny told him. "And I was not sold to you." She dared not let them see how frightened she really was. She tried to appear defiant. "Perhaps you should have looked more closely and then you might have seen what I was."

"Oh, I shall look . . . I shall look." Clarence smiled softly. "Don't worry about that. Give me time. And the right place . . ."

Fanny had to stand there and take the full force of that horrible suggestiveness. Savagely she wished she had not gone bright scarlet, not let him know how much he had gotten through to her.

She could not stand his stare any longer and turned her attention to Caroline instead. The pale gold complexion looked as smooth and perfect as ever. The tight yellow crêpe bodice revealed her as slim and lithe as a boy. Distaste must have been written all over Fanny's face, however, because Caroline suddenly smiled vividly and said, "What do you think you are staring at?"

"At you," said Fanny.

Clarence said, "She is admiring you, my dear Caro."

"That I am not!" Fanny said at once. "I do not see how anyone could admire her."

That angered Caroline. She reacted violently. "You need not stand there fancying yourself any better than me, you little fool!"

Clarence made little tutting noises at that. He said, "I really think you should let Mr. Crawley deal with Fanny, my dear, if that is how you are going to be. Sherry is more adept at it, is he not? After all, he had her doting on him so much, she quite spilled all the beans."

"Is that what I was meant to do?" Fanny asked Caroline. "Dote on him? Did you also mean to set me up as a decoy . . . have him flirt with me so as to head off any gossip there might be about you and him?" She remembered all those evenings he had openly toyed with her in company. Stupid, she thought. I was so stupid!

Caroline said, "He would not bother to flirt with you for any other reason. You did not actually think he was in love with you, did you?"

"For a short while . . . yes." Fanny gazed her out. "That is what I was meant to think, I suppose?"

"If you were fool enough." Caroline spoke sarcastically. "I did not care."

"You cared that day you let us walk to Leigh Park to dine, and we arrived late." I know how to get her rattled, Fanny thought. If I can do that, she may let out more than she wants me to know. "You cared when you thought he was truly taking an interest in me."

"Taking an interest?" Caroline laughed shrilly. "He would never show an interest in a milksop thing like you."

"Would he not?" Fanny took her time. "He showed an interest in Teresa Harley, though, didn't he?" She had been putting two and two together. "It was not Clarence's child Teresa was carrying, was it? Or you would not have been so shocked. Clarence was just going there to try and buy her off. It was Sherry who was her lover. Had he got so tired of you? Could you not keep him better occupied?"

Caroline swung her arm and slapped Fanny across the face. The slap hurt. Caroline's face slowly lost its wildness. She was like a cat after it had spat.

Clarence said, "That's enough, Caro, my dear. Good point. Badly taken. Got to think of your delicate condition, you know."

"Do I ever stop thinking about it?" Caroline threw a black look in Sherry's direction. A muscle was twitching at the curve of her jaw.

"You were clever in keeping it hidden," Fanny said.

"But not for much longer," Clarence commented. "Sooner or later some lady of the neighborhood is going to notice that dear Caro is growing a tiny bit stout. She is not yet colossal, but in a few weeks it will be impossible to hide, even from George's fuddled gaze."

"It is no wonder you were shocked that afternoon in Lowton," Fanny said to Caroline. She knew she risked another attack, but the more she kept them talking, the more she learned. "I assumed it was Clarence that Teresa Harley was looking for—that he was her lover, but he was not. I saw Mr. Craw-ley's face. I heard him use her name, but thought nothing of it. I should have known then, by the way he hurried me off under the pretense of protecting me from the row. He was protecting himself."

She looked at Sherry. His hands were shoved deep in his pockets and he had half turned away. "You do not have so much to say for yourself now, do you?" No reply.

Her attention came back to Caroline. "Did you not know where he went off to?" she asked slyly. "Were his stories very plausible? I expect they were. I expect he told you he was with his friend, Brandon?" Her gaze was clear and cutting. "I felt sorry for Teresa Harley. At least she was honest. She did not pretend to be what she was not."

Caroline's arm went up again, but this time Clarence caught hold of it. He made her sit down. "In the end," he told Fanny regretfully, "dear Sherry proved a better actor than any of us. Did you not, dear boy?" He shrugged. "Never trust a handsome face, Fanny. Let that be a lesson to you. Of course I warned Caro, often, when we lived in London, but these ladies . . ." He shook his head. "These ladies will get taken in . . ."

"You were the one who brought him home," Caroline spat out.

Clarence's smile grew more subtle. "Ah, but I did not take him into my bed. There lies the difference. You were the one who became a little greedy at that point, my dear. I did warn you about Mr. Crawley right at the beginning, but the prospect of my broth-er's money was not enough. You had to have dear Sherry as well . . . and now look what we are come to!" He was enjoying himself turning the tables on

her, Fanny thought. Now that it was his turn to cen-
sure her little weakness, he would draw the occasion
out, truly make her squirm. "One only has to remember how you met. How I came to pluck him out
of trouble in the first place . . ."

"If you think I'm staying here to listen to
this . . ." Sherry, at that point, made for the door.

"That's right . . . Run away, dear fellow, as
usual. I suppose a few home truths do pinch somewhat." Clarence watched him go, slamming the door
behind him, and then he said, "Mr. Crawley in-
dulges himself, but he does not like to face up to the
consequences."

"What kind of trouble did you find him in?"
Fanny said. Playing for time. Hoping for something
—anything—that would get her out of this mess.

"What kind of trouble?" Clarence looked at Caroline. "You see, she is curious, Caro. Our little pigeon
is curious." He picked up a corkscrew from the table, started to finger it. "Shall we tell her?"

"No. Let her rot." There were red spots on Caroline's cheeks. She almost looked feverish now.

"I agree it does not do the gentleman much credit,
but we will tell her anyway." Clarence was spinning
out his pleasure, playing with Caroline's discomfiture as he played with the corkscrew. "I found Mr.
Crawley beaten to a pulp and stripped practically
naked one night a year or two ago, in a back street
near Covent Garden. He had been in some card
game in some black hole where he had been at-
tempting to win back a vast amount he had put on
the neck of some woman." Clarence laughed. "No,
not her neck. That would not be the part of the lady
dear Sherry was interested in. Let us say, then, that
he had a vast sum on winning her favors. And he

won her. Am I telling it right, Caro? Yes, I think so. You would stop me, wouldn't you, if I got it wrong?"

Caroline's face was stony. Her eyes had a trapped look.

Clarence said, "There was only one tiny thing wrong. The lady's husband did not care for the wager. He did not care for it at all. Somebody had been vastly unfriendly and told him what was going on and where." He laughed. "The lady's husband was a boxer, accustomed to prizefights and prize money, and that was exactly what he got in the end. Right, Caro?"

A silence.

"It took three whole weeks for Sherry's face to put itself anything like right again. Might have been better if we'd thrown him out," Clarence said casually, "before Caro saw it in its proper state . . . Eh? Still, we must not be vindictive. It is such a handsome face, he believes himself justified in multiplying it wherever he goes . . ."

"Stop it!" Caroline went for him at last. "Stop it, do you hear? I have taken enough."

"So you have. So you have, my dear." Clarence leaned over and patted her arm. "What we have to decide now is what to do with our plump little pigeon. She cannot stay here, that's for sure. Not now that she knows about tomorrow . . ."

"Tomorrow?" Fanny looked at him. "What will happen tomorrow?"

Clarence laughed. "Asking questions, Fanny? Shouldn't do that, if I were you. You can't help George now, so you may as well keep your pretty little head right out of things."

"Something is going to happen to him in Leigh Wood, isn't it?" Fanny said. "Some sort of accident when he is riding. You must have been planning some part of it when Bob Steadman saw you at it."

"Clever girl. Too damned clever."

"You won't get away with it. They will be suspicious. What will you say when they start gossiping, pointing the finger?" Fanny asked.

"My dear, why should they be suspicious? Caroline and I will be here, in the house—with Mr. Crawley, of course—playing at brag and chatting as usual. When George does not come home at the usual time, we shall not show much concern at first. But then, as it grows later, Caro will begin to put on a pretty show of anxiety . . ." Clarence smiled speculatively.

Fanny said, "And if something should go wrong? If something happens to get in the way of your plans?"

"You are hopeful, dear Fanny. Much too hopeful. Nothing will go wrong. We have seen to that." A pause. "But . . . in an emergency, we should cope. We are both trimmers, Caro and I. That is how we came to fall in together in the first place. We take our chances quickly as they come. We deal our cards with both hands and look lively and hope they fall right." His little puffed-up eyes were still on her face. "Whereas dear Sherry . . . well, Caro has had to keep him held tight by the nose. He would have changed his mind a dozen times about our little scheme if we had not held him to it." The corkscrew tapped up and down on the table. "Perhaps that is why he needed his frolics in Lowton. To let off some steam . . . to pull on the rope and try to loosen it somewhat . . ." He seemed to have come to a decision. The corkscrew tapped one last time. "I have it. The lavender room."

"The lavender room?" Caroline said.

"Yes. It is right out at the back beyond the kitchens and well away from the servants' quarters. We shall put Fanny in there for the night. With her permission, of course." He grinned mockingly. "That will keep her safely out of the way of everyone, and we will get her away first thing in the morning. Deacon can do it, perhaps."

Do it, Fanny thought. What did that mean? Her heart thumped.

Caroline was sweating. She said, "How will you explain it? Her sudden disappearance?"

"Oh . . . it's simple," Clarence said smoothly. "Fanny has not been quite herself of late. Do you remember her little fit of the hysterica after the carriage accident? And have you not noticed how she has taken to going off all by herself for hours? The signs were there." His smile grew. "She has been a little nervy, had you not, Fanny? Caro had already written to your mamma expressing her worries on that point, only she had not had time to put it in the post. The letter will be produced if necessary." He looked relaxed. "And do you not remember, Fanny, on the way to church on Sunday, mentioning your desire to go back to London? You were anxious about your mamma. Young girls are prone, you know, to such nervy fits. It was the reason, I seem to recall, you were sent down to the country in the first place. Your poor mamma could no longer cope with your humors. You were being very difficult. It was thought a change of scene might do the trick. But . . ." Clarence shook his head sadly ". . . it only seems to have made things worse. So . . . if you were to take yourself off very early one fine morning, my dear Fanny, and none of us could stop you . . . people will not be so astounded. And this oppressive heat—it so aggravates the nerves . . ."

Fanny said, "He will come looking for me."

"Who will come looking for you?"

"Edward. Mr. Knight. He knows . . . he suspects your intentions toward Sir George."

"I told you!" Caroline said sharply.

Clarence ignored her. "Mr. Knight? Does he now? And what does he suspect . . . exactly?"

"That you wish Sir George dead. That you plot in some way . . . you and Caroline . . . to get his money."

"But he has no absolute proof, does he?" Clarence's voice was dangerously soft. "Not without you there to spill the beans?"

"I will get out! I will make sure I tell him—"

"It would be better, dear Fanny, if you did not." He came closer. Brought the corkscrew right up to her face. "In any case, you will be gone from here before he comes to visit."

"He will not accept your lies."

"He will have no choice."

"You cannot keep me locked up. You cannot get rid of me so easily either!"

"You think not?" The sharp point of the corkscrew touched the soft part of her neck. "That is nonsense, if you think about it, Fanny. I do not wish to be unpleasant. It is foreign to my nature . . ." He sighed and looked at her. "But if I have to—and I'm afraid that will very shortly be the case—I can get rid of you very easily. Think of poor Bob Steadman. Think of little Teresa." He made a face. "Nasty business, that, Fanny. Trouble is, I'm not squeamish. Never was. Now . . . it's almost time to dine. We'll keep you here, I think, until dusk, when we can spirit you away to the lavender room."

* * *

Huddled up for warmth on a corner of the bench in the dim, dingy room, Fanny hugged her knees, rocked to and fro, and thought endlessly of this game of charades they had all been playing.

No, not charades. Waltzing games. They had been waltzing her around in circles for weeks. Making her lose all her sense of direction. All her bearings. Laughing at her while they did it.

It was not a very big room. It had about it that sad air of neglect that went with locked doors, cold dust, old bouquets. Something over in the corner looked like a press. On the floor, under it, the thin debris of dried stalks. The lavender room.

Her eyes touched on all these things, saw nothing.

She felt drained. Her arm still hurt where Clarence had wrenched it as he had pushed her in and locked the door behind her. She could not bear to stay shut up here all night.

Shut your eyes to blot it out. No, don't do that. It will be quite dark soon enough.

A voice in her head said, You can't shut out all the thoughts.

I don't want to shut them out. Well, I do, but I've got to put them all straight first. A lot of things make sense now that didn't make sense before.

What if she banged hard on the door and shouted? The servants might hear. They would help. Annie Bates. Even Martha—if only they knew. But the lavender room was too far out into the grounds. Out beyond the kitchen wall and three stories below the servants' quarters.

Anyway, Clarence might get here first. If one of the servants had happened to hear, he would just tell them some story or other. Invent something.

Clarence's tongue was very plausible. And she was frightened of Clarence.

Better leave it until the morning then. They'd have to get her out in the morning. First thing, he'd said. Get rid of her.

That's the trouble. A sharp dart of fear. What would they do with her? Think clearly. They would not risk killing her here, so near the house. It would pose too many problems, leave too much evidence. And they would not like that, not if they wanted tomorrow's plans to go smoothly. In Clarence's language, it would overload the dice, make people unnecessarily suspicious.

She wanted Edward. His logic and clarity of mind. Edward had known all about them. Why hadn't he told her everything? He must have known about Sherry, too. It was inconceivable, being Edward, that he had not. Then why had he not warned her? That thought festered like a sore. She kept turning it round and round in her head. Hadn't he trusted her? Had he suspected her of being too receptive to Sherry's charms? Perhaps that was it . . . after finding them together like that in the conservatory the night of the ball.

But he should have warned me. You would not have believed him, would you? Sherry and Caroline? You would have laughed in his face. And if you had believed it, after a while, you could never have kept hidden your sense of shock. You would have given the whole game away. Perhaps he knew that. Perhaps that is why he did not tell you.

Edward. I wish I could ask you.

Don't think about Edward yet. What you feel for him is too strong. It might take over. You can't allow it to take over because you've got to use your head. You've got to think, clearly and concisely. Head before heart. That's the way it has to be if you want to come out of all this.

So how will they attempt to get rid of me? As Clarence had turned to lock the door on her, he had said, "I'm afraid I can't offer creature comforts. I'll leave that to Deacon in the morning. You may be going on a quiet journey with him. I hope you travel well and make no difficulties."

A journey. That was not quite so frightening. At least it offered a chance of escape. But a journey where? "I hope you travel well." A longish journey, then. To London? To some back-street room where Clarence would keep her holed up? Or would they contrive to get rid of her on the way? A little accident on the road? Mamma would not find out she was missing for weeks, if they had their way. In London they could do anything with her and get away with it. No one any the wiser. No one to know. They could say what they liked then. People would believe them.

Edward wouldn't. He would come looking. But not until tomorrow, she thought, agonized. Tonight he is dining at the rectory, and by tomorrow I shall be gone. And knowing that Edward would come asking questions later wouldn't be much comfort after you had been flung into the Thames or shot through the head like poor Bob Steadman.

Edward had been right from the very beginning. Right to hate them, mistrust them. Just as I mistrusted Clarence that first afternoon at Wentworth Street, she thought.

So long ago. Ages back. She fell asleep at last trying to remember how many weeks.

Chapter Eighteen

Deacon came for her just before it grew light. He was a little man, thin as a weasel. He would be vicious, too, like a weasel, she thought, if someone crossed him. He said nothing. Just frogmarched her across the grass in the park to the small, closed carriage that waited on the far side of the trees.

So Deacon was in on it, too.

Scattered, raw birdsong marked the beginnings of dawn. The air was raw and scattered as well. Hard to tell, yet, what sort of a day it would be.

Deacon opened the door of the carriage, released something that had been slung around his shoulders, and flung it in ahead of her. "Rabbits," he said. His first words. "For delivery."

"D . . . dead?" Fanny asked.

"Ain't likely to be alive," he replied with a harsh laugh. Then she saw the thick coil of rope with which he was going to tie her up. "Sorry," he said. "Orders." The rope twisted roughly round her wrists and then down to her ankles. He shoved her in onto the floor of the carriage, whipping the loose end of the rope to the seat struts so that she could not move or get up. "Might be a rough ride," he told her. He pulled down the window blinds. "Don't try shouting," he added, "or I'll have to shut you up."

"Orders," Fanny thought. She lay awkwardly with her head on the hard, dusty floor, heard the door slam shut and the springs of the carriage go down as Deacon climbed up in front. She thought, At least I'm not dead like the rabbits. She imagined their glassy, staring eyes and their matted fur. Hoped and prayed that they would not flop down onto her with all the bumping in the lanes.

She felt sick with lack of sleep. And with hunger. They had not bothered to feed her last night. She thought: I probably would not have eaten it anyway, the way I felt, so it makes no real difference. There was one great lurch as the carriage moved forward. To distract herself from thinking about all the shaking and rattling that her body was going through, she closed her eyes and thought about Edward and Louisa and imagined them at Leigh Park, perhaps awake in a half hour. Edward, at least. Perhaps he had farm business to see to early. He would not be a lie-abed. She sensed that. She thought about him throwing water over his tanned face and pulling on his shirt and his coat and striding down the stairs. She thought about the sureness, the decision in all his movements, and her note would be in his pocket if Annie Bates had delivered it. If Mrs. Hurst had let her go; and she thought a great deal about how it would feel if Edward appeared outside to rescue her and what he would do to Deacon and to Clarence.

Afterward, she worked out that she lay there on the floor of the carriage being shaken around for a full half hour, though she had not any clear knowledge of it at the time. The first sharp idea that they were on the outskirts of Lowton came from the rattling of other carriages and wagons now and again and a voice or two shouting and a deep church clock striking. They were slowing down, too, and it was light.

When the carriage stopped, after twisting in and out of what felt and sounded like narrow alleys, footsteps came around to the near side and she heard Deacon's voice as he opened the door. Felt him heaving at the rope, loosening all the knots with rough fingers. "Get up," he said when she was finally free.

"I . . . can't," Fanny told him. Her shoulders ached right through. Her legs had gone dead. It was a struggle to even move her fingers.

"Have to carry you, then." His voice, thin and weasely, echoed a little as if they were enclosed in some yard.

"No." She did not want that. He reeked of dirty linen. "No . . . give me a moment." All the time, her eyes were taking in what they could outside. A house. A stone wall. They were parked right up against it and against an open door. Beyond that, a dingy hallway.

She straightened her legs, dragged herself up, shook the pins and needles out of her wrists.

"Right . . . move," Deacon ordered. He half pulled her out of the carriage and straight into the house. Fanny sensed, rather than saw or heard, another person close by as she was bundled across some stone flags and through an open door.

Bang! The door was slammed and locked on her before she even had time to blink. So what now? A dog barked outside. I wish I were out there with it, she thought miserably. Even dogs have their freedom. I can't stand being shut up again.

Nothing happened then for a long passage of time, an undetermined number of hours. She found a lump of bread and some cheese on a plate in the corner and gave in and wolfed them down to the last crumb. From the sounds coming in through the dirty, boarded-up window, there was some sort of stable next door. Men shouting unintelligible commands. Boys dragging round horses with all the usual neighing and stamping. Fanny sat there and listened, telling herself there was nothing she could do for the moment. By the time they came to unlock the door, hours later, her mind had grown clearer. She knew that if they took her away from Lowton— she was certain that was where she was—she was all but finished. Sir George, too.

The scrape of a key turning. A creak. The door opened.

"Come here," Deacon said. "Now. Come on!"

His voice was rougher, as if he had been drinking. And although he was moving toward her with that new, coarser look in his eyes, she was in a way grateful that his voice was slurred, that he was a bit mouthy, almost loose in his movements.

His hand grasped her elbow. Through the hall and out to the back steps again. They were moving her, then. She wondered how she was going to give him the slip, since he had his tight grip on her arm, just under the shoulder where his hand almost reached the warmth of her breast. No good to try planning anything. Fanny took the ten steps or so from the house to the fresh carriage he was steering her toward at the far end of the alley, almost dawdling so that he might think her more pliant, and at the same time she searched with her eyes in all directions for a possible escape route.

It came almost too easily, in the form of a youth dashing out of the stable, red-faced and angry. A youth who ran ducking and weaving across the cobbles to escape the man pursuing him. He came flying toward Deacon and Fanny and tried to dive off around and past them, but his pursuer was swifter. The two of them fell in a scuffle on the cobbles. The youth tried to defend himself, but the older man sat on his chest and aimed blows at his face. Fanny saw blood come from the boy's nose.

"Steal, would you?" Another blow found the boy's face. "And lie through your damned teeth . . . ?"

The youth twisted sideways to escape, bringing him within a yard of Deacon's feet. A heave and a shifting of his weight, but it wasn't enough. When he was halfway up, the man yanked him crashing again to the ground. Fanny heard Deacon curse them, and saw him, out of the corner of her eye, prepare to step sideways out of their way.

For one second, his grip loosened on her arm. She took her chance. She brought up her elbow and dug him with it hard in the stomach. She heard him grunt. Brought her foot up, kicked him viciously in the shin. Deacon hissed like a snake and shrank to defend himself. In an instant, Fanny launched herself away from him, hit the wall in her haste and rebounded, then took off like lightning down the alley. She made for an opening she saw halfway along and ran right down it, almost stumbling on the uneven stones because she was in a panic to get away, and she did not dare believe she had done it.

Stall Street. She had come out into Stall Street. Lowton. She had been right. She breathed a sigh of relief as she slipped swiftly behind a cart that was standing by Lloyds, the bankers. She stood there for a moment in a weak state of gratitude for having got this far. The urgency which had given her the strength to run for it had ebbed away and left space for her limbs to start aching again. Her energy would come back in a minute, if she waited. She leaned against the wall, her breath coming in short bursts.

"I must think," she said aloud, "before I move. It is no use running blindly. It will only put me in worse trouble."

A voice behind her said, "Worse trouble, Fanny? What are you up to now?"

She turned with an enormous start and found Dr. Baillie standing there on the paving slabs between the steps up to the bank and one of the market stalls. Dr. Baillie with a surprised look on his face and his gray eyebrows raised.

"Dr. Baillie! It's you!" Relief flooded right through her.

"Yes. It's me." His smile was affable. "My dear, I do believe you're pleased to see me."

"I am. Oh, I am!"

"That much, eh?" His eyes took in the dust down one side of her and the disheveled state of her hair. He looked curious. "So what have you been up to this time? Mmm . . . ? All alone? Been making some purchases?"

"Not exactly," said Fanny.

The cart in front of them lumbered away. Dr. Baillie's gaze moved, too, to the market hall across the street and the ancient cross beside it. "See that stone under the cross?" he said suddenly. "The one with the strange carvings?"

"Yes." Fanny looked hurriedly along the street. She felt exposed here.

"Reminds me of the markings on a Greek pediment I once tried to bring back from the Orient. They wouldn't let me, you know. Too heavy. Cost too much."

"Oh, dear . . ." The crowd of people by the alley was thinning, and Deacon was pushing his way out. She said a prayer that he had not yet spotted her and dodged behind Dr. Baillie, gripping his arm. "I . . . I feel faint," she said. "Can we go in somewhere? It's the heat." She looked desperately around and saw

the porch of the White Hart. "In there, perhaps? I
. . . I need to sit down."

"Faint?" Dr. Baillie looked at her in a professional
way. "Have you eaten?"

"No."

"You haven't had luncheon?" He looked at his
watch. "One-thirty," he announced. "Then it's no
wonder you feel faint. You young ladies . . . !" He
took his time shaking his head. "Heads full of young
men and gimcracks! Tramping around all over the
place with empty stomachs!" His voice carried far,
like an actor's. In a moment, Fanny thought, Deacon
would hear it and look this way. She clutched at Dr.
Baillie's arm. "Can we go in?" she breathed.

"Better come in and have luncheon," Dr. Baillie
said. "I have not dined yet either. But then, I'm not a
young girl."

"Oh, but I did not mean . . ."

"Never mind what you meant." He was already
leading her up the White Hart steps. "Come along,
come along! No arguments, if you please. You are on
your own, I suppose? No one else from Cranthorne
with you?"

"No." Deacon did not count, she decided with
some irony.

"Then it is settled." With absurd, old-fashioned
gravity, he fastened her hand within his arm. "This
way. They will find me a table. They always do."

Inside the White Hart, it was dim and crowded.
The dining room of the largest inn in Lowton was a
nice-sized room with agricultural prints on the walls
and a broad elm just outside the windows. Most of
the diners seemed to be farmers. It was difficult not
to feel edgy, but Dr. Baillie, being no mean conver-
sationalist, kept the ball rolling.

"Wonderful old story about that market cross—did you know?" He watched Fanny toy with a piece of beef and a circle of cucumber. "Yes . . . it was presented to the town by a Captain in the last century. Stubborn fellow. Came back from the wars with only one leg, but thumped around all over the place with as much energy as ever. Pillar of society. Not so many about these days."

"No." Fanny felt reasonably safe in here with Dr. Baillie, but only so far as she could see both the windows and the door. She had no idea what she would do if Deacon came in. "I . . . I am sorry to have plagued you with my company."

"No plague," Dr. Baillie said in his kind, forthright way. "Not often I have the chance to dine alone with a young lady. More often than not I snatch something in the buggy while doing my rounds. You still look pale. Something wrong? The faintness coming back?"

"No. No . . . nothing is wrong."

"Have some wine. Do you good."

"No. No, really." It was the last thing she wanted. She had to think clearly. She could not tell Dr. Baillie all about it. Not at this moment. In any case, where would she start with such a story to a man who was, after all, almost a stranger. He would never believe her. He would think her a hysterical little fool. She remembered that phrase Clarence had used: nervy fits. Young girls were prone to them. That's what Dr. Baillie would think if she poured it all out.

The waiter came back, tugging at the cuffs of his shirt, to say there was lobster if they required it, and Dr. Baillie said he rather fancied some.

"I do not think I can eat any," said Fanny after the

waiter had gone. "I hope you have a healthy appetite."

"I always eat well." He looked at her. "So you
need not concern yourself, young lady." A pause.
His eyes were sharp. He was more shrewd, perhaps,
than he let on. "How does it happen you are in
Lowton on your own? It is not usual, is it?"

"No . . ." Fanny chose her words carefully. "I
. . . I meant to surprise my cousin with a small gift.
It is her birthday next week."

"Is that a fact?" If anything, his voice grew more
curious. "How did you come? In the phaeton?"

"Yes . . . well, no. I . . . my journey here was
unexpected. James . . . James had to go on. As a
matter of fact . . ." Her mind was racing into a
course of action. "I wonder if I might beg a ride
home with you? If you are going back to Stamford,
that is? If it will be no trouble . . ." Anxious eyes
met his. "Are you going back immediately after luncheon?"

It all seemed quite unreal now, but she had to see
it as reality. She glanced at the big clock on the wall
across the room. A quarter past two. She had been
working things out in her head, trying to piece it
together. Clarence had said they would all wait at
home playing brag, and the only time they played at
cards was in the evening, after dinner. Sir George
dined on Mondays at Leigh Park at five-thirty. He
always rode across through Leigh Wood. They
would do it there, either on his way out or back . . .

"Not quite at once," Dr. Baillie was saying in his
bland, professional way. "There is one more visit I
have to make. But you can wait here for me. I shall
not be long."

"How long?" Fanny said desperately.

"Oh . . . a half hour. At the most."

A half hour. Was it too long? It would have to do.
In any case, she had no other way of getting back.
As long as she could be back by half past four. A
quarter to five. In time to get Edward to ride out and
stop Sir George. The thing was, would they plan the
fatal accident for Sir George's outward or return
journey? The return journey, surely, when it would
be good and dark? Then there would be plenty of
time.

Or perhaps they would not dare to do it at all
when they found out she had escaped.

Fanny took a sip of wine. A gust of noise came in
from the hall. Farmers leaving. A delicate, dazzling
beam of sunlight came suddenly in at the window.

Everything in it turned golden. Instantly gilded.

Fanny's gaze rested on the window, on the source
of all that light. Drifted out. Stopped after a couple
of seconds. Stopped because she was frozen with
horror.

Deacon was out there. And another man. Deacon
was standing under the elm tree in the street, sweating like fury, evidently from sheer evil temper. The
other man stood saying something to him. His face
was long and thin, his skin sallow and foreign-looking . . .

"Only one thing wrong with this place," said Dr.
Baillie.

"I . . . beg your pardon?" Fanny had scarcely
registered the words. Her voice was high, but she
managed to drag her gaze back to Dr. Baillie's face.

"One thing I disapprove of. They will try to trick
it out."

"Trick it out?"

Fanny's eyes flickered back to the window. Deacon was moving now. Moving on down the street
with only the most cursory glance at the White Hart

windows. His common sense told him Fanny would never venture in there on her own. Yes, it was safe enough. He was definitely moving away.

"Trick it out to make it something it isn't." Dr. Baillie rumbled on. "This is a fine old Queen Anne place, but what do they do? Try to improve it with these damned new-fangled Greek columns and such."

"I thought you liked Greek columns," Fanny said. Her legs were trembling all over. It was a good thing they were hidden under the table. The relief was almost too much.

"I do. I like them in Greece where they belong." He fixed her with his bright, intelligent gaze. "Well, young lady . . . ? Feeling better?"

"Yes. Yes . . . much better, thank you."

"Well, next time oblige me by not trying to starve yourself, do you hear me?"

"Yes. I hear you." She smiled at him. "Dr. Baillie . . ."

"Yes?"

"Thank you. I'm very grateful." A pause. "You've been most kind."

"Hmph!" Then he said, "No doubt you'll tell me what it was all about sometime . . . when it suits you. Well, I can wait. Used to that. Ah, here's the lobster. And then I'd better cut along and see my patient."

There was a fair amount of coming and going, even with Dr. Baillie and the rest of the diners all gone. Doors slamming, shouts now and again. The chief waiter who had served them came in and out. He looked like Napoleon, she thought, a brisk little Napoleon strutting in and out like that. The would-be dictator. Had she not been left there in the corner

as a piece of luggage, so to speak, of the good Dr.
Baillie, he would have cleared her out in an instant.
She could tell by the look in his eye.

Then Napoleon had to go off on some appointment or other and there was no one left to guard the
door. Only a fat, untidy cook who slopped through
now and then, bringing all the kitchen smells with
her. It was still hot outside. Not a leaf stirred on the
elm. Fanny shifted in her seat and stemmed her impatience. It would do no good to fret about the time.
All she could do was wait.

Half an hour was only thirty minutes, she
thought, and five of those were gone already. The
other twenty-five would go by and Dr. Baillie would
not be late. He could not. He was a man of his word
and he had promised.

Chapter Nineteen

But he was late. It was fourteen minutes to four
when he came hurrying back into the White Hart.
He looked breathless, knocked up; and Fanny could
not be anywhere near so agitated with him as she
felt when every word he uttered was an apology.

"Case of fever," he said, dropping his bag down
onto the chair while he caught his breath. "Better all
week. Thought I only needed to pass the time of
day. But the fits had come back . . . never saw a
man go back down so hard. Lost all his faculties.
Doubt if he'll live . . ."

Neither will Sir George, Fanny thought, unless we can get back to Cranthorne at once.

"I'm sorry," she said. "But can we leave?"

Dr. Baillie looked at her over the top of his spectacles. He saw her impatience. "Tired of waiting?" he asked.

"No. It is not that."

"Gig's standing outside. Just got to make a little detour around by Combe End Rectory to drop off some medicine."

"Oh, but that will not take long . . . ?" Fanny said desperately. "Will it?"

"An extra five minutes to the journey. That is all." He looked at her. "Take an old doctor's advice, my dear. Slow down a little. You will be better for it. Speed is the scourge of this age . . ."

The journey back to Stamford was an even worse ordeal than the wait in the White Hart dining room. She kept thinking that round every bend Clarence would appear on the road in front of them. Or Deacon—he would have had ample time to get back to Cranthorne by now. Yet they could not be sure, she reckoned, which road she would take if she attempted to get back to warn Sir George. There was the main road they had come by or the more twisting, but shorter, bottom road; or the one that Dr. Baillie took. The road that went on a five-minute detour to Combe End Rectory and rejoined the Stamford road just before it came to Leigh Wood.

It was like one of those nightmare journeys that recur in dreams. Time seemed to split into two. The ordinary, slow progress of things out there. The horse trotting, trees swaying, clouds moving infinitesimally slowly across a broad country sky. Then thoughts, questions, speculations racing at a hundred times that speed through Fanny's head. Where in Leigh Wood? Where?

Bob Steadman had been shot at the top of the slope overlooking the lake. That must have something to do with the location. He had seen them making preparations or computations of some sort and they had killed him for it. He had slithered down the side of the slope and Taff Jenkins had found him lying half across the path just above the fringe of trees that led down to the bank.

The bank. That awful bank Sir George insisted on leaping every day. Had been warned about more than once.

Fanny felt a dreadful chill, followed by the little shock of recognition in the pit of her stomach that she had known all the time that this was the place. It was the only spot where a fatal accident would not be in the least surprising. A shot to frighten the horse at the wrong moment . . . No, not a shot. They would not risk that. Would not need to. Anything certain to make the horse shy at the moment of takeoff, at that terrible leap . . .

Think how far there was to fall. At how sharp an angle. And think of that deadly obstacle, that huge dry stone wall where it was exposed from the hedge bottom . . . Deadly.

Oh, God, she thought. He will have no chance. They will leave no evidence behind them. Whomever they pay to be down there . . . Deacon. The other, foreign-looking fellow. No, it would be Deacon. She was sure of that. It would not be in the least bit suspicious for Deacon to be there in Leigh Wood. In fact, he would be the natural person to find the old man. To race back to Cranthorne pretending to raise the alarm.

After he had made sure Sir George was safely dead . . .

But when? When would they attempt it? Sir George dined on Mondays at Leigh Park at five-thirty. Would they risk it on his way there? Too risky, surely, in case anyone should be around? But who would be around at that time of day? And the downward run was by far the most dangerous leap.

"Where are we?" Fanny demanded of Dr. Baillie. She did not know this lane half so well as the other.

"Coming round to the tail end of Leigh Wood. Almost there."

"What is the time?"

"The time." Laboriously, he heaved out his watch. "Almost four-thirty."

"Four-thirty?" Fanny said sharply.

"I will take you right to the door. Cranthorne is not so far out of my way."

"No!" Fanny said sharply.

"No?" The reins in his hand, he turned to look at her. "You do not wish to be driven all the way?"

"No." She said it with more composure, yet with more feeling. "I . . . you need not trouble yourself." She had intended to ask him to take her to Leigh Park on some pretext or other, but now she dared not risk the delay. The time edge was too fine. If Edward were out . . . if they did intend to harm the old man on the outward journey . . . Someone had to warn him. Someone ought to be up there in Leigh Wood well before five.

Dr. Baillie said, "It is no trouble." He kept the horse at a trot. "I will drop you at Cranthorne. I insist."

"No!" This time she said it with real force. "No. I do not wish to go to Cranthorne."

"Something is wrong."

"Yes." They were rounding the corner now and she saw the track up into the wood. The nearest way to get to the lake. "Yes, but I can't tell you now. There is no time. Please stop here, by the stile. I wish to get out. I . . . I wish to walk the rest of the way."

Fanny went straight up the track to the lee of the wood. She saw a pheasant fly away with a wild beat of wings and heel out across the trees. She judged that if she kept up this pace, she would be well in time to intercept Sir George, and she wished the next half hour was over and finished with.

The thick beeches at the top were almost impenetrable on either side of the path and crowned a sort of plateau or headland. Once she was there, it was downhill most of the way on all sides. Halfway down, she was almost running and could see the low, smoky mist of late afternoon beginning to gather in the valley. She could see in the distance the line of yellow that was the buildings at Leigh Park, and when she was sure what they were, and she saw them grow sharper and more defined among all that green, she felt her heart lighten, her spirits pick up.

The air in the woods, despite all that sunshine outside, was cool even to the point of being shivery. Halfway down the other side, Fanny heard a twig snap somewhere in front of her and saw a squirrel dart onto the path. For a long, agonizing minute she stopped and listened. Nothing else, though, so she moved on again and reached the small clearing where two paths crossed. She took the right-hand one that led down, then up.

She knew where she was heading. The spot where this path went over the next rise and met the path from Cranthorne. It was farther than she thought, but she ignored the leaden ache in her legs, the needling pain that was coming in her side, and she forced herself heavily up the track like a child that must finish a race.

Over the top and across a fallen tree. No sound of horse's hooves yet. There was only a long silence in that part of the wood. Odd, she thought idly, that there were no birds twittering all across those trees. Keeping to the path, she almost ran for perhaps twenty yards until she judged she was at the turning she wanted, the one that led all the way down to Cranthorne.

Something made a brushing kind of noise. Fanny looked back and thought with awful clarity how swiftly, how very suddenly, a feeling of cautious optimism could turn into a terrifying trap.

A stout man stood on the path behind her from where he had come out of the trees. Clarence, with his right hand gripped tightly around a pistol. He was smiling because he had found her and because he was aware of her fear.

His right hand came up.

The sun sifted down through a gap in the leaves behind him.

"We imagined you would try to make your way back," he said. "Just wait, I said, and she will come."

Fanny thought of Deacon rushing back to tell them. The anger and foul temper on his weasely face.

Stupid, she thought. I should have kept off the paths.

The sound of the birds began again and Clarence moved.

Fanny said, "Where is Sir George?"

"George?" Clarence laughed. "Somewhere on his

way up here, I very much hope. Caro was to make sure he left home well before five. Now, my dear, move." He motioned with the pistol. "Back toward the road."

"You would not dare use it," Fanny said.

"Try me."

It was a bluff. She took two steps forward, feeling that her legs no longer belonged to her.

"Keep walking," Clarence said.

She moved again. Clarence's face held a nasty mixture of threat and satisfaction. She looked at him. At the pistol. Tried to imagine how long it would take . . .

When she was three yards or so from him, he gave the pistol a short, sideways jerk, stabbing it into the air for her to come on past him. Not at all used to the pistol, Fanny thought, dimly reaching into her memory for something Sir George had once said: "Clarence is a damned useless shot. Always was. Big with words. Got no eye."

She said, "You are surely not going on with it? You will be very stupid if you do."

"Needs must, my dear." He was still grinning, but with a sharp little edge. "No going back. Might as well go forward."

A light gust of wind moved the branches to one side of his head, making him cast a quick glance to determine that no one was there. It was only a partial shift of his attention, but it made all the difference to the state of Fanny's mind. She twisted herself with a speed she did not know she still possessed and made for the gap in the saplings to her left.

She hit the clump of undergrowth just as the pistol went off. She came out on the other side still in one piece, except for the long scratches on one arm and ran hard, crouching low except in the hollows, and as she ran, she kept looking back in Clarence's direction.

For a brief second she saw the black of his coat between the trees, saw him break through the undergrowth after her and knew he was not going to just stand there and let her go. Running on down the slope, she also knew the only way she was going to lose him was by being sharper and faster. That would not be difficult. Clarence's weight slowed his movements. His breath would not last long, if she were not much mistaken. It would only be necessary to elude him for five minutes at the most before his strength gave out.

She made for the only spot in the wood that mattered, the slope above that dreadful leap. To think and plan which direction to take was impossible. Clarence was too close behind her for that. Her feet plunged down between tree roots and nettles, and her kid slippers were no protection against stubbed toes and sharp edges. The best way, once she got used to it, was to leap from trunk to trunk. Even so, Fanny felt branch after branch tear at her clothes.

A crack and another bullet hit one of the trees behind her. Clarence was still there, then.

Fanny ducked and dived and came over the top of the ridge.

Suddenly, from the other direction came the sound of a horse's hooves. Fanny, scrambling through the trees, dodging beneath boughs, was hard put not to panic. Between topping the ridge and halting momentarily to get her bearings, she caught a glimpse of a black horse between the leaves.

Horatio. Sir George's mount. There was that white blaze on its head. Fifty paces away and coming down hard from the Cranthorne direction. Gone again. A rush of air as the wind came. The pounding still came on, too. A flash of something in the opposite direction down by the bank.

Something brown moved in the very bottom of the ditch below the bank. A second later, it had disappeared behind a tree, but not before she had seen who it was. Deacon with something in his hand. A long loop of very fine rope. And the other end of the rope was attached to a bough on the far side of the track the horse would take. The line was loose now, but could be drawn up to neck height in a moment. In the moment that it would take Horatio to approach the leap. So that was how they were going to do it . . .

He would not see it until the horse drove straight into it. Until they were off the ground.

By which time it would be too late.

Fanny threw up her arms and shouted as Horatio came down through the trees and almost in line with her. But her frantic waving was too late, it seemed. For her cries, instead of alarming, appeared to have spurred on the rider to greater speed. And now Horatio was right on top of her in a rush of black, charging horseflesh.

One last frenetic try . . . She practically threw herself at the horse . . . Stop . . . dear God . . .

When she came to, her head was in some ferns and she seemed to be listening to Edward's voice as he leaned over her, a voice that was very rough and hoarse, almost wild, as if it were not him at all.

"What in God's name did you do that for?" he said.

"Where is he?" said Fanny. "Is he there?" She

could not seem to work out where she was. "Where is he . . . ?"

"Where is who?"

"Sir George."

"Sir George?" A long pause. "Sir George is at Stamford Rectory."

"Stamford Rectory? Is he dead? Did they take him there?" She knew she was not making sense, but it would all put itself straight in her head in a moment. When she had got herself out of this odd dream.

"No one took him there." Edward's voice was gentle now. "He rode there a short while ago."

"But Horatio is here . . ."

"Yes. He was not riding Horatio. I was riding Horatio." His hand moved up to touch the long, raised welt across her forehead. "And I could have killed you. You could have been killed leaping out on me like that. Do you know that?"

"There was nothing else I could do."

"Yes." His hand moved again. Down to her wild hair, the scratched arms. "You would say that."

"Clarence . . . Deacon . . . !" She struggled again to get it all straight, and this time the pieces fitted together. "Down there. You must find them . . ."

"Yes. Later . . ." His eyes were grim, but softened again as they saw her face. "Do you think you can move?"

"Yes." She tried it. Something hurt—the pain went right through her. Some part of her arm. She lifted her head a little to look down at it. It looked all wrong. At an angle, lying there. "Would you help me, please?"

Edward said, "I think you had better lie still."

"No. I want to get up." She insisted. She thought:

I hurt all over, but it is only the arm that aches like that. "Clarence . . . Clarence is there."

"Where?"

"Somewhere back there. He has a pistol. He was firing at me."

"He did not hit you?"

"No. I don't think so." She felt so bruised that she wondered how she could tell if he had.

"No one is there now." His eyes raked the hillside.

"Are you certain?"

"Quite certain."

"Deacon was down there . . . by the bank." She told him what she had seen.

"He is not there now."

"Then they will have heard the commotion. They will know that it was you on Horatio and not Sir George."

"That is a pity." His eyes held regret. "I was hoping to catch them at it."

Fanny said, "You came on Horatio on purpose . . . you intended to ride into their trap? But they might have killed you!"

"I doubt it." He got the full force of his conviction into his voice. "I am not an old man."

"So what do you think they will do now?"

"I imagine Clarence will cut and run. You look very white."

"I am not white. I am black and blue." She attempted to make light of it without quite succeeding.

"What did they do with you? Where did they take you?"

"Only to Lowton. I took the first opportunity to run." She looked at him. "Did you receive my letter? Did you visit Cranthorne this morning?"

"Soon after breakfast. I did not like the sound of your letter."

"And what did they say to you?"

"They told me you had gone back to London."

"And you did not believe them?"

"What do you think?" His eyes interrogated her. "However, I let them believe that I did."

"And what did you do next?"

"I watched the Hall for the rest of the day. I saw Deacon come back in a great hurry. Then, about midafternoon, Mr. Crawley left in almost as much haste." Edward's voice was dry with irony. "I have no great acquaintance with the gentleman, but it was clear that something had altogether rattled him. I followed him as he rode toward the village and I cornered him as soon as we were clear of the house."

"Cornered him?" Fanny saw the look in his eyes and guessed what that meant.

"Mr. Crawley soon talked. It did not take a great deal of persuasion." The faintest of smiles touched Edward's mouth. "I heard how they had found you out and spirited you away. After Deacon came back with the news that he had lost you, it seems the thieves began to fall out. Clarence insisted on going on with his plans, and Mr. Crawley thought it too dangerous and decided not to be around to face the consequences. So he left."

"Did not Caroline try to prevent him?"

"If she did, she failed. Or perhaps she thought he did not mean it. As it happens, it was fortunate for us that he did mean it. I extracted a great deal of information from the gentleman. I found out where they planned to attack Sir George, and as soon as I knew that, I intercepted him and persuaded him to change mounts with me."

"How did you do that?" Fanny asked. "He is always so stubborn."

"I managed." Edward's smile was a touch sad. "He is not what he was. I told him our plans for the evening were changed. That we were both dining at the Rectory to discuss the state of the church roof with the Elthams. And I told him I thought my horse was going lame and asked if I could take Horatio to deliver a quick message to Taff Jenkins. So George rode off down to the village and I took Horatio up into Leigh Wood at his usual time . . ."

Fanny said, "And that was when I ran out at you."

"That was when you ran out at me."

She said, "It was all my own fault. Getting into such a fix like that. I was so stupid. I tried to confide in Sherry. I told him everything." An ache passed through her head.

Edward saw her wince. He said, "Does it hurt?"

She said, "Yes." She was not thinking about her arm. "Clarence . . . he must not get away."

"He won't." Then he looked over her shoulder and said, "Someone is coming."

Fanny froze. Clarence? Deacon?

It was Dr. Baillie. He walked briskly down over the track before either of them noticed him. Said, "Good heavens, young lady, what have you been up to this time? Looks like you need my professional services. Heard some shots. Thought there must be something funny going on, so I decided to come up and see for myself." He looked at them both and saw Edward's arm still firmly round Fanny's shoulders. "Well, then, Edward—move out of the way for a moment, would you, dear boy? Give the girl some breathing space." He took his first squint at Fanny's arm. "Humph! Broken," he said. "Told you where all that haste would lead. Better get you back to the house." He glanced up. "Saw that gamekeeper of George's skulking away across the field just now. Something obtuse about that fellow. In a great hurry. If you will get out of the way, Edward, we will see if she can stand up."

Chapter Twenty

Edward did not trouble himself to follow Deacon, who was small fry. While Dr. Baillie undertook to care for Fanny, he went off on Horatio once more in the direction of Cranthorne. It was another half hour or so before Dr. Baillie drove Fanny back to the Hall in the buggy.

They bowled up the long drive and stopped in front of the pillared porch. Deserted. Like the day she had first arrived. A strange kind of silence hung over the place. A kind of waiting. Waiting for what?

Dr. Baillie climbed out of his seat and helped Fanny down. He looked at the house. There was no movement anywhere.

They tried the hall first, Dr. Baillie's hand lightly on Fanny's good arm, warning her lest she should take it into her head to dash off again on her own once more. He moved lightly, for a man of his size, across the black-and-white tiles toward the staircase.

The drawing room was uninhabited. An ormolu clock on the mantelpiece started to strike six. Fanny would always remember the sound of its chimes.

They turned toward the library. Went slowly, steadily toward the double doors on the far side with the plinth above them and the busts on either side. Again, the doors opened silently. Cooler in here. The windows were all closed, the curtains half drawn against the remains of the day's heat. No one in there. All silent as the grave.

The dining room came next. As they approached its door, Fanny suddenly had the wild idea that they would all be sitting in there as they usually did at this time of the day: Sir George at the far end, Caroline next to him lightly handing out the apricot tart. Clarence and Sherry would both look up as the door swung inward and they came in. The conversation would stop.

The door opened in reality. Fanny saw the long, polished mahogany table. Empty. Nothing laid. A bowl of roses. A chair pulled out. A fly buzzing. No dinner. No people.

She wondered suddenly what had happened to the servants. The smell of early evening was starting to creep in. No voices to be heard, just an eerie, hollow silence filling the corners with a sense of danger.

"Sit down and rest," Dr. Baillie told her. "We will see to that arm."

"In a moment," said Fanny. The arm had been put into a makeshift sling. She could stand the pain until she had found out what was happening. She walked out of the dining room and over to the alcove below the staircase, to the table that stood holding more flowers and the silver cigar box.

"Better to see to it now," Dr. Baillie said. He looked troubled, wary, as if remembering the brief, low conversation Edward had had with him earlier in Leigh Wood.

Fanny turned her head, suddenly listening.

Movements upstairs, a voice up beyond the carved bannister rails. She found she was holding her breath and made an effort to get her pulse back under control. Another voice, a movement, a board creaking . . . and easing his way backward on the landing from the passage that led to Caroline's bedroom, not seeing anyone below, was Clarence. His arm was half raised, half pointing in a gesture that Fanny recognized. He continued to edge backward quite slowly, stealthily. Feeling his way back.

Fanny looked at Dr. Baillie. Back up at Clarence's pistol. At the direction in which the pistol was pointing.

She dared not move.

The pistol was pointed at Edward. Edward was up there, too. Slowly, cautiously, one step at a time, he was moving toward Clarence with open loathing in his dark eyes.

"Don't come any farther," Clarence said. "Stay where you are. Don't do anything. Caro, what in hell's name are you waiting for? You'll get past him now. He'll let you. He will be forced to or I'll put a bullet through him." To Edward he said, "And don't think I won't, my friend. I've nothing to lose, and come to think of it, I'd rather enjoy it."

Fanny made a quick, instinctive move toward the stairs, but Dr. Baillie's arm came out to block her way.

"Come on, Caro! What the devil are you waiting for?" said Clarence with sarcastic urgency. A movement behind Edward and Fanny saw her cousin standing pressed flat against the wall. Her face bore an odd mixture of cunning and apprehension, quite different from her usual light expression. She knew she had to move past Edward, who was blocking the passage, to escape with Clarence, but she was terrified to attempt it.

Clarence took a step back toward them and waved the pistol again. Caroline half moved and half slid gingerly along the wall. She took a step, two steps. No move from Edward yet, but his eyes must have made their mark on her, for she hesitated once more.

"Caro, move!" Clarence said with a gritty edge to his voice. This time Caroline obeyed him in earnest. But her very haste served to undo her. Her foot seemed to catch on something in the carpet. Edward saw it and seized the moment. Lunged for her as she half stumbled into him, and with a sharp push, he threw her at Clarence.

It seemed for a split second that Clarence would go down as she hit him, but he regained his balance, thrust her away, and tried to aim the pistol once more at Edward. Actually fired it. But Edward was no longer there in the center of the landing. He was on top of Clarence. He went charging straight at him with all the force of his broad shoulders, and although Clarence attempted to dodge him with a swerve to one side, both men went back hard against the paneling. The muzzle of the pistol jumped, went off with a crack and a spark and soft, blue smoke drifted down into the hall.

A half scream came from somewhere inside Fanny, but then she saw that the bullet had gone into the ceiling.

Edward swung round on Clarence in a sort of fury and with the power of his clenched fist knocked the pistol from his hand so hard that it spun across the carpet to the top of the staircase.

For a brief second Fanny saw Caroline move, leap like a deer to pick it up, but Edward was faster. Caroline was half crouched and coming in low. He

caught her on the shoulder and she jerked back into
the bannister rails. He swung back again in the other
direction, for Clarence was coming again, put his
immensely fit frame up as a barrier against the older
man and at the same time put his knee up, drove it
into Clarence's stomach.

Having all the wind knocked out of him was an
experience new to Clarence, and although he got up
again, he did not have any bounce left in him. His
breath was coming back in great, fast puffs that took
all his time to control, and his legs were sagging and
would scarcely hold him up.

He still came rushing back with a grunt, however,
and got back the advantage by using his immense
weight to slam Edward's head back against the
heavy paneling. At the same time, his hands came
up in a stranglehold. Fanny thought, Edward's
stunned, he's out cold, and her hand gripped at Dr.
Baillie.

Clarence with a sideways lunge went to pick up
the pistol. A turn and a grin and he was lifting and
aiming. Squeezed the trigger. Squeezed hard.

Fanny shouted a warning, incoherently . . .
screamed his name. "Edward—!"

But as the gleam of satisfaction reached Clarence's
eyes, Edward's fist came up and caught him by surprise. Clarence spun and stumbled; the pistol went
off with another crack.

Clarence stumbled on and fell. The thin blue of
Caroline's light muslin was spattered with blood
when the smoke cleared a second time and Fanny
saw her cousin's neck, too, streaking with red.

Caroline . . . Oh, God . . . ?

It was not until Clarence dropped the pistol that
they saw clearly the result: Caroline falling, shot
through the heart. Clarence still sprawled against

the stairs gazing at her, disbelief written all over his
puffy face.

Silence.

It ended all at once, with Edward dragging himself
upright, swaying a little, grasping the huge, carved
knob at the top of the staircase and speaking in a
voice half blurred with strong emotion.

"You'd better get up here, Dr. Baillie." He bent
down and took up the pistol. "I think it's too late,
but you'd better try."

Fanny observed all that evening's happenings
with a strange sense of detachment. The magistrate
came and went. Clarence was taken away. Caroline's
body was removed, too, and the servants returned
from the back part of the house where Edward had
sent them.

Someone—Mrs. Hurst, she decided later—came to
urge Fanny to eat, but she would not, could not. It
would have choked her, she said.

Shock came out in all sorts of ways. She kept
thinking, all that night, that she heard her mother
fussing around and calling for her. The Hall seemed
cut off by the darkness of the park all around. Each
room cut off from the next. Even her mind seemed
quite self-contained and strangely empty. She
seemed to have three choices: not to talk; to talk too
much; or to walk round and round the room talking
to herself in her head until she had got it all
straightened out.

The latter she did first. After that, Mrs. Hurst
came and Fanny did not say anything at all. She just
sat there, refusing the food on the tray in bare
monosyllables, staring at the little gold flecks on the
top of the beef broth, and waiting for Mrs. Hurst to
stop patting her on the shoulder and making little

clucking sounds and saying things like, "There, there, miss. It's no wonder you are numb—but I daresay it is all for the best." Or, "You never know about folk until all the cats come out of the bag." That was the nearest she ever came to any mention of Caroline. Then, "Mr. Clarence always did cause trouble. But that is all over now. Now we shall get back to a bit of peace, I should think."

Then it was peculiar, but as soon as she met Edward, Fanny could not stop talking. It was an odd sort of instinct to pour everything out—almost an attempt, absurd and exaggerated, to entertain him with all the tiny details. She remembered thinking, in the back of her mind, that he would think her quite mad or simply hysterical, but as soon as they were sitting down opposite each other in the drawing room later that evening, the silences, no matter how brief, all had to be filled with words. Mostly trivial, a lot of them totally out of character. But her tongue, once loosened, would not seem to stop.

Sir George had been put to bed upstairs. Louisa had been over and had gone again. She had agreed with her brother that the old man was not in a fit state to stay up with them all evening, and Dr. Baillie had given him a sleeping draught. Tomorrow they would start the long process of getting him back to his old self again, or as near to it as they could hope for.

Fanny sat in the center of that huge room, rather stiffly, like a doll on the long, shiny sofa, great stretches of blue satin on either side. She had almost never sat there before, she kept thinking, without Caroline's light laugh over there in one corner or without Sherry's drolleries or Clarence's nasty comments over there in the other. It was eerie. All open. All empty. She was glad they were gone, but she had not yet got used to the fact. She could not have sat there again with them, she told Edward in a great hurry, but she felt . . . she did not know. There seemed a kind of insecurity in the very silence. In a way, she felt lonely. Her brain felt unsettled.

Edward looked at her and said, "It will take time for it all to register."

"But it has registered." She looked back at him, then away. "Every little bit of it. I know it all by heart, I have gone over it so much. Caroline is dead. I did not like her when she was alive, so it seems wrong to mourn her. And yet she was my cousin and it seems wrong not to. And Clarence is under lock and key at Westbridge . . . Is that not where you said he is? And Sherry has run off somewhere to get out of it all. And Sir George is safe and sound upstairs . . . and we two sit here. So that is the end of it, is it not? But it still feels . . . unbalanced. I still feel unbalanced."

He did not answer. She felt uneasy with him. She did not find his expression easy to read. She had worked herself up to believe that he was going to come and comfort her, but he did not seem to be in that kind of a mood at all. Her entire set of responses had been based upon what she had seen in his eyes this afternoon in Leigh Wood: gentleness, warmth, passion even. But since she now saw none of those things in his face, since he now appeared only correct, very formal, almost distant, how could she know how to respond to him at all?

So she talked. She unearthed all sorts of silly trivia and laid them before him. If she once departed from this flow of quick, bright conversation, she might lose all her control and go to pieces entirely. She fell into the subject of her adventures in Lowton with as much haste and lightness as some joke about the weather. "The object of it, I suppose," she told him, "was to dump me where no one would find me. I had quite decided on the bottom of the Thames as my ultimate destination, but I daresay they would have had a dozen other suitable locations in mind."

Edward said, "Clarence did not tell you where Deacon was to take you?"

"I don't think Deacon was going farther than Lowton. There was another man waiting by the second carriage when I escaped in the alley. The man I saw Deacon talking to outside the White Hart. I should think they had paid the second one to take me on somewhere." She flung him a fleeting glance. "I kept hoping you had got the note I gave Annie Bates and that you would come looking for me."

"I did receive your note. That is why I went to Cranthorne so early the next morning. They told me you had suddenly taken it into your head to go home. That you missed your mamma. That she missed you and that you got up at the crack of dawn and left."

Fanny gave an odd laugh. "You would find that very comical if you had met my mamma. The only reason she would miss me would be that I was not there to give a good scolding to. Or to blame for everything that went wrong. And she likes me to be there so that she can rail about my papa. She is fond of doing that. She thinks me very like him, you see. That is probably very true. I am proud to be like him, no matter what she thinks. But she would not miss me for anything else. She thinks that I cost her too much and she resents me for being young and for not having a dozen or so handsome young men hanging around. That is what she was like when she was young, she tells me. She had dozens of admirers and made the biggest mistake of her life by choosing my papa." She was looking down with a firm little frown. Her voice had risen, despite her efforts to appear detached, and she suddenly became aware that Edward was still not saying anything. So she thought she had better startle him into replying by bringing out the one question that she had wanted to throw at him ever since it was all over. She looked up and straight across at him and she said, "Why did you not warn me about Sherry? You knew it was he and not Clarence that Caroline was . . . was involved with, and yet you did not say a thing. You let me go on barking up the wrong tree. If you had warned me, I might have guessed a great deal more about his nature. He was always so plausible."

"I'm sorry. I should have told you." Dark eyes gazed at her. He was very still. Very set.

"He was so charming. I might not have been half so susceptible to him if you had warned me."

"Susceptible?" That forced some sort of emotion out of him.

"Yes." She stared back. Then decided to be strictly accurate. "No. I did not mean that, exactly. I meant that I would have seen what he was earlier. You should have warned me. It was not fair not to." She stopped, but there was still a lot of raw tension in her.

"I thought it too dangerous. I did not think you could—"

"What? Hold my tongue?" Her tone was flippant, but her face in that moment was angry and insistent. "If you thought that, then you should not have told me any of it." It may have been the precarious state her nerves were in, or the fact that he still had not moved or come across to her as she wanted him to, but all at once she felt reckless. "Didn't I prove myself trustworthy enough? I suppose you thought me too young and silly—"

"I thought nothing of the sort—"

"You need not explain. I know exactly what you thought." Fanny did not know anything of the kind, if truth were told. She had no idea what was going on in his head, but there was this sudden, perverse pleasure in making him feel guilty. It would serve him right for suddenly being so noncommittal; it might puncture some of his awful formality.

"I almost told you that time you stayed the night. But then Louisa interrupted and I thought it best to leave it for the time. I thought it would put too much of a burden on you, if you want to know the truth." His voice was perfectly modulated. "I wasn't sure if you could take that particular bit of information for the moment. I thought you would not be able to go on playing their game if you knew—"

"I suppose it never occurred to you that I might confide in Sherry, get myself into real trouble, as I did?" She had not meant any of this to come out tonight, but her feelings all kept tumbling out, her pulse beating faster.

"It ought to have occurred to me. But I thought your instincts would tell you not to confide in him too much, not to pour it all out—"

"I had to pour it out to somebody. And you were not to be found!" Her voice wobbled dangerously. "You were too busy with other things."

She heard him say, "Fanny . . ." He sounded impatient.

"It does not matter," she said hotly. "Sometimes, when I think of it all, I wish—"

"Yes?" He spoke gently, as if keeping his temper in check.

"I wish I had never known her. Caroline." Perversely, she went on, "I wish I had never come here."

A silence. A long silence. Then he said, "Do you mean that?"

"Of course I mean it. I never say things I don't mean." Her eyes came up and met his. Unnerved by the long, powerful glance, she swallowed hard and turned swiftly away, so that he could not see her tears. She got up and walked over to the window. No one had bothered, tonight, to pull the heavy draperies. Outside, the park lay bathed in dull moonlight. Tired, disoriented, disappointed that he had allowed her to quarrel with him, she realized that all she wanted in the world was for Edward to put his arms around her and hold her until his warmth drove all her tears away.

But he did not come. The silence went on and on. And then she felt very cold and so exhausted that all she wanted to do was lie down and sleep. And when he said goodnight and she went upstairs on her own, that is what she did. She slept without dreaming for almost twelve hours. But it did not make her feel refreshed.

Chapter Twenty-one

Fanny got the feeling over the next couple of weeks of living in a vacuum, one day running smoothly and a little aimlessly into another, the mornings all crisp and bright and frosty, the afternoons turning quiet and golden and mellow.

Sir George did not really seem to need her there. In the aftermath of Caroline's death and his brother's arrest, he seemed bluff, more rational and yet curiously solitary. He talked to her, communicated, yet deliberately shook off any attempt to comfort with a show of hearty well-being. Sometimes Fanny even thought that her presence there might remind him of Caroline. Perhaps that was why he would not confide in her.

Edward and Louisa came to visit them every day. Formal, kind occasions. Then there was the funeral, a quiet affair. Everyone thinking, no one saying much. Edward visited even more often after that, but it was only to inquire after the state of Sir George's health. Fanny felt sure of that. He was still so impersonal. She had a sudden insight that now that there was a different set of circumstances, everything was going to be different. She thought and, in fact, knew that she and Edward could never go back to the casual warmth of their earlier friendship.

That was why one September morning, quite suddenly, she decided to return to London. Edward had called. There had been much the same short meeting in the drawing room as usual. Now he and Sir George had gone out riding, and Fanny had come back to her room. She sat there looking in the mirror. Soft, sun-speckled hair that had grown fairer since she came to Cranthorne. Green eyes with

darker flecks the color of pondweed. A square determined chin which gave the face some substance. She
tried seeing it from Edward's point of view, but
could not manage it at all. Too boring and ordinary,
she thought: she was not beautiful. Only Sherry had
said that, and everyone knew now what he had
been.

As she stared into the mirror and the green eyes
stared back, she felt all at once quite unnecessary in
the house. She felt that her life had moved in a circle; she had returned to some starting-point, in this
old-fashioned, square little bedroom that looked out
over a hazy park. Perhaps it had all been a dream—
all those emotions with Edward, Caroline, Clarence,
the shooting. Perhaps it was just time to move on
into another day, another place, another life.

If Edward just did not care . . . She swallowed
and looked at the face in the mirror again.

Yes, I'll go home, she thought.

She announced her decision when Edward and
Louisa were there the next morning. She told them
quite simply and boldly, "I think I must go home.
I've been here so long. My mamma will expect me
home." She did not look at Edward.

"No need to run off," Sir George said with a sort
of a cough. As though perhaps to counteract the impression that he held her at all responsible for Caroline's behavior. He gave her a rapid, curious glance.
"Stay as long as you like."

"Must you go?" Louisa said. Her gaze strayed
across the room to her brother. "I thought . . .
well, we thought . . . We have just got used to
your being here. We should miss you."

At last it was Edward's turn to speak. He had been
standing with Sir George by the window and now
Fanny saw him turn and fold his hands behind his

back. "Have you heard from your mother?" he asked abruptly.

"Yes." Fanny grew nervous. "Yes, I had a letter from her yesterday."

"And what did she say?"

Fanny fidgeted. She wished she had not told him all those things about her mother that time. It put her on sticky ground now. She put up a hand, began to straighten her hair. Edward followed her every movement with that dark, impassive gaze. She said, "Mamma . . . Mamma thinks it is time I was home." It was not the truth. The bulk of Mamma's letter had consisted of shocked amazement at the news of dear Cousin Caroline's death and then had gone on to heap abuse on Sir George's head for not looking after his wife better and for trumping up what she supposed were ridiculous charges against poor Mr. Clarence Stanhope.

"So you intend to go?" Edward said.

"Y-yes. Yes, I think so. If that will suit."

He did not reply. There was a silence like that which falls when no one can think of anything to say.

Fanny said, "I have been here almost two months." Her disappointment made her awkward. Yet it was stupid, she supposed miserably, to expect him to add his own pleas to those of his sister. To care if she stayed at Cranthorne or not.

"Is it really that long?" Louisa said.

"Yes. It is that long," said Fanny. "After all, I only came . . ." She stopped herself in time. She had been going to say that she only came to keep Caroline company for a week or two. Now she went scarlet and finished, rather tamely, ". . . I only came for a short stay." She looked at Sir George and he said, without changing his expression, "Time goes on." Mumbled again, "Got used to having you here, miss, but you must please yourself, of course. Can't stay forever, I daresay."

Another silence. All the time, Fanny kept hoping to hear Edward ask her to change her mind, stay a little longer, but in the end all he said was: "Which day did you have in mind?" His expression was not warm or interested. His face was dark and still, with something more intense underlying the stillness.

"I . . . had not really thought." Fanny said it hurriedly, but then squared her chin. "But Friday, perhaps." Today was Wednesday.

"That soon?" Louisa exclaimed.

"Yes. I think so." Fanny felt a little surge of panic. Her voice wavered, but she told herself it was no good to take half measures. If Edward did not care, then he did not care and that was all there was to say. The sooner she was gone, the better. "I can take the Oxford coach again from the inn, can I not?"

"That is the usual route." Politely, Edward agreed with her. His mask of reserve was still in place.

"Then that is decided. What time does it leave?"

"You will need to go at ten in the morning," he told her.

"Then that is perfect," said Fanny.

"If that is what you wish."

The streets outside were just long rows of windows, her mother's temper as variable as ever. It must have been about three weeks after Fanny's return to Wentworth Street that she fully realized how lonely and desolate she felt. What an utter fool I was, she thought, harboring the hope that Edward would come up to London to find me. After all, she told herself, who could blame him for not coming near me again when one considers with all the clar-

ity that time and distance lends, what a member of
our family, Caroline, had done, or tried to do, at
Cranthorne?

At first, she had tried to imagine all sorts of trivial
reasons why he might call on them at Wentworth
Street. To return some little item or other that she
might have left at Cranthorne. To deliver a note
from Sir George asking after her health. Such far-
fetched notions had only been a temporary comfort.
After two weeks—two weeks and a half, to be pre-
cise—she knew he was not going to come. Examined
through the glass of reason, such ideas shrank to
their true size. Examined in the light of day, there
was no hope at all that Edward would come.

She had flattered herself—why not admit it
frankly?—that he had felt love, tenderness of some
sort, toward her. Well, his feelings had obviously
not been so strong as to make him want to ally himself, to mix with, a family such as her own. Could
she blame him for that? Yet she did blame him. It
hurt so much to think she would never see him
again. Never see that tender spark in his dark gaze.
Indeed, she was so ridiculously hurt, bereft, that she
could scarcely think of him without wanting to
burst into tears.

She was too proud to write to him. Or to Louisa,
though this latter would have been perfectly per-
missible. Indeed, Louisa had written Fanny a short
letter—rather a disappointing one, when it came to
it. After asking politely about Fanny's health, Louisa
had said:

> *Sir George goes on famously now, I think. He seems
> all at once, this last week, to recover with an extraordi-
> nary force and vigor. Monday was wettish. Yesterday
> Edward was over there and the lanes were very sloppy, he*

says. In the village there has been a spate of weddings—
they are all getting fixed before the winter, Miss Rush-
worth says. Miss Austen visited yesterday . . .

Miss Austen . . . That put paid to Fanny's pleasure in receiving the letter. And was Miss Austen to
be one of the autumn brides? Was she to be married
to Edward with all the fuss and ceremony in Stamford Church that two such wealthy families could
provide? There came a queer sort of cramp in the pit
of Fanny's stomach at the thought that the next letter to arrive might even announce such an event,
and it was a pain such as she had never known before. It meant she could do nothing, concentrate on
nothing.

She could not have described her state of mind to
anyone. It was a kind of continual agony of waiting
and watching. Every step out on the street, every
knock on the door, every sound, every voice caused
her to start, drop her work and go to the window.
Every hour that passed seemed endless.

One afternoon, she felt quite unwell. It was the
strain of coping with her mother's tactlessness. Her
head was all aching. She did not seem to be able to
collect her ideas together at all or take in the sim-
plest, down-to-earth talk. She did not feel alive because there was no one in the house to make it feel
alive.

She was sometimes certain he would come. At
other times, she knew he would not.

It would have been easier if her mother did not
always ask such bruising questions. She came into
the room and found Fanny staring blankly out of the
window. Mrs. Milbanke said, "One hears nothing
but sighs! Believe me, Fanny, you will do no good
sitting there in the dumps! If I had half as much to

be grateful for as you, I am sure I should not be sitting there like a lumpen thing. It seems to me that Cranthorne did you no good at all. It seems to me you are worse than before you went! Be so good as to tell me, did no part of it suit you? I am sure Cousin Caroline's shocking demise is not at all your concern. That is for Sir George to worry about and I hope he does. I am sure it will serve him right. He should have had more sense than to marry such a young girl. And I did warn you, to be sure, about that branch of our family. Caroline's father was always a rogue. Your dear father always said so. It is one of the few bits of sense he ever spoke."

If Fanny did not answer, then Mrs. Milbanke grew even more persistent. "Well, I did not expect you to give me a civil answer! I mean, that would be just too much to expect, would it not? I am sorry to have to trouble you with my conversation, Fanny. I realize it is probably much too dull for you here now, after all the pleasures of Cranthorne. But I do not know why you should be so very secretive about everything . . . It would not hurt you so much to tell me . . ."

"There is nothing to tell . . . !" Fanny said, avoiding her mother's gaze. Her voice was unnaturally controlled, her eyes desperate.

"It is a good thing some of us make the effort to be civil," Mrs. Milbanke said, sniffing. "Of course, no one knows the effort it costs. Several times, Fanny, I have thought it would be better if you had stayed at Cranthorne altogether."

"I wish I had," Fanny was heard to mutter.

"That's right—show your bad humor!" Mrs. Milbanke touched all the cushions, set them straight. "You are of no use to me here, that is certain! The only thing that sustains me is the thought that your sister, Clarissa, will be old enough in a year or two to talk to her mamma as a loving daughter ought. Keep yourself to yourself . . . see if I care!"

"I will talk to you if you talk about other things," Fanny said behind ground teeth. "I do not wish to talk about Cranthorne all the time!" She threw down her cross-stitch.

Mrs. Milbanke said, "Pray calm yourself, Fanny. There is no need for such violence! I am sure I do not know where you get it from. At least, I do know, but I am quite aware that you will jump down my throat if I say it was your only legacy from your father. He was exactly the same. He would leap at me with his tongue as soon as I uttered a single word. But I shall not allow you to get to me—that is just what you want . . ."

Then inertia took over. Fanny would start the day in a patient state of mind, but minute by minute all her energies seemed to slip away from her. She was obliged to go out of the room not to snap at her mother's sillier remarks. Mrs. Milbanke was the vainest and most difficult woman upon earth, Fanny thought. There were times she wished with all her heart she could just walk out of the front door and away from the house and never come back.

She was reflecting on this fact the morning that Edward eventually did come. There was a faint haze of fog in the street that morning, though the sun shone as brightly as any of the days in the summer. Outside, there were damp, gingery colored leaves lying in little heaps under the black railings. The same gingery leaves hung in thicker numbers on the chestnut tree in the pavement, only they remained brighter and more glowing. Beautiful blotches of color and winter on the way. The people going past fewer in number and the windows beginning to be in need of a fresh coat of paint. All as it had been, and would be, as long as life in this house went on.

Fanny had no real reason any longer to sit there in reach of the windows, although she would not yet stop herself doing so. The day belonged to a bunch of them, all alike; barred from all life and light. The fire was not yet lit. The walls looked smaller than ever. The children were thumping around in the room overhead and Mamma was out in the hall, talking to the maid and all Fanny could hear was the long, rambling complaint about some chair or other that had been discovered with a half tin of beeswax left open upon it for the first person that came along to sit down upon. Fanny could imagine the lines of sullenness on the girl's face as she answered back, although she was a pleasant girl, if treated pleasantly. If Mamma only had the sense to talk to her the right way . . .

There was a brisk rap at the door and Mamma began saying, "Who can that be? Lizzie, wait a minute before you answer it. Give me the polish! And if it is that Mrs. Godwin, say we are not in. Do you hear? I cannot bear with her grumbles this morning—"

Fanny was still motionless when she heard his voice. His presence and his deep voice must have rattled Lizzie at first, that much was obvious, because her thin little tones floated back into the house with a nervous stammer. "Wh-who shall I say, sir? Mr. Knight? B-beg you to stay there, sir, while I see . . ."

And then Mrs. Milbanke's voice in a soaring whisper from the back lobby. "Who did you say,

Lizzie? A Mr. Knight? We do not know any Knights. It is some mistake. Pray get rid of him . . ."

Fanny moved then, faster than she had ever moved in her life. The feeling of disbelief and delight which had threatened to take her legs away was quickly overcome. She was in the hall before Lizzie had had time to get back there herself.

She said, "Mr. Knight!" Caution was all gone. Her delight had to show.

"Miss Milbanke." He was equally formal. Excruciatingly so. And he looked so tall and broad in the familiar blue-black coat with the velvet lapels. They both hesitated, then both spoke at once.

"You are well?" Fanny asked.

"Thank you. Yes."

"And . . . and your sister?"

"Louisa is well, too. She sends her regards." A pause while the maid scuttled away. They stood there stupidly, staring at each other. Fanny said, "Will you come into the drawing room?"

He followed her in. Mrs. Milbanke, coming into the room behind them, was as quick as ever to see that something was awkward and to jump in and say so. "My dear Fanny," she began, "what are you doing standing there in the middle of the room like a loon? Ask the gentleman to sit down, pray, if he is come to call. Lizzie says he is from Cranthorne, but nobody has told me about him. Are you a friend of Mr. Stanhope's, sir? Of Mr. Clarence Stanhope? He was a great favorite here, before this unfortunate late incident." She fumbled for her handkerchief. "Mr. Clarence Stanhope came here a great deal, you know. He was quite a friend of the family, poor man."

"I am a friend of Sir George Stanhope," Edward Knight told her.

"Of Sir George?" Mrs. Milbanke was genuinely taken aback. "Well . . . I do not know what to say about that! I do not, indeed! I was saying to Fanny only yesterday, I find it a very odd thing for a gentleman—or a supposed gentleman—like Sir George to allow them to stick charges on his brother like that—"

"Mamma . . ." Fanny was mortified. She did not know where to put herself. She knew what Edward must be thinking about her mother's loose tongue.

"And as for all this gossip about our cousin, Caroline, I do not know how people can bring themselves to pass round such scurrilous stuff!" An elephant could not have stopped Mrs. Milbanke now. She was determined to air her opinions. "Fanny could no longer stay there, of course, after the tragedy. With dear Caroline gone . . . We should not wish her to. Indeed, I would not allow it."

"Mamma . . . !"

"You cannot conceive, of course, the excessive hauteur with which some of the upper families view those who are . . . shall we say . . . a little newer to society. That is what is at the bottom of all the talk, after all. You may depend upon it. It is nothing but jealous gossip." Mrs. Milbanke's eyes were sharp and curious. "Where did you say you are from, sir?"

"From Stamford Parva, ma'am. I am a close neighbor to Sir George Stanhope."

"A close neighbor?" Mrs. Milbanke went on staring at him hard. She did not care for his dark complexion, his stern look. One could almost see her bridling at it. Not a hint of solicitude or charm in the gentleman, one could hear her thinking. Not at all so easy-talking and gracious as dear Mr. Clarence Stanhope. As if on cue, she went back to her favorite.

"Mr. Clarence Stanhope was always so civil," she sighed. A pointed look here in Edward's direction. Another great sigh. "So compassionate! But there, it is always the same. The good do not prosper, you know."

"Mamma . . . !" A great paleness had come over Fanny's cheeks during all this. "Perhaps Mr. Knight would like some tea?" She flashed him an agonized look.

"Tea?" Mrs. Milbanke flared up at this. "I do not think you need to remind me of my duties, Fanny. I will ring for Lizzie."

"Perhaps . . . perhaps you ought to go and search her out yourself, Mamma. You know she will not answer. She is almost always outside at the back at this time of day exchanging news with the Gilsons' cook."

"To be sure . . . !" But Mrs. Milbanke still did not go at once. Once more, she fixed her regard on Edward Knight. She could not make him out at all. She said in a piercing tone, "You will have heard a great many of these stories, I daresay, sir, about Cousin Caroline—it gives some people great satisfaction. They find it vastly entertaining to say she was an adventuress, to view our family in this mortifying position. But I do not mean to let them get to me. Fanny may disagree, but it is when I am most severely tried that I am at my most unaffected . . ."

When her mother was gone out of the room—as soon as the door was firmly closed behind her—Fanny felt a little more tranquil. At least, until Edward came across the room and sat down next to her on the sofa. His eyes were keen and strong. There was a long, difficult silence, then Fanny said stiffly, "You must not mind Mamma. I'm afraid she has always been like that. I can do nothing about it. She does not listen to me at all."

Edward said, "You look tired." The clock ticked. He sat there against the shabby cushions and looked at her broodingly. "Are you well?"

What a question! How could she answer it, Fanny wondered, without giving away the truth?

"Sir George is improving," he went on.

"Yes. Louisa said so in her letter. Please thank her for writing."

"Ah, yes . . . the letter." Without moving, he gazed at her. "You did not answer it."

"I . . . I could not think of anything to say."

"That I don't believe."

Worse and worse, Fanny thought. He was reproaching her for a breach of etiquette. She sat there miserably staring at the carpet.

"So I was forced to come here and pay you a visit," he said.

Fanny said nothing.

Then Edward said, "I wanted to know if you were fully recovered. Are you? Have you forgotten your ordeal at Cranthorne?"

"Forgotten?" How could she have forgotten any of it? Nothing else had been in her head since she had come home. "I . . . have forgotten the worst parts of it," she said at last.

"And what are those? The worst parts?"

"I . . . would rather not talk about it. I should like to forget it all."

"All of it?"

His expression confused her and she rushed on, raising her voice: "Some parts. It was not all . . . so unpleasant."

"Which parts were not so unpleasant?" He was persistent. Her face flooded with color. She brought her fingers up to her brooch. The pearl brooch that Annabella Austen had belittled. The thought gave her something else to talk about, a new path to lead the conversation into. "How is Miss Austen?" she asked brightly, completely ignoring his repeated question.

"Annabella? She is well, I think."

I think. Two little words that could mean so much —or so little. Fanny pushed back her hair. "Don't you know?"

"Why should I know?" He had that closed-up look on his face that she had seen once or twice before. It seemed to say, Keep out. Private property.

Fanny said, "I . . . I thought you and Annabella were friends."

"We are friends." He paused. "As much as anyone could be a friend to Annabella."

What did that mean? Fanny looked away. Then she added, for the sake of something to say, "Miss Austen has powerful connections. I should think that would mean she has a good many friends."

"You can be friends with Annabella as long as you do not contradict her. As long as you let her have her own way."

"I see."

"Do you?" Edward sat looking at her. A silence. Then he seemed to make up his mind, and he reached out with his hand and trapped hers inside it. "Fanny, what has Annabella Austen got to do with any of this?"

"Oh . . . nothing." But she could not keep up the carelessness. She might as well be honest. "I understood there was some understanding between the two of you."

"Understanding? Between Annabella and me?" He seemed almost ready to laugh. He considered her for some seconds without speaking and then he said, "Fanny, how did you manage to outwit Clarence and Caroline when one half of your brain can make such a ridiculous assumption as that?" He added in a reasonable voice, "Let's just get this quite straight. Exactly what kind of understanding did you think I have with Annabella?"

"The usual kind." Fanny kept her chin high.

"And what is the usual kind?"

"Well, that you and Miss Austen are . . ."

"Yes?"

"That you are . . ."

"What?" He was not helping her at all.

"That you are to be married. One day." Her face was red.

"Married? To Annabella?"

"Yes." She glared at him.

Now he did laugh. "Oh, Fanny . . ." He spoke gently, but Fanny felt quite breathless. "I can understand you wanting to run away back to London because I am too old for you or because I had put you in a situation that strained you to the limits, but . . ."

"Too old for me?" It was her turn for incredulity. "Who said you were too old for me?"

"It's obvious, is it not?" he said. "You are nearly twenty. There are at least twelve years between us."

"And is that why you became so cold and distant after Caroline's . . . after the worst of it was over?" She felt a tightness of the throat.

He looked at her. "It was one of the reasons. The main one, perhaps." He seemed strangely stung. "I was not cold. I have never been cold toward you."

"It felt cold," she said simply. "You changed. I don't understand why. It was as if, after it was all

over—the business with Caroline and Clarence—
you made up your mind to drop my acquaintance."

"Drop your acquaintance?" He looked at her in
disbelief.

"Yes."

"But I came to see you every day."

"You came to see Sir George. It is not the same
thing."

Edward said, "But you were included in my concern!"

"Was I? I could not have guessed it."

"But you were the one who decided to drop the
acquaintance! You made up your mind to come back
to London."

"Only because I thought you did not care whether
I was there or not."

"Oh, Fanny . . . you are being incredibly
dimwitted."

"Don't call me dimwitted! It is not true. It was *you*
who was dimwitted." Her eyes were suddenly filling
with tears. "I needed you. I needed someone to comfort me and you would not do it."

Keeping his eyes fixed on hers, he said, "I would
not do it because I might have been taking advantage of your state."

"Of my state?"

"Yes." It was a statement so firm and positive that
she glanced up in surprise. "You were distraught and
highly volatile. It was natural under the circumstances. I felt for you, but I was suddenly aware how
vulnerable you were."

"I was not so very bad," Fanny told him. In an
attempt at dignity, she said, "I thought I managed
pretty well."

"So you did. But you also told me you wished you
had never seen Cranthorne. That shook me. I

thought you might mean you wished you had not seen me, either."

"It was a stupid thing to say. I was not myself that night."

"Exactly. So how was I to tell what you really thought? What you wanted? I decided it was fairer to keep my distance, to leave you . . . not to say anything more than was strictly necessary until you were more yourself . . ."

"But I did not want you keeping your distance," Fanny said unsteadily. "You were so unresponsive . . . it made me very unhappy."

"Unresponsive?"

"Yes."

"You think that?"

"Yes." Fanny did not move, though she had started to tremble a little.

A muscle at the side of his jaw was twitching. "You really think that?"

"Yes." She sat there defying him until he reached for her face and forced her to look at him. He looked . . . impatient. There were black flecks in the brown of his eyes. Men explode so suddenly, Fanny thought. She was astonished at the fierceness of his gaze.

He said huskily, "I'll show you how unresponsive I am." His mouth came down on hers. The kiss was long and passionate, but when his hold on her loosened at last, he whispered, "Forgive me." He pushed back the wildness of her hair. "You look frightened—"

"No." She could not let that idea stay in his head. She was not at all frightened. The shaking in her limbs came from something else entirely. "No, I'm not frightened," she said shakily. She sat there looking at him. "I didn't think you would ever come here."

"Did you want me to?"

"Oh, yes," she said. "Yes, I did . . . ," and she put up a hand, half smiling, half uncertain still, and touched his face. This elicited another long moment of incoherent passion. "I will be frightened," she whispered at last, "if we go on much longer."

Edward let her go reluctantly. He smiled and said, "I almost asked Louisa to come and speak for me. Explain how I felt about you . . . ask if there was any chance . . . But that would have meant explaining to Louisa how I felt, and I didn't know how to do that either."

"I am sure Louisa could not have done it as you have done," Fanny told him with a smile. "I am glad you came yourself." Slyly she added, "I am not sure you have told me exactly how you feel about me. Not in words, at any rate."

"I love you, Fanny. Is that clear enough? I have wanted you every single day since you left Cranthorne. But I waited. I made myself wait all this time before coming to see you. I wanted to give you time to know your own mind. You were so young. I thought . . . forgive me . . . I thought you might be, well, susceptible."

Fanny said, "Are we talking about Sherry?"

"Partly. You admitted you were taken in by him. That you found him attractive, too."

"Only at first."

"I realize that you changed your mind later . . ."

There was mischief in Fanny's eyes. "I should warn you that with you it was the opposite. At first I found you abominable and then, after a while I began to like you."

"Only like?"

She put her head on one side. "By the night of the Assembly Ball, I will admit to wishing I could stop thinking about you for at least two minutes of the day. And then I was so mortified when you walked into the conservatory and found me with Sherry like that . . ."

Edward said, "I wanted to knock him through the wall."

"I did not know what you were thinking. Your face is such a blank sometimes."

"If it was blank, it was because I could not show what I was feeling." He touched her hair. "You were so beautiful that night. At first, when we met, I thought you quite plain—"

"Thank you!" She could not resist teasing him now that he was again holding her close. "I am not sure I like that at all."

"You were not plain. You blossomed in the sun. I watched it happen over those few weeks. You loosened your hair and your skin turned to pure gold and . . ."

"Yes . . . ?"

"I wanted to kiss you every time I saw you. Every time you looked shocked or worried about what you heard about your cousin, you made me feel old and cynical. But at first, I dared not believe such innocence could be real. I thought, if you came from Lady Caroline's family, you had to be tarred with the same brush. I was amazed when I found you were not. And I hated you being there in the middle of that den of vice with your huge green eyes and that clean look you have . . ."

Fanny said, "It was not all so bad." She hesitated. "In Sherry's case, I think he did try to be kind at times. I still cannot help feeling he was not so bad as the other two. Oh, I know he had great faults, but he would not have been in it so deep without Clarence and Caroline."

Edward said, "Mr. Crawley was a piece of flotsam. He was washed around by every tide . . . by stronger currents. At every point of his life, he took the line of least resistance." He said, "Clarence Stanhope was the mind behind it all. Clarence always gathered people around him that he knew he could manipulate. And Sherry was easy to manipulate. Clarence picked him off the street in London and kept him on a sort of rein. Do what you are told and you will have an easy living. Sherry was lazy. Easygoing and charming, perhaps, but his idleness made him easy fodder for Clarence and Caroline."

"But Clarence did not intend the . . . the alliance between Sherry and Caroline?" Fanny asked. "Surely not? It brought untold complications, did it not?"

"Luckily for us, as it happens," said Edward. "Caroline was another matter entirely. Clarence could not always control her. He needed her for his plans to get Sir George's money, but it had to be very much on Caroline's terms. If she could not have Sherry at Cranthorne, she would not marry Sir George."

"And that is where I came in," said Fanny. "People would not get suspicious at the length of Sherry's stay at Cranthorne if . . ."

". . . if you had not been there to give his visit a seeming purpose." Edward went on looking at her. "A young, beautiful girl . . . What could be more natural than that Mr. Crawley should be attracted and should linger."

Fanny said, "And then if they only made it obvious to me how unmanageable Sir George was . . . how he drank and beat Caroline, they would hope, I suppose, to have had me tell the magistrate after Sir George's death what a hard time they had with him. And to think I almost swallowed it all at the beginning. As my mother swallowed all Clarence Stanhope's lies and flattery." She glanced at him sideways as she spoke. "Edward, she does not mean to be offensive when she runs down Sir George and takes Clarence's side. She gets things wrong. She cannot help it. My father suffered from her indiscretions all his life." She looked down at her hands. "You would have had much in common with my father. He would have been to your liking."

"I am sure he would." Edward smiled. He said steadily, "Your mamma will be to my liking, too, as long as she comes to visit but once a year." He watched Fanny's face change. He said, "Fanny, you will marry me? It is what I came to ask. You don't have to give me an answer now. You must come on a visit to Leigh Park. We should get to know one another better before you give me an answer."

"I think we know one another fairly well already." Her face flooded with light; she was teasing him again. "Does it mean a great deal to you?" she asked. "That I should marry you, Edward?"

"Do you need to ask such a question?"

Fanny tried to ignore all that intensity. "You will need to have strong nerves if I marry you," she told him. "They will talk, after all that business with Caroline. They will say I am after your money and I shall probably make the most terrible blunders in society and Miss Austen will never forgive you."

His strong arms encircled her. "I love you. Miss Austen may go to the devil." At first, the kiss was gentle and sweet, but then stronger forces slowly took over. Fanny melted into him, her arms wound themselves tightly round his neck.

The door opened. Mrs. Milbanke's voice said, "My dear Fanny, whatever is going on? What do you think you are doing?"

Fanny came swimming back to reality, and then she gave back to her mamma the obvious answer.

"You do not like me to be dull," she said, "so I am entertaining the gentleman."

And from one look at Edward's face, she knew he was not going to contradict her.

A Message To Our Readers...

As a person who reads books, you have access to countless possibilities for information and delight.

The world at your fingertips.

Millions of kids don't.

They don't because they can't read. Or won't. They've never found out how much fun reading can be. Many young people never open a book outside of school, much less finish one.

Think of what they're missing—all the books you loved as a child, all those you've enjoyed and learned from as an adult.

That's why there's RIF. For twenty years, Reading is Fundamental (RIF) has been helping community organizations help kids discover the fun of reading.

RIF's nationwide program of local projects makes it possible for young people to choose books that become theirs to keep. And, RIF activities motivate kids, so that they *want* to read.

To find out how RIF can help in your community or even in your own home, write to:

RIF
Dept. BK-2
Box 23444
Washington, D.C.
20026

Founded in 1966, RIF is a national nonprofit organization with local projects run by volunteers in every state of the union.